QUAKE CITY

Praise for St John Karp

Radium Baby

"A devilishly rich, satisfying scientific confection."—*Kirkus Reviews*

"Much like a brilliant episode of *The Simpsons*, this story synthesizes a greedy fistful of whimsical elements to hypnotic effect...Karp throws historical elements in with robots and giant hornets, keeping it all fresh by writing with acrobatic aplomb."—*Open Letters Monthly*

Skunks Dance

"It's refreshing for me, a lover of the absurd, to find a new novel by St. John Karp...Karp is a nerd after my own heart, with soft spots for pigtails and superheroes. He's delivered an emotionally-resonant dollop of day-glow Americana without relying on the clichés that YA books—and too often reality—insist kids live by: smoking, drinking, and navel gazing. Has Karp written the book he wanted to read? Surely. Are there any teens in the audience not racing toward adulthood? If so, they'd be the treasure to find."—*Open Letters Monthly*

"[A] truly addicting story. In alternating chapters, we follow two stories. I cannot say which I found to be more addicting, as both really pulled me in. Both stories were made up of strong characters, drastic events, and highly entertaining moments. Throughout it all, the two were intricately connected, the link between the two making for one highly entertaining read...I had so much fun with this one. Honestly, I cannot begin to explain how enjoyable this one was, not without giving away spoilers—something I refuse to do. Thus, the only thing you can do is give this one a read yourself."—*Bibliophile Ramblings*

"As highfalutin and entertaining as any tall tale told around a prospector's fire, St. John Karp's *Skunks Dance* is a young adult mystery with its roots in California's gold rush days, and with a resolution as elusive as a glimmer in the pan...*Skunks Dance* is solid, sarcastic, and bombastic young adult fare, certain to satisfy the appetites of all youngsters who have a taste for adventure."—*Foreword Reviews*

By the Author

Radium Baby

Skunks Dance

Quake City

Visit us at www.boldstrokesbooks.com

QUAKE CITY

by

St John Karp

2020

QUAKE CITY
© 2020 By St John Karp. All Rights Reserved.

ISBN 13: 978-1-63555-723-7

This Trade Paperback Original Is Published By
Bold Strokes Books, Inc.
P.O. Box 249
Valley Falls, NY 12185

First Edition: August 2020

Credits
Editors: Jerry L. Wheeler and Stacia Seaman
Production Design: Stacia Seaman
Cover Design by Tammy Seidick

Acknowledgments

I want to thank everyone with whom I've ever had a terrible date. Our brief time together was so grim that you made me long to be embraced by the loving arms of a pyroclastic flow, but without you I'd have no good stories. Please consider embarking upon a new career as a piñata, telegraph pole, or crash test dummy.

ANDRE

8:09 p.m.

"I don't want to go to a party," says Tom.

I arch an eyebrow at him skeptically. Yesss, look at this. No human can withstand the eyebrow. I am crueler than Cruella de Vil and more magnificent than Maleficent. Tom shrieks and withers under the shade my eyebrow is throwing at him, begging me for mercy, apologizing through his tears for being so depressingly heterosexual and refusing to go to one teeny tiny party.

Or at least he would be. If he was looking at me. But he's still lying on my couch with his head on the armrest, browsing *KinkBitches.com* on his phone. I hold my eyebrow arched like that for a second in case he looks up and I can pretend I've just done it. Come on, Tom. Look at me. *Look at me.*

My face muscles start spasming. I drop the eyebrow and rub the side of my face, pretending it never happened. I don't know why I bother trying to have facial expressions for Tom. He even ignores the one I call "The Judgment of Meredith." Lookit. See? It's all in the eyebrow and the lips. Before you even realize what's happened, I have become someone called Meredith. You don't know anything about Meredith, but you know she's *judging* you. She is judging you for all your dumbass ideas and your weird music. I imagine Tom has just told me Grace Jones is a second-rate singer. Come the fuck on. Who doesn't like Grace Jones?

She's a goddess. Fucking Tom. He wouldn't know sexy if it came on his face. Who does he think he is, anyway?

"Fuck you, Tom," I shout. "You think this is all about you, but it isn't. You know? It just isn't."

Tom is so startled he loses his grip on the phone and drops it on his nose. I would laugh, but Meredith is too angry with him.

"What'd I do now?" he says, giving me a sideways scowl.

"You know what you said, you son of a bitch."

"All I said was I don't want to go to a party." Oh right, the party. I put my angry face away for the time being, but the ghost of Meredith still haunts my eyebrows.

Tom's all right looking, I guess, if you're into that kind of thing—though his hair is always too long, and his hands are too rough from climbing mountains or wrestling goats or whatever it is straight people do all day. Now he's trying to act like a party is such a huge deal. If he's going to crash on my couch and mooch my hospitality for a week, the least he can do is come with me.

I know how much hotels cost in San Francisco. Tom's saving a fortune, which means he owes me like a thousand dollars payable in chocolate and wine. Has he even said thank you? What do *you* think? He just lies on my couch all day stinking the place up with his hormones. He's coming to this party if I have to break his legs and *roll* him there in a wheelchair.

"Tough," I say. "You have to go. There's only one key, so you won't be able to get back in without me."

"So, I won't go out."

"What if there's a fire?"

"Then I'll *die*," he says.

"I don't even know what you're saying to me right now. Why you gotta be so freakin' weird about it?" I turn away from him to check my hair in the mirror. "Maybe we'll run into someone I know," I say. "Like my girlfriend, Amy."

I check my phone, but Amy hasn't texted me back. She hasn't been returning my texts for a week now. And then today she deleted her social media accounts. It's almost the kind of thing you could put down to being on her very long, very colorful shit list, but she's done this before. And I'm the only reason she's still here.

I go into the bathroom with a can of hair spray so Tom won't get suspicious. I jam my finger down on the nozzle to cover the sound as I call Amy. The air is filling up with hair spray. It's making my nose itch. I can practically feel the ozone layer shrivel up and die. But no one picks up. I dial again, just in case, and suddenly there's a voice on the other end, and I'm so surprised it takes me a second to go, "Amy?" And she pauses, like she's really thinking about answering.

Then she hangs up.

I march out of the bathroom in a cloud of hair spray fog and throw the can into the laundry hamper. "I can't do this right now."

Tom says, "What? It looks good."

"Yes, it does," I snap at him, but I secretly double-check my hair in the mirror. Does it look good? I guess so. I tease it a little bit until it has that nice, unaffected look. It's not so bad. Maybe I can do this. I give myself a side-on to make sure everything's where it should be: skinny black jeans, tight white T-shirt, and a black blazer with lime green crosshatching I got at a thrift store in Camden a few years ago. It's a good ensemble. And I've got them good Mexican genes, so in juuuust the right light, you can see through the shirt and see the outline of my nip-nips.

"Do these jeans make my ass look big?"

I can tell he's not looking, but he answers. "Massive."

"Good," I mumble back. "But booty massive, not bootsy massive, right?"

"Bootsy? What the hell are you talking about?"

"Never underestimate the power of the ass."

"I never have," he says.

I turn to give him a view of it and flex one cheek after the other, doing an accent: "Tohhhm. Look deep eento mah aye. Ah vill heepnotize you vith mah sexy powerrrr." But he's not paying any attention, so I do another voice. "Oh, well, what's this? My stars, I appear to have dropped my handkerchief. I better bend over and pick it up before I get an attack of the vapors." I bend over in front of him and give him a face full of my magnificent ass.

He looks at me and says, "What kind of a party is this, anyway?"

"It's a *gay* party."

"Urrrgh," he says, rolling his face into the sofa. "What you mean is there's no chicks and I'm gonna spend the whole time being letched on by queens. What am I supposed to do all night?"

"Oh my God, it's like you have no idea how this even works. Listen up, Thomas. Women love the gays, and more importantly they don't seem to mind that we don't give a flying fuck about them."

"What?"

"It's like you and lesbians. They have what you want, but you're not allowed to have it. We're what women want and it makes them insane. Who can blame them? Smell me. How can anyone say no to this?"

I thrust my neck at him so he can properly appreciate how magical I smell. He wrinkles his nose. "It's burning my eyes."

"What? What are you saying? This is Jimmy Choo. A friend of mine once wore this, walked into a room full of tits, and came out sucking the only dick in the whole place. Maybe I'm not wearing enough." I fumble for the tiny bottle of *very* expensive fragrance and spray a cloud into the air. With grace and poise, I waft myself through it. The droplets land on my skin, cool and refreshing, making sure I'm sexified enough to withstand a night of sweat and cigarette smoke.

"You look like a fish," says Tom.

I look over. Here I'm trying to impart my wisdom, and he's lost in his phone again. I snap my fingers at him. "Tom? Thomas? Tom-boy?"

Tom's eyes dart up from his phone. "Sorry, I thought you were gonna be a while."

"How dare you. You lie there humping my sofa and drooling over digital pussy when I'm offering you the real thing."

"What are you even saying to me right now—" he starts, but he stops himself. I'm standing here with a big openmouthed smile on my face just to rub it in. Can you believe it? He's starting to talk like me. Maybe he's not completely hopeless after all.

"Can we discuss what just happened?"

"Can we not?" says Tom with a pained look.

I'm basically a merciful god. I decide not to rub it in too much. "What I'm saying, Tommo, is that the club is going to be full of lady-girls, all horned up and nowhere to go. There might be other straight men there," I say, waving my hand dismissively, "but you have a gay wingman. Harness the power of the butt-lovin's. I give you my personal guarantee that you'll be swimming in tits by the end of the night."

Now he starts cracking up, apparently for no reason. Maybe he's having a breakdown.

"*Swimming*," he gasps, a little too melodramatically if you ask me. Take it easy there, Liza, you're not up for any Oscars. "Like there's a pool full of disembodied tits? Is that how this works?"

"An *Olympic*-sized pool full of tits," I say, trying to impress him with the scale of what I'm offering him. But now he's just being dumb.

"Is that what you think straight men want?" he asks, then goes all serious. "Wait a minute. You think you could pass for straight, don't you?"

"Hells damn yes, I could pass for straight."

"The shame!"

"Look, I'll do it right now." I drop my voice to sound like a stupid jock. "Dude, that's totally baller, I'm hella down for some beer pong, I'm gonna saddle up that poontang and ride it over the mountain Gangnam Style with a tuba fulla brewskis and...

all right I have no idea what I'm saying any more." My straight impression died a sudden death. But between you and me, for the first two, maybe two and a half seconds, I shone like a star.

"It's uncanny," says Tom.

I nod. Clearly I'm starting to get through to him.

The last thing I need is an ascot I tie at a Scooby-Doo angle around my neck. And maybe a hat? Is tonight a hat night? I'm not really feeling it, but the outfit looks like it's missing something without it. I try on a red fedora with a broad brim. I turn to Tom. "What do you think? How do I look?"

He looks up from his phone. "Like Liberace, only gay."

I still need to teach Tom he shouldn't try to be funny. He's not as good at it as I am.

"I choose to take your raging jealousy as a compliment. Aren't you getting ready?"

"I *am* ready," he says.

Can you believe it? He's lying there in his baggy running shorts and black tank top like he was raised by wolves. Though he does actually look okay in them, in a perverse gangbanger/frat boy kind of way. I swear with a bit of grooming and a nose hair trimmer, he'd clean up to a seven. Maybe an eight with rounding.

But I'm not going to let this fly. "I see what you're trying to do," I say. "You're going to make this hard for me. It's fine, I like a challenge. You can dress like a Soviet bag lady if you like, I'm still going to get you laid by the end of the night."

"With a girl, right?"

"If you insist. Honestly, I don't know how you *ever* get laid if you're this picky all the time. Sometimes I don't know why we're even friends."

"I make you feel less like the crushing inevitabilities of life are bearing down upon you."

Yeah. He's a real funny motherfucker. "All right, then. Let's go."

❖

My apartment is on Mission Street between 24th and 25th. It can be kind of a janky neighborhood, and the shouting keeps you up until about 3 a.m., but I like it anyway. Every couple of years, the cops try to clean up the streets between the Mission Street BART stations, like they're trying to ruin the neighborhood or something. Like just a few years ago they put up these pee-proof concrete walls around the BART stations. I read an article about it. If you try and pee on them, it's got this special coating that makes it reflect back and splash all over you. So one night I had to try it out, you know?

I'd had a couple of drinks, and there's no way in hell I'll ever use the BART toilets in case I get pregnant off a toilet seat, and the wall was just there. It was for science. Can confirm, that shit actually works. I had to walk all the rest of the way home smelling like piss, but then no one notices that kind of thing in the Mission anyway. Because you can clean it up all you want, but the Mission is always gonna be a butthole. If you get rid of all the drugs and hookers, what do you got left? Leave it alone, this is the way we like it. Besides, I only get mugged like once every six months. I dunno who carries anything important in their wallet anyway.

We grab dinner at a pupuseria, then walk up 16th toward the Castro. It's all hipster stores selling records and zines until you get past Dolores and start seeing super buff men coming out of gyms with rainbows in the windows. Some of them are kind of cute, but some people just get so big they turn gross. How are you supposed to hug someone who's just a big pile of lumps? Plus there's something about working out that turns people's heads into giant tomatoes.

We turn onto Market and see Harvey Milk Plaza at the end of the block. The giant rainbow flag is flying over the intersection of 17th and Castro. It's still early, so there aren't many people on the balcony of the Lookout yet, but that chill is already in the air and it won't be long before the bars are full. Then we turn left onto Castro where the MUNI turns. On the corner here is a bar called Twin Peaks, which people call the Glass Coffin because it has huge glass windows and everyone in there is about seventy-three years old.

"It's so depressing in there," I tell Tom. "Like having a drink in a room full of mummies. I know this one guy Kelvin says he loves it. Says it's the one bar where he's guaranteed to be the youngest and most attractive person in the room. Between you and me, I think sometimes he hooks up with one of the retirees. But if they creep on you too hard, you can always outrun them." I do an impression of an old man with a walker, and I can see one or two people inside the Coffin scowl at me.

"I dunno," says Tom, "it looks all right."

"Shh. Shut your damn whore mouth and stand there and look pretty. You don't know what you're talking about."

"Aw, you think I look pretty."

"No, I don't," I said. "You look gross. You are a gross person now. I think about you when I've drunk too much and need to throw up."

At first, Castro Street looks like any other street in San Francisco. The Mission is kind of the hipster capital of the world, so when you come from that direction there's nothing weird about lampposts covered in posters for concerts or stores selling artisanal cookies. It just takes you a second to realize the artisanal cookies are in the shape of penises and the posters show enough skin to get you arrested pretty much anywhere else in America. I guess it's true what the Nob Hill Theatre used to say: you can't spell "artisanal" without "anal."

Some of the crosswalks here are normal, but some are done with rainbow inlays in the asphalt. On one corner, there's a memorial for someone killed in a car accident or shot by a cop or whatever terrible thing's happened now. On the other side of the road, there's a guy with a sign selling rings and braided bracelets and other bits of cheap crap you'd only get when you're drunk or high. The only hardware store in the neighborhood is run by lesbians who know exactly how to help the clueless gay men who can't figure out how to fix their leaky faucets or jump-start their cars. There's porn in most of the windows you can look through, but at the Castro Theatre they're advertising a sing-along screening of *The Sound of Music*, and tomorrow they're showing an all-drag remake of *Whatever Happened to Baby Jane?*

I can tell Tom's all at sea, so I ask, "What?" A naked man at least sixty decides to walk past right now. There's a lot of sagging all of a sudden. Too much, some people might say. "Ahh, it's a lot all at once," I say, a master of sympathy. "It's all right, I remember my first time. Actually that's a lie, but I can pretend it's true. Look at my face. Do I look sincere? I can fake almost any emotion. I bet you're feeling comforted already. Have I soothed your doubts with my understanding face? I can see I have. Now don't be surprised if no one wants to talk to you. You are depressingly heterosexual. I feel like putting up a lot of shelving whenever you're around. It's enough to make me cry. Think how the rest of the Castro will react to an outcast like you. San Francisco can be a very cold town, but I promise this is only the tip of the iceberg. Stick with me and I'll show you how it's done. Thomas? Hello? Tom-boy?"

I turn around and realize I've lost him. It takes me a second before I find him talking to two strangers who are *chatting him up.*

"It's your first time here?" one of them asks. "That's so awesome. You'll have a great time. What are you doing tonight?"

"We're going to a club," Tom says. "Andre really wants me there. I'm kind of his wingman."

Are you hearing this right now? Now you see what I have to put up with. I will find a way to make him suffer for this.

The stranger turns to his boyfriend. "That's the cutest thing I ever heard! Can we keep him?" He's got his arm around Tom, and he's pawing at Tom's disgustingly flat stomach. And he's just standing there and taking it. Unbelievable. For a second, it looks like Tom might go with them. And they're actually kind of cute, which makes it worse. Don't they know he's *my* hopeless case? They can get their own Tom. This one's mine, bitches. The stranger turns back to Tom. "Do you work out? You feel like you work out." What the eff? I heard subtler flirting in *Leather Boys with Big Toys, Volume VII.*

I grab Tom and pull him out of their talons. "Sorry, we really gotta go."

"Too bad," says the stranger. "You wanna hold on to him, though. He's a real keeper!"

A real keeper. *Tom.* I can't even trust the gays in my own city.

"He was nice," says Tom with a big, goofy grin on his face. "Do you think he was hitting on me?"

"What? No, he wasn't. Why would anyone hit on you? You don't know what you're talking about."

"I think he was hitting on me."

"No, he wasn't. Now shut up your big stupid head and come with me."

"Is that a sexy store?" he asks, pointing at the Sausage Factory.

"What? No. See what I mean? You can't even tell the difference between a sex store and an Italian restaurant. I went there once. They serve wine in cups, Tom. *Cups.* I ask you."

"How about that one?" He's pointing at a building with sort of curly Chinese roof and cheap, painted lettering in the window that says, "Ambassador Ming's Garden of Terrestrial Delights." From here we can smell incense, and there's like a voice in the distance. Maybe a rumble. I dunno, I'm not stopping in every damn shop in the Castro just so he can gawk at the Tom of Finland books. I am so ready for a drink, and I can already see the corner of Aunty Bob's Quake City Club on the next block.

Anywhere in the Castro is going to have a hard time standing out. You're in the middle of the rainbowiest place on Earth where the shop windows are crowded with what you *hope* are novelty-size dildos. You can parade up and down Castro Street wearing nothing but Christmas tree lights and a pink strap-on attached to your head like a kinky Dalek and no one's gonna bat an eyelid. So, what did Aunty Bob's do? They painted it black, inside and out. They even painted the windows. They did such a good job there isn't even a little gap where the window meets the frame. When you go in, you're in Aunty Bob's now. You leave the rest of the world at the door.

It's on the corner of the street, and it's got some words painted on the side in a weird language. It looks like Spanish that's all eff'd up, but I like the font—kind of a Gothic thing with all the squiggly bits inside the letters so you can't tell the difference between a G and a Q. The door is the only place any color leaks out from, but you can tell it had to bounce around a few corners to get there.

It's this weird thing with Aunty Bob's. You got to go through like a maze to actually get in the place. I guess it's supposed to make you feel disoriented going in. It sure as hell makes you want to hurl on the way out. There's two bouncers, the scary-looking one who makes problems go away, and the hipster-looking one, who I guess is just there to look like a big douche nozzle. He checks the IDs. He has a mustache with twirly tips that go almost as high as his eyeballs. I try not to but I can't stop imagining what it's like to kiss that, or have those furry, twisty tips tickling your butthole, and then I really do want to hurl. All the mustache grease and stray bits of hair, and food and snot that gets stuck in there. Gross.

I try to avoid looking at the scary one, especially after Kelvin told me if you look a bear in the eyes, he can steal your soul. I thought it was a joke, but he said it was true. He said he has an ex who was a power twink until he accidentally locked eyes with a bear's reflection in a mirror in the bathroom at Toad Hall. Six months later, he'd put on sixty pounds and grown a pelt of hair from his shoulders to his toes. And you know how Kelvin never lies.

Mustache-man says, "You're rockin' that hat, buddy." Of course I am, I *invented* hats. Who does he think he is, anyway?

I don't need your compliments, just lemme in the club, door-jockey. "Where did you get it?" he asks.

"What?"

"Who gave you the hat?" he asks again.

"It's mine. I bought it."

He looks at me weirdly, like he's trying to catch a spy. "*You* bought it?"

"Yes. And it's not like it's any of your business or anything, but I'm wearing the hell out of it. Are you the hat police now?"

He checks the time. Suddenly I realize how long it's been since I saw anyone wearing an old-school watch, like one that doesn't even talk to your phone. It's a weird one as well. It has too many hands. I guess it must be expensive. I can't imagine why the hell else you'd wear it. He says, "All right, go on. Your friends are waiting for you."

"How did he know we're meeting people?" I whisper to Tom, but not quietly enough.

"This isn't my first time," says the bouncer, pushing me toward the door. "Get along, little doggy."

"What did he call me? Did you hear that? Punk bouncer, thinks he owns the whole club."

"Forget it, Andre. It's the Castro."

I shrug. Maybe he's right.

We navigate a few turns around the corners of the entry hall. The walls are painted completely black, so it can be hard to figure out where you're supposed to turn. I've seen more than one person smack their head against a wall they couldn't see. Since then I think they've tried to put up some posters to make the corner more obvious. One has a picture of a buff Asian dude in a mankini and it says, "Not your grandma's Singapore Sling." It's almost as blinding as the black paint. Hell, even Tom is a more attractive prospect than a man in a mankini.

We step on the dance floor, and I think the party must have started a while ago because it's already full of people. The strobe lights freeze everyone in time, which makes them look slow-motion one minute and sped up the next. I think the club turns those lights on so you can't see how bad people are at dancing. Everyone looks cool under a strobe light.

The bar is straight ahead of us on the other side of the dance floor, and there's a stage on the right where one of those bargain bin San Francisco drag queens is doing her bit. I know this one—Lucinda Fanny. She auditioned for RuPaul once and got rejected, which she managed to turn into her own TV special, but it's streaming on Hoodoo or Zipadeedoo or something so no one's seen it. Now she's up on stage emceeing with the same super annoying nasal voice she always uses. At this point I can't tell if it's the character or if she needs some kind of urgent sinus operation.

That happy wave hits us, the expensive perfume mixed with the sweat of the dancers and the sugar from the overpriced cocktails. Cotton candy–smelling clouds rise up from people vaping at the bar, and I can just about smell the fresh cigarette smoke from the open section at the back. I hate it, but it wouldn't be Aunty Bob's without it.

"Oh shit," I say. "Ian's on bar tonight."

Tom follows my gaze and sees Ian, the bartender, mixing the worst drinks in town and charging too much for them. They're awful, but he does make 'em strong, and Ian's the only bartender that'll mix me one of my specials. But Jesus fuck he's a bag. Of. Dicks.

"I don't care what the drinks are," says Tom. "I can drink *you* under the table." And then he looks down at me meaningfully, as if my height's supposed to prove anything.

"Oh, you think you can outdrink me? Is that what you think? Can you even hear yourself? You are ridiculous. But since you offered, the first round is on you. Wait, wait," I say as he starts for the bar. "I don't want any of your candy-ass Bud Light or shit. Tell 'em Andre's here and wants two of his special drinks.

They'll know what you mean. You got this, Tom-boy." Tom starts to edge his way around the dance floor toward the bar, and I add under my breath, "You'll never make it out of here alive."

I look around the crowded room for a second trying to find any sign of Amy. She might be hard to find because she's so short, but then she's usually giving some moron the business so she tends to stand out. I bite my lip. I can't see her anywhere. Stupid. I don't know what I was thinking. A club's probably the last place she'd be. I just don't want to be one of those people on the news who says, "I don't know why I didn't notice. All the warning signs were there," the day after they find her alone in an apartment with her face being eaten by cats.

Then I hear someone shouting, "Andre! Behind you!"

I turn around with relief. For a second, I think I might have found her. We actually met in this club, though it was years ago and everything's changed since then. San Francisco's a different city. Apparently, I was angry about something and was trying to climb over the bar to punch the bartender. I don't remember that, but that's how Amy tells it, and she's not the kind of person who'll make things up. She'll tell you what a dickhead you're being right to your face and she'll rub it in for years after, but she's not like Kelvin.

You can never tell what's true when you're talking to him. By the end of the conversation, you won't even know your own name. But Amy? She's a real friend. She took me to Squat and Gobble and made me drink coffee and eat bacon cheeseburgers until I calmed down. I still don't remember what I was so angry about, but she's like a rock. She just listened and made me feel like I mattered. She's so sensitive. That's how she was such a good listener.

I heard someone say once that they were born without skin; they had nothing to protect them from the world. I didn't realize at the time, but that's Amy. Then when it was her turn, I tried to be there for her. That's what it's like with friends you really care about. Though I still made fun of her all the time. And I'm pretty sure I accidentally pissed in her sister's bed once.

I don't know why I thought I'd find Amy. It wasn't even a woman who shouted my name. It takes me a second to recognize my friend Wes sitting at one of the little tables against the wall with two girls I don't recognize.

You know that thing where there's a mixed-attractiveness couple? You don't get them too often, but you see them around every now and then and you wonder, *How does that even work?* Like that model who's in all the Plus de Merdre designer clothing ads. You could dress her in a burlap sack and she'd still look gorgeous, but I saw a photo of her with her husband once and I was so startled I snorted up some of my coffee, spit it back into the cup, and kept on drinking it to steady my nerves.

She's got the looks, she's got the money, she's got the fame, so what the hell is he bringing to the table, that's what I want to know. Turns out he's a writer, so I thought maybe he's really good at that, but I saw one of his plays and I fell asleep somewhere between the first ten minutes and the third hour. Maybe he's hung like a racehorse, I dunno. It's a mystery.

Anyway, these two girls are one of those couples. It's too early to figure out what their deal is yet, but it only makes sense she's got *something* going for her, right? One is thin and petite. She looks like maybe she's part Indian because she has light brown skin and beautiful eyes where the skin gets darker around them. The other one looks like she could stand to lay off the Bacardi Breezers and figure out the way to the gym. She's wearing an unfortunate outfit that shows off a lot of epically sloshy boob. Is that a thing? Maybe that's a thing.

Wes, on the other hand, looks like he lost an argument with his hairdresser.

"What happened here?" I ask him, grabbing his head like a crystal ball and hating him for being this attractive even with super short hair. "This is a tragedy. Who did this to you?"

"We did it like a month ago. We had kind of a 'Vote for Pedro' moment and shaved it all off."

Wes is one of twins. Identical. And believe me, there is nothing I wouldn't do to be the meat in that sandwich. *Nothing.* I wonder from time to time if they ever jack each other off.

"Devin too?" I ask. He nods. Fuck, two sexy short-haired twins. I can't stand it. "You look terrible."

"Shut up, what do you know? You're only a designer. I am an artist," he says, indicating himself like a princess.

"What are you trying to say?"

"What was your degree in again?" he asks. "Coloring-in?" I stick my tongue out at him, and he says, "Here, lemme introduce you to Regan and Val. They're a bit dispossessed these days since the Lex closed down."

"Good riddance," I sputter. "That's where I had one of the worst dates I ever went on."

"Maybe you weren't her type," said Val. Deadpan. I hate that.

"Will you get a load of this one?" I say to Wes. "Got kinduva a mouth on her."

Out of nowhere Val grabs me by my lapels. She's got a big disgusting Band-Aid on her neck with a bit of blood seeping through the padding. And pus. Is that pus? Oh my God. I try to step back, but before I can do anything she kisses me right on the mouth. So many different thoughts go through my head at the same time. Her lips feel soft and squishy like I'm kissing a rotten avocado, and suddenly my nose is full of the flowery smells of her lipstick and perfume. My dick turtles up. Then, before I can hurl up into her mouth, she lets me go and smooths out my jacket.

"You don't know the half of it," she whispers.

Wes is already laughing his ass off, and Regan looks as stunned as I feel. I look down at my cock. "I think you killed it. I'll never get an erection again."

Tom stumbles into me and says, "Andre! Thank God you're

here." He bursts out into a huge grin, and I can already tell he saw me get face-raped.

"Thanks for nothing! Where were you when I needed you? Who's supposed to protect me from man-starved lesbians?" I look at him for a second and realize he's come back empty-handed. "What happened to the drinks?"

He looks over at the bar in a weird way. "Shit, I'm still getting them. I need to find that guy with the mustache."

"Like the bouncer?"

"The bouncer…" he says, confused. "No, he was already here when we came in." He sees something, then ducks back into the crowd. I turn to look at Wes and the lesbians, but before I can say anything, Tom's back with two Andre's specials.

"That was quick."

"Was it?" he asks. Fucker is up to something, I know it.

"What's that supposed to mean? Is that some wisecrack about me being sexually assaulted in the mouth?"

"What are you talking about?" he says, all innocent. A likely story. He gives me my drink. I'm going to enjoy my first one of the night, but I know I've got to pace myself. Andre's specials are like tits and balls—one is weird, two is good, and three is just unnatural. I swirl it a bit, watching the clouds of purple dissolve in a miniature tornado. This looks like a good one.

The next thing I know some lard-ass has barged into me from behind and my drink goes all over my fucking hand. It drips on my shoes, and I try to steady the glass without getting the rest all over me.

"What the fuck?" I say, turning around. Wouldn't you know it. It's our fortune-telling bouncer with the twirly mustache. He looks wasted now. He's sweated straight through his shirt, and his mustache is all eff'd up.

He looks at me with his big, crazy eyes and grunts, "Get out of my way."

"You need to calm the fuck down," I say, but he's already

pushing his way past other people. That's when two cops grab him from either side and force his arms behind his back.

"What are you doing?" he says. "Get your hands off me." He catches sight of me again, and I can see his bloodshot eyeball go completely mental. "It's the *hat*," he says. He's screaming now. He's screaming so loud people are looking over from the other side of the club, and I can hear his voice tearing at his throat.

Then he's out the door. I turn back to the others.

"Well?" Tom asks. "What's this about your hat?"

"Fuck if I know."

There's a noise behind us, and we turn around to see that mental bouncer again. He broke away from the two police, but they're dragging him away again. I don't catch the last thing he says, but he's raving some apocalyptic prediction about two o'clock. Something's gonna happen at two, I guess. The end of the world or the invasion of the crab people. Or maybe he's just completely batshit crazy.

I turn back to the others again. "I have seen people tripping balls, but that was a lot of fucking special all over the place."

"It *is* a cool hat," says Regan. "Can I try it?"

"Sure…" I mumble, too distracted to think of a real answer. I hand her the hat and she puts it on.

REGAN

9:48 p.m.

4 hours 12 minutes remain

The hat fits me pretty well, considering Andre has a head the size of a chihuahua. I tug the brim down over one eye and give the boys a good look. "What do you think? Do I look like Carmen Sandiego? I feel like I just stole the Eiffel Tower."

Wes's eyes go wide. "Oh my God, you really do."

Andre is still trying to lick his spilled drink off his arm. "Who?"

I bug my eyes out at him and watch him react. He doesn't know what's going on. The little chihuahua is a bit slow. "You're killing me, whatever your name is."

"*Andre,*" he insists.

"Whatever, it's shameful. And you call yourself a hipster."

"I don't call myself a hipster—"

I hear Val mutter, "They never do."

"Can I have my hat back?" the chihuahua asks, making a grab for it. But I'm too fast for him.

"Noooo, just one more minute. I haven't even got a selfie yet."

Val takes out her phone and offers to do the honors. I push my chest out, which elicits a devious smile from Val. The flash goes off. What can I say? I know how to look good in photos, and Val is waaaay too easy to please. I'm wearing my red leather bustier, the one that makes me feel like a jolly nineteenth-century madam, which I really might have been in a past life. You know, I like to keep the customers satisfied, but the welfare of my girls always comes first. And the welfare of *my* girl is the most important thing of all. Give Val an eyeful in this bustier, and she'll be drooling for the rest of the night. She probably needs a proper kiss to take away the taste from the last one. Andre's looked super limp. It gives me a shudder just thinking about it. I pull her to me by the hand and kiss her like she's supposed to be kissed.

I can hear Wes whooping in the distance, but Andre just goes, "Gross." What are you gonna do? Some people are beyond help.

I put my arm around Val and take a second to admire her. She really is beautiful, even with that Band-Aid on her neck. Can you believe it? Stung by a wasp when she was coming up the driveway this afternoon. Val has the worst luck, but I wouldn't care if she were the Elephant Man, she'd still be a knockout to me. She's wearing a '20s-style black flapper dress with her hair in a bob. I didn't think I'd like it on her, mainly because she said she was going to look like a sexy Ayn Rand. But I do. Whaddya know, apparently Ayn Rand is my type now.

I think she needs someone like me to draw her out a bit. If she had it her way, she'd still be at home playing games on her laptop. And I know she can be a bit off-putting at first. A lot of people don't like her the first time they meet her. I know I didn't. But I like people who know what they want, you know? Have an opinion for once. I don't have time to watch you figure it out. I guess what I'm trying to say is, there's a lot more to Val than most people realize. Just give her some time, and you'll see.

Val looks annoyed at the brim of the hat. "You can't hardly even kiss in that thing. Where's that ass-flap Andre? Give him his stupid hat back."

Wes looks around. "He went to get a new drink. I can't see him." Then he smirks and says, "Did you call him an ass-flap?"

Val nods. "He was annoying as fuck. Did you see the way he talked? Head flapping and honking like a Muppet."

Wes furrows his brow. "That is my friend you're talking about."

"I'm sure Val didn't mean anything," I say, but Val won't take the hint.

"I'm not saying anything bad about *you*," says Val patiently. "Just that you're friends with a Muppet."

"I liked him," I say. It's not too bad, I can probably turn this thing around. "He was stupid, but he was kind of cute, like an adorable little Pinocchio pretending to be a real boy."

Val shrugs and changes the subject. "You look pretty in that hat. I'm thinking maybe we could use it later, *Carmen*."

I take a moment to savor the shiver that runs down my spine. "I don't know about that," I say coyly. "You're going to have to find me first. Where in the world could I be?"

"You dress like Carmen Sandiego," she says, nipping at my lip. "And I'll dress up as Waldo."

I start giggling so hard it breaks the moment, but I don't care. "If we do that," I gasp, struggling in Val's arms, "we'll *never* find each other. We'll never have sex again."

Wes interrupts us. "I'd be all right with never *hearing* about it again. But Val's right, that would be the best role-play. You need to film it and put it up on the internet because I guarantee there's some Rule 34 for that shit."

"What's Rule 34?" I ask, and Val starts coughing and laughing at the same time.

"Babe, I don't got time to explain it to ya."

I don't get the chance to respond, because the beat changes suddenly and my ears prick up. "Holy crap! I love this song. Come on, let's eat the carpet."

"Cut the rug!" says Val, taking my hand and running out on the dance floor with me.

"I know what I mean."

Val makes a "stand aside" gesture, and then she starts

busting some wicked moves. The '20s outfit makes it look like a Charleston or something. I laugh and try to copy her, but her legs are going too fast for me to keep up. I stop trying to dance like a flapper and do my own moves, which I'm not ashamed to say are pretty decent when I've had a few drinks and the music is good. God, I love her. There are those moments when you suddenly feel like a million bucks and everything just seems all right. We could be the only people in the world, just Val and I dancing together in outer space.

"Oh hey," says Val. "There's Muppet-man."

I look over and see Andre having a really pissy-looking conversation with a preppy type near the bar. The boy turns away from him a bit too suddenly and jostles Andre, and now he's wearing his second drink of the evening. Val bursts out laughing.

"At least he's wearing a white T-shirt!" I say. "Not a complete waste of a drink."

"Yeah, I didn't really need to see the Muppet-man wet T-shirt competition."

"Now her, on the other hand…" I nod toward a woman at the bar—a bit of a hot mess, but damn she would fill out a wet T-shirt like a pro.

Val presses her mouth into a line. "I didn't know that was your type."

"Maaaaaaybe there's a lot you don't know."

"Seriously though? I can't really see it."

"What's that supposed to mean?" I demand. She's always doing this. I've let one too many of these little insinuations go by, and they are really starting to irk me. If she has something to tell me, she can go ahead and say it.

"Come on, just look at her. One drink and she's anyone's. I didn't realize you were that shallow."

"Shut up, Valerie."

One of the dancers elbows me and shouts right in my ear, "Calm your tits or take 'em somewhere else. We're trying to dance."

Not a bad fucking idea. I push my way through the crowd. Behind me, just before I lose her, I can hear Val telling that guy to go fuck himself.

Wes is sitting by the wall and Andre is still at the bar, so I skirt Muppet-man and make for the beer garden. I run through the narrow hall at the back of the club and up a few wooden steps. The air hits my face. It's night now, and the air is cold. It feels good at first, but I'm too steamed. The tips of my ears feel flushed and chilly at the same time. I tell myself just to breathe. Bad idea. I catch a lungful of cigarette smoke. I can't even enjoy standing outside without a tap on the shoulder from the cancer brigade.

The beer garden has a couple of wooden picnic benches on the left, which are packed with super twinky types clustered around the ashtrays, their skin glowing in the light from the lamps. There's a bar on the far side of the courtyard, and between me and the benches is a long wooden staircase that goes up to the second floor. It looks sturdy, but narrow. I can see people squeeze by each other on the landing and for a second it looks like one might fall over the handrail and flatten me. I move out of the way, but the shadow has already passed.

I get an itchy feeling on the back of my neck and realize Val might follow me out here. I hope she does. But I can't shake the worry that she might have just gone home instead. It wouldn't be the first time. When she loses interest in something or she thinks there's nothing for her to do, she'll just go. Usually without telling anyone. And I'm not the kind of person who makes girls jump through hoops for me, I swear, but if she goes home now this thing is over. Yeah, Val can be prickly, but you can work through stuff like this if your girlfriend is willing to meet you halfway.

But at the same time, I'm not ready to talk. Not yet. I dash up the staircase and push past someone as he's coming down. I hope I've been fast enough to give Val the slip.

The upper floor of Aunty Bob's has another bar, but no dance floor. This area is more of a lounge. The walls are lined with pleather-upholstered booths in semicircles around the tables. Most booths look full already. You know how it is when there's an early bird land grab. A couple of people in the middle get the prime real estate and can spread out as far as they like, while the rest of us have to jam ourselves onto the end of the bench clutching a drink in our hands because there's no more room to rest it on the table. At least it's a bit quieter than it is downstairs, and that clingy tobacco smell doesn't seem to come up this far.

I turn to the bar and come up short in front of someone. I nearly have a heart attack. It's Val.

"How did *you* get here?" I demand.

"Up the stairs," she says, like I'm stupid for asking. "Where did you go?"

"I came *here*. To get away from *you*."

"Me?"

I grab her face in a loving squeeze. If it gets any more loving, it will pop her eyeballs straight out of her head. "Listen to me very carefully, my love. I'm not trying to get rid of you, but right now I really need you to leave."

"What does that mean?"

"Why are you still here?" I shout.

Val looks around nervously, but no one's heard me. The bar is too noisy. "You want me to go?"

"Yes!"

"Like, now?"

I can't believe what I'm hearing. I focus on the sting on her neck and, not for the first time, I wonder if that's what it really is. Without warning I jab my finger into it.

"Ow! What was that for?"

"You're still here!" I feel sorry for what I did, but not too sorry. I guess she wasn't lying about the sting.

She looks hurt now, like she has any right to, but at least she seems to be getting the message. "Oh. Okay. I'll call you, all right?"

"No, I didn't mean—" But she's already turned around and is halfway gone. What did she mean, I'll call you? Is she going home? She'd better not be going home. And she'd better not call me, either.

I try and take a deep breath, and I turn back to the bar. The bartender is serving someone ahead of me, so all I can do is stand and wait, gripping the brass handrail to stop my hands shaking, trying not to look like I'm standing here on my own. I start to twist my hand around the rail and relish the feeling of the friction pulling at my skin and the pressure that's turning my knuckles white.

After a few minutes that feel like hours, the bartender finally comes over to me. "What can I get you? Specialties tonight are the Flaming Queen, the Top Bottom, and the Wrinkled Retainer."

By the time I've heard myself say it, it's too late. "What's in a Top Bottom?"

The bartender smiles. "On a good night, me."

"Walked right into that, didn't I?"

"It's the little things, ma'am."

"So, *how do you make* a Top Bottom?"

He smiles again, and I realize what I've done. "A *lot* of rum," he says with a wink.

"What do you have in the way of gin?" I ask, practically having to pry my mouth open to force the words out. I'm determined not to give him the satisfaction of laying another one on me.

He roots around under the bar for a minute, muttering, "Gin...Gin..." before producing an unlabeled bottle of clear liquor. On the side, someone has written "GIN?" with a sharpie. "We have gin," he says.

I just blink at him. Fuck it. I don't even care any more. "Well, let's have one of those then, shall we?"

I pay the man but leave a conspicuously small tip. Let's see how he likes that for a double entendre. I turn away from the bar and check out the rest of the room. I could go over to the little standing table by the entrance, I guess. There is a free spot in the corner next to the woman who looks like—shit! It's *Amy*.

I turn around quickly and hope she hasn't seen me yet, but I know she has. I can feel her dull glare burning into the back of my head. I know she's going to corner me and ask me why we never went on a second date, but I don't know her well enough to tell her she's a big bag of mope.

The date didn't even start off too bad. We went to a December Fairground concert, and I love their music so much I bought a T-shirt at the merch table. Amy started out by hitting the bar pretty hard, ordering whiskey and bitters and muttering something about, "I'm gonna need a few of these, I can tell." Then like three songs in, she leans over to me and goes, "This is fucking awful."

"Come on," I said. "Let's go closer to the stage."

"Why? Are they handing out lobotomies?"

"They're not that bad," I said.

"No, I guess compared to nuclear war or children with leukemia, they're not that bad. My appendix burst when I was fourteen and I nearly died of septic shock, and this is definitely better than that, almost."

"Well, what do you want, then?"

"It's supposed to be a date. I want to talk to you."

"Just ten more minutes, I swear," I said, and she looked at me in a way I never want to be looked at again. I don't know what it was—pity, disappointment, arrogance…and disgust. I shiver. I'm not going to say I'm an angel, but I deserve a hell of a lot better than that.

If I don't look back, I can pretend I haven't seen her, though I know she's still watching me. I walk casually over to the booths and wonder what the hell I can do next that's not going to look stupid. I can't lose all my dignity by perching on the edge of the booth like I'm at the kids' table. But then I catch sight of a one in the far corner with only an older Asian woman sitting in it.

I guess she's like fifty. She's wearing mom jeans and a baggy T-shirt. Her hair is long, stringy, and gray, and there's something weird about her face. She looks crabby, but at the same time the lines on her face make her look like she's about to laugh. The only things on the table in front of her are a glass of white wine on a cocktail napkin, and a shoebox.

"Excuse me," I say. "Is anyone sitting here?"

She doesn't smile, but her voice has a gentle humor in it. "No. Take a seat, why don't you? *I* don't bite."

Don't think I didn't notice the emphasis she just put on "I." And her accent surprises me, too. I don't know why I assumed she must have been born overseas, but she's obviously not foreign. She must have been born here.

"Thanks," I say. "Neither do I."

"Well, that's good to know. My name is Madeleine."

"Regan."

She nods. "And this is George."

I look around, but we're still the only two people in the booth.

"George?" I ask, looking to see if she might have been indicating someone nearby. "Is that your son?"

"*No*," she says as if I'm stupid for asking. "I named him after Mr. Bush. Although between you and me, I think that's giving Mr. Bush all the best of it."

Something catches my eye, and suddenly my attention is on the table. It looks still now, but I know I just saw the shoebox move. I take the first sip of my "gin" and savor the burn. It really is the worst. Perfect.

Now that I'm looking more closely, I can see someone has punched a few holes in the lid of the shoebox with a pencil. I shift in my seat a little bit, and I can feel the cheap pleather sticking to my thigh.

"George is, uh…George is in the box?"

Madeleine nods. "Want to see him?"

She doesn't wait for me to answer. She sets her wineglass

down and pulls the box toward her. Then she begins to lift the lid. I'm holding my glass tight now, wondering if this might be the last thing I ever drink. I take a good mouthful and keep it there, not knowing whether to swallow now or wait to see what comes out. I realize I must have bitten the inside of my cheek recently because I can feel the gin burning at the ulcer. When did that happen?

The lid finally comes free.

At first I can't see inside. The lights are too dim, and then they're strobing, and then they're dim again. All I can see is a shadow in a nest of shadows. For the first time Madeleine grins, and her eyes almost get lost in her face. I remember when I used to smile like that.

Slowly she lifts George out of his box.

I swallow suddenly, and the burn fades.

"Oh!" I breathe with relief. It's a spider! Like a tarantula or a huntsman—the kind you'd put on a burglar's face in a *Home Alone* movie. "Oh hey, George. Hey there. He's beautiful. Ha, I thought you were going to be one of those weirdos who keeps cockroaches or something. Bugs really freak me out."

She seems almost completely absorbed in passing George from one hand to the other in gentle, fluid motions. "Oh no, nothing like that. He's an absolute sweetheart."

"I'll say he is. Where's he from?"

"Indonesia. Do you want to hold him?"

I nod and put my drink down. I reach out and Madeleine transfers George onto my hand. I giggle. It tickles when he walks up my hand to my wrist. "Whoa there, cowboy," I say, maneuvering him onto my other hand before he gets all the way up my arm. "I'm surprised they let you in here with him."

Madeleine shrugs. "I'm sixty-three years old. The bouncers look tough, but they're tadpoles. What are they going to do?"

I don't want to say goodbye so soon, but I guide George back into his box anyway. "My ex used to keep a bunch of these in big glass tanks. She had this piece-of-crap apartment in Fremont, but I guess it's an expensive hobby."

"It can be," says Madeleine.

"So, how did you wind up here? I mean, no offense, but this doesn't really seem like your scene."

She stares at me in a way that makes me really nervous. I start to panic and add, "Because of the lights, I mean, and all the noise…"

"And because I'm so old? Just because I've got one foot in the grave and the other one on a banana peel doesn't mean I don't enjoy a drink and the musical stylings of Lil' Kippa. Besides, I like being in the company of young people. It's good for the soul."

"Well, what do you think about the upcoming generation? Is the world in safe hands?"

Madeleine paused for a moment over her last sip of wine. "It's nice to know that the children of today are going to fuck things up as much as we did. That comforts me in my extreme old age."

I have to laugh. "I did ask." I figure I can offer a gesture of goodwill. Maybe I'll prove our generation doesn't completely stink. "Here, let me get you another. What are you drinking?"

She asks for a Chardonnay. I take her empty glass and head over to the bar. It's relatively quiet at the moment, so I grab a spot next to a couple engaged in some industrial-strength flirting. I order another wine, and while the bartender pours it I can overhear the couple next to me turn their attentions from each other and on the crowd.

"Have you seen Kingsley tonight?"

"Downstairs, I think. He was pre-gaming, so he's in a bit of a two-and-eight."

Eeeee, the second one's English! I love that accent. He's super pretty, too. I should say hi. I should say hi and pretend like I'm English, too. I bet he'd never even know.

"Did you see Grandma Moses over there hogging the whole booth? I think everyone's too scared to sit next to her."

"I'm pretty sure I saw her in *The Mummy*."

"Yeah? Who was she?"

"The mummy," cracks the English one. He looks like a boiled potato. God, how did I think he was cute.

"What's the deal with that box?" says his man-wife. "That's some serious Log Lady shit right there."

"*Hey, fucko!*" I grab Madeleine's wine off the bar and throw it in the American's face. "Here's a bright idea—mind your own goddamn business."

He stands there gasping for a second, holding his hands in the air like he doesn't want to touch anything. "What the fuck's wrong with you?"

"You wanna go, twinky? I can break you like a Kit-Kat." I grab him by his two hundred dollar T-shirt and twist it up in my fist.

"Get off me, you psycho bitch."

Then before I can react, the English one grabs the hat off my head.

WILL

10:25 p.m.

3 hours 35 minutes remain

"Got your hat!" I shout at her. Before the hormonal steampunk even realises what's going on, I've scarpered. Johnny's still at the bar with a slack smile on his face and a few drops of white wine hanging off the bottom of his chin. The boy probably doesn't know if it's safe to laugh yet. If he giggles now, that steampunk's gonna slap him, but I'm not sticking around to find out. I'm already halfway across the room. I throw a look behind me, but the steampunk isn't going to let this go. She's right behind me, tits heaving like she's gonna try and knock me out with 'em.

I hit the door and start pounding down the stairs. It's dark. My feet are going too fast for my brain to follow. For a second, I feel like my feet are in the air, like I'm going to fall and the stairs won't be there to catch me, and I'll keep falling and falling, maybe forever, before I pulp myself on the concrete below. But my feet know the way. They meet the wooden staircase, and I can feel the whole thing shudder underneath me. I land on the concrete at the bottom, and I can't move for a second. My legs are stunned by the impact, but I'm relieved to feel the ground under my feet. Then I'm moving again. I feint back and hide in the corner of the patio underneath the stairs. There are two picnic tables taking up most of the space, but the lights are dim and there are plenty of dark corners.

I'm down on my haunches now, back up against the cold brick wall. I look up and see lights shining through the stairs above me. I wait and watch. If I can throw the steampunk off the scent and trick her into going back into the club, she'll never find me. She could spend all night picking through that dance floor.

But the footsteps aren't coming. I keep my eyes on the stairs, but the steampunk isn't following me.

Her loss, eh?

I stand up cautiously and step out of the shadows into the weak light from the lamps in the awning. I put on that hat and grab the brim like I've seen them do in old movies. It ain't half bad, this thing.

"That is fierce," says a voice from one of the tables. "It makes you look like...oh, what's her name?"

"Jessica Rabbit?" I ask.

"No, Margaret Thatcher."

"Figures," I say, wrinkling my nose. "I half-inched it off a steampunk Nazi. At this very moment, she's probably going Belgrano on the boyfriend." I watch this bloke's face, but he's gazing at me blankly like he's still waiting for a punchline. Americans. If you don't do a ba-dum-tss at the end of a joke, how will they ever know when to laugh?

I take a gander back at the stairs. What *has* happened to Johnny? I was hoping I could sneak back up after I gave the steampunk the brush-off, but I never counted on her not coming after me. Johnny should have come looking by now.

Something's struck this bloke at the picnic table because he gasps, "Are you *English*? I love your accent." He clears his throat and a little part of my soul dies. I've been in this country long enough to know what comes next. "I say," he ejaculates in his poshest voice. There's no point telling him I'm a Londoner. He'll only give me another blank look. "Spiffing game of tiddlywinks. Would you care for a spot of tea?" I nod patiently until it seems like he's done. I open my mouth to say something, but then he shouts, "MOVE YER BLOOMIN' ARSE." Aha. So, we know he can do Cockney when it's from a musical.

"First rate," I say. "You know what you should do, mate? You should visit London and try that out. I bet you make it the whole trip and no one rumbles you."

"Really?" he says. And now you see why I have to humour them. Look at his little face, all lit up and excited. He thinks I'm complimenting him, poor bastard. You don't blame a kid for doing a bog-awful drawing. You just put it on the fridge and say well done, you. He nudges the bloke next to him, who's watching him with an indecent amount of enjoyment. "See? Can I say it? I told you I was a natural." He turns back to me. "I am a performer, you know. I'm at the SF Dance Academy."

"You're a dancer. That must be why you have such a flawless mastery of accents."

His mate tells him, "You just did a video shoot with P. Diddy, didn't you?"

The dancer mmmms ambiguously.

"Really?" I ask. "Are you famous?"

"I don't like to talk about it."

His mate chips in. "He's suspiciously quiet about the whole thing. I think P. Diddy sexually molested him. Lucien, if you don't speak out, people like Diddy are going to keep getting away with it. Now, show me where the rapper touched you."

I snigger, and his mate catches my eye with a mischievous smirk, but I can tell the dancer's made up his mind to ignore me. "If you can dance, you can act. It's all the same muscles."

"You'd be a great brain surgeon if you really wanted," says his mate.

The dancer nods thoughtfully. "I would. It's steady hands. My body is my instrument, and I have to train to control it."

"Right now, his testicles are doing somersaults and you can't even tell. Most people just mistake them for very excited tumours."

The dancer turns back to me and points to the seat opposite him on the bench. "Sit down, sit down, will you. I can tell we're gonna be friends. This is Kelvin, and I'm Lucien."

"Will," I say, taking a seat but keeping one eye on the stairs in case the steampunk comes back for an encore.

Lucien definitely moves like a dancer. He's not especially long-bodied, near as I can tell, but he's compact and deliberate, like he's making a conscious decision about where every part of his body is going to move before he moves it. Then when he reaches for his drink or waves his fag in the air to emphasise a point, he carries out his plan perfectly. He understands irony like an American, but he might actually have a point about being a brain surgeon. I can see those precise movements coming in handy. You don't want the man in the white coat getting twitchy when he's wrist-deep in your cerebral cortex.

I've got to admit, I've got a soft spot for people like Lucien. They've got that sort of feckless charm. I wouldn't want to get hitched to a Lucien, but they're usually good for a laugh. Kelvin, on the other hand, is a weird one. One of those people I can never really read. His face is expressive enough. I just can't tell what's in the undercurrents. He does have this permanent twinkle in his eyes that sometimes makes it as far as the corner of his mouth. I can't tell if he and Lucien are a couple, but either way if Lucien is the one steering this ship, it's only because Kelvin is letting him.

Lucien taps his fag over the ashtray with his forefinger. He's one of those people who hold their ciggie up in the air like a '40s film star. Bette Davis without the eyes.

"How long have you been in San Francisco?" Lucien asks.

"About five years. I was working in London before I moved, but you know all the really good tech jobs are in Silicon Valley."

And here's the other thing I can see coming a mile away. Lucien narrows his eyes at me suspiciously. "Oh, you're one of *them*."

"Ruining the tone of San Francisco," Kelvin chimes in, "what with your money and your gentrification. I used to be able to walk down Mission Street and find all the crack and hos and crack hos I ever wanted. Now I can't even piss on the walls. It's a disgrace."

"Yeah," Lucien says. "But since you're up to your tits in moolah, I'm gonna let you buy me a drink. Sex on the Beach," he adds, shaking his empty glass at me.

Kelvin rolls his eyes, but I don't say anything. The dancer obviously doesn't know what a real drink is, but I like him and I need to get something for myself anyway.

I take his glass and head over to the bar at the back of the garden. A few people are hanging around, but I'm lucky and no one is waiting to order. I get myself a beer and order Lucien one of his Sex on the Beaches. I can just about see the bartender raise an eyebrow at that, but I shrug.

There's two blokes sat next to me who look like they drive Volvos. You know the sort. The short one has Disney prince hair and clothes from Abercrombie & Fitch. The taller one is more of a jock, with a long, straight nose and hair that spikes at the front like he sprayed it and ran into a brick wall. I dunno what I expected them to be talking about, but I guess I'm surprised to hear they're talking art. I don't understand it all. Something about Neoclassicism, whatever that is.

A third one sidles up to them, and this one's kind of naff-looking, like a kicked puppy. He's not part of the conversation, but he wants to be. He opens his mouth to try and inject himself into the discussion, and I hold on to my hat. This ain't gonna be pretty. "I really like Romanticism," he says.

The awkward silence makes me really glad I don't know anyone involved. I try to keep my eyes ahead of me, but my ears are straining to hear every word.

"What?" says the short one, and I can't tell if it's because he couldn't hear over the music or if he can't believe what the naff one said.

"I like Romanticism," he says, and I feel like that was a bad move for him. Shoulda known when to shut his gob.

The short one smirks. "And what makes you think you like Romanticism?"

Ohhhhh shit, son, it is *on*.

"I know it can be divorced from reality," says the naff one defensively, "but that's the point. It has an elevating effect without having to rely on, like, specific contemporary or historical references. It transcends the context of its composition. You know?"

"Escapism," says the taller Volvo driver. He manages to look angry and bored at the same time. How is that even possible? His eyebrows are knitted together, and his mouth has a cruel twist, but he's not even looking at the naff one. He doesn't even think he's worth telling he's wrong. He's telling his friend instead. "It's puerile. We get infantilised enough by popular media without letting ourselves be coddled by *pop* art like Romanticism."

I'm suddenly on the side of the naff one. These twats are vivisecting him.

"It has no structure," adds the shorter one. "No message. It's just comforting eye-candy. You might as well go to the county fair and buy a painting of a unicorn in pink and glitter."

"You don't *really* like Romanticism," says the taller one. "You just think you do because you don't know better."

The naff one is trying, but it's like watching one of those zombie ants that's been taken over by a brain fungus. You just want to step on the bloody thing to put it out of its misery. "It's not that I don't like Neoclassicism or Impressionism, I just think they're a bit inaccessible, you know? They don't inspire anything in me the way—"

The shorter one cuts him off with a laugh, but he's not even laughing *at* him. He's laughing to his friend, like they're sharing a joke about a really ugly shirt in a shop window.

"See what I mean?" says the taller one to his friend. "People don't want to have to think. They just want something pretty to look at. That's why Facebook is full of pictures of cats and baby hedgehogs. 'Just hang in there! Jesus loves you.'"

"I mean I'm not a fan of *cat* pictures or anything, but art can have different significance for different people."

No, no. Dig *up*, stupid.

"Oh my God," gasps the smaller one between gusts of laughter. "He's a Postmodernist as well. I can't believe it."

I throw my money on the bar, grab my drinks, and get the hell out of there. Let 'em keep the change. It's better than being forced to watch those two stuff a kitten into a blender. There's only so much I can take.

I get back to the table and hand Lucien his drink with relief. They'll never know how glad I am to see them again.

"You look like you've seen a ghost," says Lucien. Then, in an unidentifiable accent: "Did a dingo eat your baybeeeeeee?"

Kelvin shakes his head. "Dude, wrong country."

"Lies, I am a master of accents. You heard Will. He agrees, and he's a real live English man."

I figure now's a good enough time to try and deflect the conversation around to Lucien. "Are you in any shows at the moment?" I ask him.

"I'm in *The Rocky Horror Show*."

I'm about to say that's cool when Kelvin says, "Ask him who he is."

Lucien gives him another one of those looks, but even he knows it's too late. He holds his head up high. "I'm playing the Criminologist."

"Who?" I ask.

"Why does everyone say that? It's a very important role."

"I'd love to come see it," I say. "I'm sure you're great."

That seems to calm him down a bit. Don't get me wrong, I do want to settle him down, but I pray I don't actually have to see that bloody show. It's one of those things, innit? You can't get through the night without promising to read a couple of books, watch a TV show that's now in its seventh series, and go skiing at Lake Tahoe, wherever that is.

"Well, at least that would be putting your millions of dollars to good use," Lucien concedes. "You might as well help a starving artist afford the rent in this city."

Kelvin checks his phone and says, "Seventeen minutes and forty-eight seconds."

"What?" asks Lucien.

"The time it took you to mention the rent in San Francisco. Don't feel bad, it's a statistical inevitability. You just Godwinned the conversation."

I have to jump in now. "Except it's not Godwin's Law, is it? That's how long it takes to mention Hitler. This is more like Kelvin's Law. You Kelvinned the conversation. You Kelvinned it so hard, it won't walk straight for a week."

"Yeah?" says Lucien. "Well, how about I Lucien your ass. How about that?"

"Loosen his what?" Kelvin asks, and I smile at Lucien's attempt to sound tough. He doesn't have the personality for it, know what I mean? It comes off more like a hissy fit. Cute in its way, but light beer is more threatening.

"I don't think The Boy would like that," I say. "He doesn't like it when I don't share."

"Will!" he says in that surprised-slash-accusing way where his voice goes up and down like a roller-coaster, ending high. "Wiiiiiilllll! You never said you had a 'The Boy.' You just got a little bit more interesting. Is he here?"

"He *was*," I say, checking my phone. Not a dicky-bird. I write *where r u* and turn back to Lucien. "I kind of lost him after he got into a barney with a lesbian."

Kelvin winces. "Oooh. Those don't end well. Lesbians win by default. It's like a law or something. I read that in a book. I am practically a lawyer."

I smile at the thought of Johnny hitting anyone at all. I saw him try to tenderise a steak once. He looked like a toddler hammering on those wood blocks.

My mobile buzzes. I check it quickly. It's from Johnny, but all it says is *fuck fuck fuck*. Maybe the steampunk really did slap him about. I feel suddenly guilty for leaving him up there alone. I'm about to go back and see if he's all right when I get another text: *feorge esccaped*. Then: *grge escapped*. Then *gorge*.

I'm no expert, but I'm starting to get the impression something's up.

RUN AWAY— his last text. Bloody autocorrect. Boy's not making a lick of sense.

"So, tell us about him," says Lucien. "What does he do?"

"He's an engineer."

Kelvin rolls his eyes. "Oh yes. We were forgetting the rule against dating outsiders. Gotta keep the bloodlines pure."

"I guess. But he's a front-end guy."

"I'll bet he is," says Kelvin. I'd hold it against him more if I hadn't made the same joke myself about a hundred times.

"All JavaScript. I don't understand most of it. He might as well be a lion tamer."

I double-check that last message. *RUN AWAY*.

"Maybe I'd just better check on him," I say. "See if he's all right."

"Only if you bring him back here!" says Lucien. "We need to get ourselves a look at your man."

I agree and go back to the stairs. I'm almost at the top when the door flies open, and Johnny comes barrelling down the stairs. He ploughs into me so hard we both fall against the handrail. For a second, it feels like we're about to tip over. The concrete below us looks very far away. My heart seizes up and I grab on to Johnny, but we're safe.

I feel a breeze in my hair and notice Johnny's knocked the steampunk's hat clear off my head. I hold on to the handrail extra tight and look down into the shadows. Lucien is moving over to pick it up.

LUCIEN

10:58 p.m.

3 hours 2 minutes remain

I straighten up, and I can feel the pull in my hamstring. It still hasn't healed from that music video I did. I told everyone I know I was gonna be in a video with Diddy, and all my friends kept going, "Oh my God, you're gonna be famous, can I come meet him?" And I was all like, "Maaaaybe. Let me run it by Diddy. You can't just ask famous people like us to pose for a photo, that's so rude." And maybe it was a stupid idea, but I thought for a hot second, I'd be a famous dancer and get more music videos even though I don't really want to do music videos. I'm more of an artist, and I want to choreograph my own shows because when I'm on the stage it's like a thirty-minute expression of who I am, a way to get out all the things that are always only on the inside.

And then I met Diddy. He was a lot hairier than I expected. And he had those gross, grabby hand-feet. And he was about two feet high.

"Where's Diddy?" I said.

"Here he is," said his agent.

"*P.* Diddy?"

"No, Diddy Kong."

Diddy Kong. It wasn't a rapper, it was a *monkey*. Fuck. My. Life. I bust my ass all day at dance academy just to be in a music video with a monkey. A monkey with an *agent* and about two million followers on YouTube. I don't even know why I try, I should just quit dancing and buy a monkey and go on the internet. The monkey was all right, I guess, except his little grabby hands still really freaked me out. His agent asked to see the routine I'd been working on, and I showed him, and he went, "Aw, yeah, Diddy's really going to like that. Do you think maybe we could work a banana in there or something? Last time we shot a video with a banana it got 200,000 likes."

That's when I pulled my hamstring. Turns out that little monkey bitch has got some moves. I couldn't let him steal the show, so I reached a little bit harder than I should and danced for the rest of the shoot on a bad leg because you can't let the monkey smell your fear. So, now there's a video of me on the internet back-up dancing like a psycho for a monkey with a banana. I can never tell anyone. And oh my God, I can *never* tell Kelvin. He'd never let me forget it.

I rub my thigh. I try to forget about it for tonight. I don't need to think about all the ways a monkey could ruin my career before it's even started. But the *Criminologist? Really?*

"I think you dropped your hat," I say, looking back at Will all the way up there on the stairs. He's got the lights behind him, so all I can see is him looking down with his arm half around someone who has the shadow of a total babe. I don't know who I'm jealous of more.

I sit back down next to Kelvin. I don't realize how big this stupid hat is until I try to find somewhere to put it. Oh look, that'll bug the crap outta Kelvin. I drop it on his head.

KELVIN

10:59 p.m.

3 hours 1 minute remain

"Here, you need something to give your face some character."

I pull away from Lucien, but he's already got the hat on my head. I adjust the brim a little. Gotta Bogart that shit up, yo.

"My face has plenty of character," I say. "Why do you think I never chose a life of crime and scurrility?"

"You were never a criminal," says Lucien, and I can hear that note of incomprehension with juuuuuust a hint of doubt. That makes it all worthwhile. Sometimes I can't tell if he's doing it because he really gets it and enjoys the game, or if he's just a bit dense. In the end, though, I don't think it matters. I like him either way.

"That's what I said. I was too recognizable to pull off any great heists. Look at these features. Do they not arrest your attention? Are you not hypnotized by my striking countenance? Can you even imagine trying to get a lineup of suspects who look like me? Impossible. I am a fulminant, a bolt of lightning that blasts the blackened earth with its uniquity."

"I'm going to get a photo of you and Diddy and tell people it's a spot-the-difference."

"Really?" I say. I'll be honest, I'm a little bit taken back by the surprise compliment. "You think I look like Diddy?"

"You have no idea," he says.

Maybe he's still talking, I'm not sure. I'm a mite distracted by Will and his fender-bender. They look like they know each other. Must be this much-ballyhooed front-end boy. They come down the stairs and sit at the bench on the other side of the table. At first, the friend is on the inside, but then he seems to get an attack of claustrophobia and wants to be on the outside. He swaps with Will, but now he's on the outside he feels too exposed. Will still looks a bit rattled by the head on, but on the whole he's still got his equilibrium. There's something afoot with the new one, though. He keeps checking the top of the stairs. Squirrelly motherfucker.

Will says to him, "What's the *matter* with you?"

Now I realize the friend is holding on to Will's arm. A bit too tightly, by the looks of it.

"Remember that...*thing* I told you about?"

"What thing? That stupid spider phobia?"

"It's not a phobia if it's a rational fear," says the friend a little too quickly, like he's said it before.

"We're at Aunty Bob's," Will protests. "Where are you going to—"

"The Log Lady had it," he gasps. "That's what she had in that shoebox. Who the actual fucking hell brings a tarantula into a bar?"

"George..." Will says.

"We're all going to die..." moans the boy.

Lucien decides it's been long enough since anyone paid any attention to him, and says, "Well it's great to meet you, George. I'm Lucien and this anonymous, unrecognizable master of disguise is Kelvin."

See what I mean? Not as dumb as he seems, sometimes. New theory: he plays dumb to lure me into a false sense of security and then catches me with my guard down.

"*I'm* not George," says the boy. "I'm Johnny."

"So, who's George, then?" Lucien asks.

I have the same question, but no way am I letting Lucien get away with this. I hold out my hand and, like a champ, he shakes it. "Hi," I say. "I'm George. Nice to meet you."

"You're Kelvin!" he protests.

"No, no, you're thinking of Lucien."

"*I'm* Lucien!"

I shake my head sadly. "Is that what Kelvin told you?"

"What's going on?" he shouts, on the verge of hysteria. "I feel like I'm taking crazy pills."

Johnny looks around the top of the stairs. "George is...*up there*."

I lean in close. I'm genuinely fascinated now. This just has to be good. "Who is George?"

Johnny doesn't seem to be able or willing to say it, but when I look across to Will, he beckons me closer. I stretch over the table and Will whispers it to me. This is *juicy*. If this gets any stranger, it's gonna be better'n mah stories.

"On the loose?" I ask, leaning back. He nods gravely. "*Log Lady*?" I ask.

Will gives me a "don't ask" kind of look. I don't have the first clue what's happening on the second floor, but I decide not to give Will the third degree. Damn, that's good. I wonder if there's any way I can work that into the conversation.

"Look, I don't have the first clue—"

"You don't have a drink!" Lucien barges in, throttling my wit in its crib. I'll get him for this, you see if I don't. In the meantime, is it worth making another attempt? Or has the moment passed?

Lucien is right, though. Johnny exited stage left pursued by a bear so quickly he left his drink upstairs. Will suggests they go get a fresh one from the bar in the corner, but not before he scopes it out to make sure the coast is clear. I know that look. I've seen it before. He's avoiding someone, maybe an ex. Or a hookup.

Johnny looks like he could use a drink. He also thinks he's safest out here, away from George's lair on floor two and the claustrophobic dance floor. Of course if George really *is* on the loose, the last place he'd want to go is a noisy space jam-packed with people. Chances are he's living it up right here in the beer garden, but I keep that to myself. Good thing *I* don't have any irrational fears. Except maybe saltwater taffy. And who's to say that's not rational?

Will and Johnny get up, and Will suggests they get something strong to calm Johnny's nerves. Well, they've come to the right place. "Strong?" I say. "If you really need a jolt of Dutch courage, get him one of Andre's specials. It'll knock your dick into your watch pocket."

"Is that good?" Will says with some very rewarding bewilderment.

"Good? What's goodness got to do with it?" I turn back to Lucien to find him staring at me.

"You are such a retard," he says. I point to myself questioningly. "*Yes,*" he says. "You are Doctor Who in the retardis. You are retardosaurus rex. They wanted to put you in the retard class but you were just too damn retarded." I take a happy little bow, or at least the best I can manage while I'm sitting. "You know Andre's special is gonna kill him, right?"

"That or it will fuse with his DNA and create some kind of rampaging mutant destroying the entire Castro. Then he'll kidnap you and climb to the top of the Transamerica Pyramid. Then the Blue Angels will shoot him down, and when he hits the sidewalk he'll explode and die. *Then* how you gonna feel, huh? Huh?"

To be honest, I could tell Lucien tuned out halfway through, but that's only more motivation to push him farther and farther until I get a reaction out of him. He just takes a placid sip from his cocktail and says softly, "I'm gonna tell him to land on your apartment."

I don't know why I don't hang out with Lucien more often.

A loud crack blasts through the beer garden. Everyone jumps. A few people lose drinks. Lucien's clutching his pearls, but I notice he hasn't spilled any of his cocktail despite how dramatically he swooned.

"That frightened the skaboopy out of me," he says.

"What in the name of flying rainbow Jesus was it?" I ask.

"Probably Johnny starting to hulk out," he says in the derpy voice he does when he's imitating me.

Seriously though, what the hell *was* that? It was like a lightning strike right overhead. People are looking around, confused about where the noise came from. A lot of them seem to be looking at the outdoor speakers like it was a glitch in the sound system, but I'm positive it came from the direction of the bathrooms. From what I can see from here, no one inside seems very troubled by the noise. Probably too loud to hear anything at all.

"I'm gonna check it out." I step over the bench and make for the door.

"Be careful," he calls after me, suddenly serious.

I wander over to where the bathrooms are. They're inside the club, just around the corner from the short hall. The back of the bathrooms have windows onto the garden, but the doors are on the far side facing the club. When I get there, there's one nebbish-looking guy waiting outside. By the way he's hopping from one foot to the other, I'd guess he's been waiting a while.

I go for the door but he says, "Excuse me, there's a line!" He's shouting over the music—probably didn't even hear the noise himself.

"Is it full?" I ask.

He nods anxiously.

"I just want to look," I say.

He gives me a weird look. "Okay, but I'm still next."

I push open the door and step inside. I get my confirmation I'm in the right place. There's a smell. I mean more than the usual one of prodigious sprays of urine that somehow manage to hit everything except the target and combines with the urinal cakes to form an even more deadly mutant stank. This is different. The air is sort of tingly and has that sweet, acrid smell you get around bumper cars. It's getting up my nose and making it itch. I go to scratch it and I flinch. A blue spark just jumped from the tip of my finger to the end of my nose. What the hell? It stung a little, but I guess I'm more surprised than anything else.

On the wall to my left is one urinal and a toilet stall. On the right is a sink with a busted-ass soap dispenser on the wall. Instead of fixing the fancy dispenser, management has opted just to put a disposable hand pump on the edge of the sink. I can tell from here they're out of paper towels, and there isn't a hand dryer in sight. That *is* weird. I would have bet anything that sound was an electrical fault, like maybe one of the dryers exploding.

I check the sink and the pipes, but there's no sign of anything electrical except the lights, which look like they're working just fine. The pipes are all intact, too. There's nothing that might have made a noise like that—no exploded hand dryers, no detonated time bombs, no immolated fireworks.

In fact there's no one in here at all.

I step back out into the club and ask the guy waiting, "Did you see people go in?"

"Yeah. What are they doing? I'm bursting."

"It's all yours, buckaroo," I say. And because I feel like a buckaroo needs a garnish, I take off that amazingly ridiculous hat and slap it on his head.

FRANCIS

11:25 p.m.

2 hours 35 minutes remain

Buckaroo? I think as the strange man leaves. I want to go after him and give him this hat back, but I can't right now, I really need to use the bathroom. But then what if he does want his hat back? I might have to carry it around all night until he comes to get it. And what happens if I don't have it any more? He might be angry. He seemed like he might be unstable. What's the sign of a sociopath? It's a retarded sense of empathy. But how can you tell? Do they have facial expressions? Did *he* have facial expressions? I can't remember. He might have done this on purpose, just to give himself an excuse to punch me. There's no telling what he might do.

How long would it take the bouncers to save me if I got into a fight? Too long. I should just run away as soon as I see him coming. I can't win a fistfight, but maybe I can run faster than him. But he's tall—he's like a cross-country runner. God, what if he is a runner? I won't stand a chance. What am I doing? I'll never be able to outrun him. I'll just be a hat thief, and I'll get into a fight and then I'll be dead. But God, at least I'll get to urinate before I die.

I push open the bathroom door carefully. I don't want to interrupt the people inside. He said it's all mine. What did he mean? I'm dying to go, but there's nothing worse than having to wait behind someone at a urinal, pretending you're not watching someone with his penis in his hand while he's releasing a stream of urine right in front of you, all the time trying desperately not to accidentally catch a glimpse of *it*. What would happen if someone thought I was peeking?

Actually something *is* worse than standing behind someone at a urinal—being stood behind when *you're* at a urinal. Once I had to use the old trough the Castro Theatre used to have, and that wasn't by choice, I can tell you. The line went out the door, around the corner, and up the stairs, and the stall doors stayed shut and stayed shut and stayed shut until I thought they'd taken up residence there. I *had* to use the trough.

As soon as I stepped on the platform, trying to keep my shoes out of the damp splatter on the tiles, one of the stalls opened up behind me. By the time I turned my head it was already taken again, so there was no escaping The Trough. Waiting for me like a crooked yellow grin. Laughing at me as I unzipped and pulled it out, wondering what size it's going to be this time. It was a cold night, but then it's always cold in San Francisco.

It was too small, I know it was, and I *knew* that guy on my right had seen it. How could I tell him it's usually bigger? My eyes darted to one side, but I forced them back ahead of me. I *refused* to look at the man on either side. But at the same time I had to ignore the one behind me, watching, waiting, *judging*. Nothing came out. I froze. Didn't know what to do. The longer I waited, the more I felt them staring at me to see what I would do. I couldn't fail. I couldn't let them *see* me fail. In the end, I waited until the men on either side had rotated out, shook it once or twice as if I'd just gone, and left. That way each of the sets of strangers would think I'd peed during the other set's watch.

I think I handled that pretty smoothly.

But now, as I enter the bathroom, I see my fears were misplaced. There's only one urinal, and there's no one at it. There's only one stall too, and no one's in that either.

For a second, I'm more relieved than anything else, but then I stop in confusion. I look around for another door or anywhere else they might have gone. There's nothing except for a small, high window on the far wall that opens onto the beer garden. It's the kind that opens outward at the top and hinges on the bottom, like a transom. The gap is nowhere near big enough to squeeze a person through, and if they'd tried, their weight would have broken the glass or the hinges or *something*.

And yet I know when I came in here the first time there were two people—one at the urinal and one in the stall. I waited outside the door the whole time, and the only person who went in or out was the man with the red hat.

But there's something else different now as well, a sort of burnt smell in the air. It's not the cigarette smoke from outside, though I can smell that, too. It's something that tingles. It makes the hair stand up on the back of my neck.

The door behind me crashes open, and before my brain can catch up with my body, I'm making a dash for the stall. I slam the door shut behind me. I hope I've been fast enough to avoid being seen, but then in frustration I silently curse myself for hurrying too much. I probably slammed the stall door so hard he heard me when he came in.

It doesn't matter. I'm bursting, and I'm alone here in my little stall, protected from the world. So close to home. I ease the cheap plastic lock into place in case it makes a sudden noise and draws more attention to the fact I'm here. The door is sealed. I'm safe at last.

I turn to the toilet bowl. Don't ask me why but I'm wearing these briefs that don't have that penis flap at the front. That means to urinate standing up, I either have to perform some acrobatics and pull down the front of the waistband by manipulating it through the little window of my pants fly, or I can simply drop both my pants and underpants to my knees. This latter option can be more fraught with risk. I have to be sure to avoid letting my pants touch the floor, where I shudder to think what they might touch, but it does have the advantage of letting me urinate unencumbered by any unnecessary acrobatics.

I opt for dropping my pants and try not to pay too much attention to my penis and testicles. It's another chilly night, and the presence of someone else in the bathroom is only making me more apprehensive. My testicles have retreated up toward my abdominal cavity in an attempt to regulate their temperature, while my penis looks white and withered like that of a naked child at a public pool. The effect is not helped by the fact that I have no body hair. One man with whom I had a regrettable one-night stand remarked that I looked like a shaved cat. I didn't know how to respond to that, so I didn't.

I reach out to hold it and—ow! What on earth was that? A spark just jumped from my finger to the tip of my penis. I can feel it still, a tingling, burning around the head. I look around in case I'm touching a live wire or something, but everything looks normal to me.

Then a whisper comes. "It's that Romanticist again."

I must have made a noise in my surprise. And suddenly I realize who just came into the bathroom. It's *them* again, the ghouls from the bar. They're on the other side of the stall partition, and they have just recognized me. One of them is at the urinal, and the other sounds like he is waiting by the bathroom door. I can't tell which is which, but under the gap at the bottom of the partition, I can see the right shoe of whichever one is at the urinal. I wonder if I can just wait in here until they leave.

The one at the urinal shifts his stance, and then I hear him say to his friend, "He's taken his pants all the way down."

I look down and realize they can see the top of my pants from under the partition. They know I'm naked while I'm peeing standing up. At this exact second, they're picturing my butt sticking sadly out from under the hem of my shirt while I clutch my withered penis between my fingers.

The other one suppresses a snicker. "Hey, sorry about

earlier," he says, even though I can tell he's not. "I didn't mean to scare you away."

The one at the urinal whispers something to his friend, but I can't make out what it is.

The other one's apology seems to demand a response. "That's okay," I say and wish I hadn't. I could have pretended it wasn't me. Now I've confirmed it.

Maybe he meant it. Maybe I misjudged him and he really was apologizing, but I would have preferred to forget the whole thing happened and pretend they didn't exist.

The one at the urinal finishes up and goes to wash his hands. His friend takes his place at the urinal and starts to urinate. That's when I realize I've been standing here this whole time and have not even started yet.

I try, I really do. But you know how it is when you're stressed. My bladder is stretching out like an overfilled water balloon and the deluge is pounding at the gates of my urinary sphincter. I whisper to it inaudibly to convince it to relax. It quivers. It bows like a failing dam. But it does not fail. *Just open. Just open and we can all be happy.* I push, begging anything to happen, but it's as if pushing only knots up my urethra harder and puts even more pressure against my bladder until I feel certain I'm about to rupture something and flood my internal organs with urine. The second one's strong, confident stream splatters into the urinal, and it's like listening to a powerful fire hose. That is how a real man urinates, but I can't produce a single drop.

The pressure keeps building, and now it feels like my own will is no longer responsible for containing it. Paradoxically, the pain lessens a bit as my bladder floods past danger point. I know I have even less time now.

I hear him finally zip up and wash his hands. He's going agonizingly slowly. If I can hold on for just a few more seconds, I'll hear that bathroom door open, the monsters will leave, and I can finally undo the knot in my urethra. But that sound never comes. I wait and wait. Then I hear one whispering something I can't quite understand to the other. Probably some crack about how I've been standing in front of this toilet for minutes now without making a single sound. They're not leaving. They're never leaving. The only way I can possibly save any face now is to flush, exit the cubicle, and act like I've done my business. Just like I did at the Castro Theatre.

I flush the empty toilet and exit the stall. There they are, standing by the towel dispenser with expectant smirks on their faces. The second they see me, they both crack up all over again.

"What?" I say hotly. "What is it now?"

That's when I realize I'm still wearing the red hat the stranger put on my head right before I came in. I catch sight of my reflection in the mirror above the sink. I look ridiculous.

I briefly consider taking it off, but I have nowhere to put it, and it doesn't seem right to leave it here. Taking it off would only be an admission of weakness.

I wash my hands stoically and go to wipe my hands. I pause for a second at the dispenser—there are no towels left. With as much dignity as I can muster, I wipe my hands on my pants. The two are watching me every step of the way. I pass them as I make for the bathroom door. Right before I open it, I make a half turn back to them and bid them good night: "Gentlemen."

I step out into the club again. The beat is pounding so hard I can feel it bounce around my bladder like quake vibrations. It's throbbing inside me. The beat is almost enough to unlock my sphincter through its visceral power and cause me to wet my pants. Me, a twenty-four-year-old man wetting himself in the middle of a nightclub. It doesn't bear thinking about.

Something is wrong.

For some reason everyone in the room is looking at something behind me. I look back, but there's no one there. I turn back to the crowd and realize everyone is looking at *me*. I glance down as subtly as I can to make sure I've zipped my fly back up. I have. I look back up, maybe too quickly. Do they know I was just checking my own crotch? What are they staring at? It doesn't make sense. Maybe they've figured it out. Maybe someone told them. They must know.

"Well come on up, honey, don't be shy," says a voice that's all nose. "I don't bite…hard!" The voice booms around the whole club. On the stage, an aging drag queen beckons me to join him.

I shake my head in horror. This can't be happening. Hands reach out to pull me toward the stage. I hear the bathroom door open behind me, and the two Neoclassicists step out. There's nowhere to hide. For lack of a better option, I'm letting myself be shepherded onstage. I'm trying to make my brain work, to figure a way out of this, but I can't. Nothing is working because my bloated bladder is filling up all the space in my head.

I climb onto the stage with difficulty. Any pressure on my midsection right now will be a catastrophe.

The drag queen grasps my arm in his claws and pulls me upright. I'm standing here in front of everyone, lights in my eyes, skin burning and holding a swimming pool in my bladder.

"Where are you from, sweetie?" he asks, then pushes the microphone at me. It is shaped like an erect penis. Suddenly the terror grips me that I might clench so hard I give myself an erection.

"San Luis Obispo," I mumble into the glans.

"Aww, is this your first visit to civilization?"

A movement at the foot of the stage distracts me. The monsters have made their way to the front to witness my humiliation firsthand.

"No, I—"

"What do we do with virgins?" shrieks the drag queen. He's reaching for something in his purse.

The two in the front row are almost horizontal with laughter.

The drag queen withdraws a big, pink ray gun from her handbag. "Hold still, beautiful. Glitter don't hurt. Just don't get it in your eyes or you'll get a big ol' case of pink eye."

"Shoot him!" they shout. "Shoot him!" Their faces flash in

the strobe lights, smooth, pretty, distorted into ugly shapes, their eyes compressed into slits, their teeth glistening, lips pink and soft, curling, cruel.

An ominous rumble reverberates across the stage. It thunders in my bladder. Now I know I'm going to die.

I stop trying to hold it back. I'm ready, I'm *ready* to piss myself right here and now on this stage if it means I'll save my own internal organs.

The monsters whoop and yowl in the front row, falling over themselves with evil laughter. I clench my hands into fists. Red palms. White knuckles. If I could punch, I would kill them with my fists alone. I don't care if they *are* stronger. I have the rage and I can take them down with me. There's a stabbing pain in my guts. It's too late for me now. I'm already dead, but I *will* kill them. I hurl myself into the crowd and land on top of the taller one. He goes down with me on top of him.

"What the fuck?" he screams, squirming underneath me. He can't make much progress with me sitting on his chest. His head is right between my legs.

"You want a piece of me?" I screech. My head is burning. Flames. Flames on the side of my face. "Hit me! Go on!"

He catches me in the stomach with his fist. Hard. The force against my sphincter is unbearable, and for a moment it feels like it's suddenly, mercifully, burst. And then the pressure is finally released, and I'm so relieved it hurts.

There's screaming. And someone knocks the hat off my head.

LAWRENCE

11:46 p.m.

2 hours 14 minutes remain

The hat seems to skeeve a lot of people out. I don't know why. It wasn't even touching the puddle, and anyway, urine is sterile. You could chug a gallon of the stuff, and you wouldn't catch anything from it. I don't know why you'd want to unless you're heavily into water sports, but you could, and between you and me, I know a couple of people who would.

More people than you think are adult babies. That's people who wear diapers and suck pacifiers and, yes, they will even piss themselves so their "parents" can change them. And scold them for being a stinky baby. You can see them walking down the street at Folsom, but if you're smart, you'll take my advice and won't look too closely at their diapers. You won't like what you see, even if it does happen to be clean. Which it won't.

Though I've gleaned from babyfurs that shitting the diaper is a notorious *faux pas* in the wrong circles. I was talking to the host of a crinkle party, who was furious that one of his guests had taken a dump in his bed. I didn't find out whether that dump was in a diaper or not, but I'm okay not knowing some things. I don't like to yuck other people's yums and if you get a hard-on whenever you smell talcum powder then I'm not going to tell you it's wrong, but thank you no, that particular vintage is not for me.

I check the inside of the hat and find the label. It's a cheaper brand, but I could already tell that just by feeling it. It's not fur felt. It's wool felt, like those cheap costume hats people wear to parties. Still, it's not a bad hat for the price and I think it gives me a nice profile, so I decide to keep it. It wouldn't be hard to mod it, maybe put some wolf ears sticking up through the brim, then I could wear it to Further Confusion next year.

I can tell you from experience walking around is a lot more comfortable with a partial suit, or even just ears and a tail, than it is wearing the whole fur suit. You sweat. A lot. I'll step out of my custom commissioned fur suit looking like I just ran a marathon. I've even seen people have sex in them, which is another league of athleticism entirely. I, on the other hand, prefer to have my reproductive organs free and unfettered, although on the downside you don't get to dress up as your actual fursona. I suppose it depends which one means more to you—your fursona or your electrolytes.

I am standing to one side of the dance floor looking for anybody I know. The crowd filled back up as soon as Mr. Robinson cleaned the urine off the floor and now things are starting to get crowded. I really want to find that pretty steampunk girl again, but she said she had to go to the restroom, and I haven't seen her since then. She probably got sidetracked.

I wonder if I should go find her. It seems all too likely she has become embroiled in some quagmire of a conversation from which she is unable to extricate herself. I would want someone to give me a convenient excuse to leave, but then I doubt I'd have a problem outlining for the other person exactly how insufficient their attempts at conversation really were. I'm sure she was smiling at me.

I hide my face as I catch sight of Andre on the other side of the bar. Mercifully, there are enough proles in the way that I think I have maintained my anonymity, but for one moment I fear he may have caught sight of me when he appears to squint in my direction as if *I'm* the one who's done something wrong. Then he's gone, and I can't see where he went. That is unlike him. While I am able to move in and out of crowds with the artistry of a cat burglar, Andre tends to make a scene and carry it with him wherever he goes. It is unlike him to vanish so effectively into the night, as it were.

I inch around the corner of the bar, being cautious that I will still be able to keep myself anonymous should he suddenly reappear. But he has not jumped out at me yet. And now I see a door recessed into the wall, painted black, marked "PRIVATE." It seems almost impossible that anyone should want to consult that buffoon on any matter of business whatever, let alone something related to the operation of an establishment like Aunty Bob's. I happen to know the proprietor, and he certainly has more business sense than to invite random customers into his inner sanctum. And yet where else can Andre have gone?

I make my way inconspicuously to the door marked "PRIVATE." I catch the whiff of cigarette smoke not coming from the vapers in the club. Someone is smoking inside. Menthols, unless I am very much mistaken. It is impossible to hear anything through the hubbub, but it is extremely fortunate that *I* am here to take care of the matter. I keep a "camera bag" at my side at all times for precisely this kind of undertaking. This is where I keep all the devices I use during my off-hours when I occasionally moonlight as a private detective. I can't say that it is frequently edifying work, but I always enjoy being able to apply my skills to solve a problem. From the bag I withdraw a small black cylinder that attaches almost unnoticeably to the door.

Now I can stand back a bit so I don't look too suspicious. I take out my phone, put in the earbuds, and connect to the microphone. Now we're cooking with gas. I can hear everything going on inside the office.

Andre's in there all right. And so is Mr. Robinson.

"What do you know about him?" asks Mr. Robinson.

"I never met him before."

"Never?" There is a pause. "You know I could have you barred from this club."

I can't help smiling. The thought of an Andre-free haunt in the Castro scarcely bears thinking about. I wonder if there's anything I can do to shit the bed—diaper off—and blame the turd on him.

"This is bullshit. I already told you, I never saw him before. What do you want? Who is that guy even?"

"Trouble. Maybe dangerous trouble, I don't know. But after all these shootings, I don't like to take any chances. This is *my* house, do you understand me? And if anyone threatens me or my family, I will eat them whole and shit out their skulls.".

"Shootings?"

"Now you understand. What I want to know is why he was so interested in you."

"I don't know. I don't know anything. What do you want me to say?"

"Don't lie to me."

"Are you for serious right now?"

There is a long pause.

"All right, I believe you. But something stinks, and I don't like it. Who did you come here with?"

"I was hoping I'd find Amy tonight. Have you seen her? Short, dresses like a lesbian. *Is* a lesbian."

"That isn't what I asked. Who did you come here with?"

"Tom-boy? He's harmless."

"How well do you know him?"

"We met online—" Mr. Robinson must have interrupted him with a look because Andre rushes to add, "Everyone meets online now. He's a good guy, I promise. But y'know, don't tell him I said that."

"How well do you know him?"

I am startled out of my concentration when a meaty forefinger taps me on the shoulder. I look up from my phone and see the bouncer from when I walked in, the extremely nonverbal one with the swollen eyeballs and hairy teeth. I reluctantly pull out my earbuds.

"Two-drink minimum," he says, like those are the only three words he knows. I recognize this strategy. He's decided he doesn't like the look of me hanging around, so he's trying to get me to move along. Little does he know with whom he has chosen to tango. I am not so easily moved, hustled, or shooed.

"I don't drink," I say. "I told you before, my judgment must remain untrammeled at all times."

"Two-drink minimum," he says again, as if it were a valid counterargument.

"I'm telling you I don't drink, and when I do I must have complete equilibrium of mind and body to appreciate the subtle bouquet of the liquors. The idea that I would drink anything concocted in this swamp is making my anal sphincter contract in horror."

"Two-drink minimum," he says, and this time he looks like he means it.

"Well, if you insist," I say, humoring him. "I suppose I could manage a tipple."

I start toward the bar when I remember the microphone still attached to the door. A glance back tells me the bouncer is still there, staring at me with pop-eyed incomprehension. I turn back. I'm out of range of the microphone. Best forget it for the time being and collect it later when no one's looking.

Despite the growing crowd, I'm just about able to get to the bar. I slam my hand down a couple of times and say, "Barman! I shall have a *dry* martini. Do you know how to make a *dry* martini?"

"I know how to make a martini," he says.

"After you pour the gin, I want you to bring the glass into proximity with a bottle of vermouth and show it the label. *That* is how you make a dry martini." I smile and wait for him to laugh, but he doesn't. That does not surprise me somehow. He is even more of a troglodyte than the neolithic bouncer. He is working at a bar, after all, and doesn't even know how to make a proper martini.

"Do you want well gin or—"

"Or! Or!" I say before he can get any further. Well gin! You can drink well gin if you like, but we all know those are the same people who buy wool felt hats and piss themselves in nightclubs.

"Do you have Monkey 47?" I ask, knowing he won't.

"We don't have that," he says stoically.

I huff. "Well, I suppose Tanqueray will have to do."

The drink lackey goes to mix me my martini, and although I make a show of not paying any attention to him while he's doing it I am actually watching him very closely. Sure enough, he dumps a gallon of vermouth into the shaker. Typical. My martini will be ruined.

I pay him, but make very sure to collect my change. The man doesn't deserve a tip if he's going to go murdering a perfectly good martini with an overdose of vermouth. And look at these nasty, cheap Spanish olives. I hate this drink already and I haven't even tried it yet.

As I take my first sip, I catch sight of someone I know from FC. Ashen is sitting at one of the tables by the wall with a few other people whom I don't recognize. I attempted to flirt with Ashen a couple of years ago at the Critterlympics, but he was still transitioning and was not ready to date anyone yet. That was shortly before I caught him with his hand down someone's pants at the Saturday dance, but I don't hold it against him. I know people have to lean on their polite fictions in the name of diplomacy. I just wish they wouldn't bother with *me*.

I wander over to them and call out, "Ashen!" He doesn't look up at first, but when I call his name again, he looks over and sees me.

"Hello, Lawrence."

"It's been too long," I say, parking myself in a spare seat and placing my wretched martini on the table. "I've been very busy lately."

"I've been—" he starts, but I'm not finished yet. Ashen's a nice guy, but he has to learn not to interrupt all the time.

"I spent all last weekend LARPing in Mendocino. I was a Dragonborn foot soldier. I'd have preferred to be an archer, but the guild's equipment is woefully inadequate and they ran out of bows, but I've used them before and they are impossible to work with anyway. So, it's night on the first day of the campaign, and I persuade our generals to stage a night raid on the Blood Elves' castle in order to recapture the Starlightstone of Elamar. The Blood Elves didn't see us coming. We crept through the forest and surprised them. Most of our troops attempted to storm the drawbridge, but I feinted back and went around the side of the castle. When one of the watchmen spotted me from up on the ramparts, I managed to convince him I was a Blood Elf scout returning with information about the Dragonborns' battle plans. He allowed me into the castle where I gave him the slip. As I wandered through the hallways, you *would not believe* who I found—the king! He had his back to me and was watching the main door anticipating news of the Elves' victory. I could hear our troops were being beaten back, and it looked like the Elves were about to win. That's when I tapped him on the shoulder and said, 'You may consider yourself assassinated.'"

Everyone has gone quiet, and I can tell they're hanging on to my every word. I'm about to continue the story and tell them how I located the jewel in the castle's booby-trapped vaults, but the music stops abruptly, and we hear this over the speakers:

"Why can't you treat me like I would be treated by any stranger on the street?"

"Because…"

And then the whole club stops what they're doing and chimes in: "I AM NOT ONE OF YOUR FANS!"

Then the music launches into Whitney Houston singing

"I Will Always Love You," and everyone starts laughing and chatting again.

I turn to one of the people sitting with Ashen and say, "That's a great movie. Do you know what movie that's from?"

He says, "Yeah. I was quoting it."

"It's from *Mommie Dearest*," I say, in case he just knows the quote but doesn't know the movie itself. "It's about the relationship between Joan Crawford and her daughter Christina."

He looks at me strangely. Possibly he is a bit simple, though I will concede he is rather attractive in a conventional sense. He has a perfect amount of scattered blond stubble and a cute little nose that's turned up ever so slightly at the end. When he talks, I can just about catch a glimpse of the teeth between his lips. They are like smooth white pebbles on a beach beneath a burning sunset. I find myself hoping he will smile so I can see them emerge. But he is not smiling for some reason.

"I'm Lawrence," I say, holding out my hand and doffing my hat to him.

He looks impressed at how fluidly I did that, and he shakes my hand. "Benny," he says.

"Benjamin! It is indeed a pleasure to meet you."

The conversation seems to have slowed down now. He's at a loss for words, no doubt. I've given him more than enough opportunity to speak, but now it seems like it's up to me to breathe some life into things.

But before I can say anything, he surprises me by asking, "Are you watching the new season of *Drag Empire*?"

I shake my head. "I don't like drag."

"Why not?"

"Well, since you ask," I say now that I'm sure I have his rapt attention, "it's just not interesting. What's supposed to capture my attention—watching men put on makeup for an hour? Or watching them parade around in heels and fake breasts? There's nothing funny about it because none of them are any good as comedians. The only joke they're making is, 'Look, I'm a man dressed like a woman.' There's no wit or intelligence in it, and it isn't remotely attractive. Who gets turned on watching a bunch of men dressed like Baby Jane? And that's leaving out the fact that drag is incredibly sexist. It's the equivalent of blackface in all significant regards. It's a grotesque, exaggerated representation of the appearance of another group of people in order to mock them. It's a minstrel show. If you cared at all about feminism, you would be more like me and take no interest in it whatever."

He looks at me and asks, "How do you know Ashen again?"

"We met at FC two years ago," I say, and I can see Ashen giving me a look to try and shut me up. But what right does he have to tell me to be quiet? I am who I am, and I'm not ashamed of that. I will not bear pretending to be something else.

"FC?" Benjamin asks.

"Further Confusion. It's a furry convention in San José every year," I say, shifting in my seat to rearrange the semi I can feel creeping unbidden into my loins.

"Ashen, you never said you were a furry!"

I can sense where Benjamin's conversation is going, and I have to derail this train of thought immediately. "We're not all perverts. It's a legitimate subculture for the appreciation of anthropomorphic media."

"And porn," says Ashen. I almost nod, but I catch myself. Before I can respond, Ashen continues. "There's a saying, by and large furries are bi and large."

Benjamin starts howling with the laughter of someone who doesn't understand what wit is.

"They also say," Ashen gasps, "that if you want to get laid at a furry convention, the odds are good but the goods are odd."

Benny—if that *is* his real name—is now laughing even harder and looking at me very pointedly.

Don't think I don't know what's going on. Ashen, the traitorous Quisling, is trying to wash his hands of the whole fandom so he can look cool in front of his friends. I'm furious to feel myself flushing. I hope the others can't see. It's obvious that

Benny thinks those "jokes" were a reference to me. I don't know why I should care what this mediocrity thinks. It's not like I was trying to hit on him. He's not that attractive anyway. His snub-nose is extremely aggravating, and I'm positive I can smell the breath coming off his moldy tongue.

I shiver and take off my hat.

BENNY

12:11 a.m.

1 hour 49 minutes remain

"Here," he says, jamming the hat on my head. "Take this. It's cheap and ugly, like you."

"What the fuck?" I say, trying to get away from this neckbeard.

"You're an ugly little—" He's saying a bunch of stuff right now, and I don't understand *any* of it. He's probably making it all up anyway, like that dumbass story he just told us about the Dragonbutts versus the Twink Elves or whatever. But I catch enough to know what he's calling me, and *no one* calls me ugly.

"I'm not ugly, fat ass. You look like the northern end of a southbound camel."

"Oh sure, real classy," he says. "Thank you, William Shakespeare. Won't you furnish us with another one of your nuggets of wit and wisdom? Please, your adoring public awaits." People are starting to look in our direction. The Dragonbutt is making a scene.

Well, he wants a nugget, Imma squat over his face and deposit a nugget right on it. I tip the hat at him and say, "M'lady."

He turns as red as a smacked ass. It looks like he's getting ready to stand up, but it might take him a while because he's so big and the tugboats aren't in the harbor. I decide to let him stew while I get another drink. No one messes with this bitch.

The bartender sees the hat and looks pissed off for a second, but then he sees my face. "Oh, sorry. I thought you were someone else."

"I know ex*act*ly who you mean," I say with a glance back at the Dragonbutt. Now it looks like he's chewing out Ashen. I can't read lips, but I'm pretty sure Ashen's telling him to suck a bag of dicks. "Is he for real?"

The bartender nods sadly, and I can tell the Dragonbutt must be a regular. "What can I get you?"

A few people around the club have been drinking these weird-looking drinks I never saw before. It's got to be something good.

"What's that pretty purple sparkledrank?" I ask, pointing at one nearby.

"That's Andre's special."

"What's in it? No! Don't tell me. I don't need to know how the sausage is made."

I wink at him and he smiles back. He's kind of a cute one, too—super buff, almost like a bodybuilder, and his arms are covered in geometric tattoos. Nice chest. He is wearing the hell outta that shirt. He's maybe in his late thirties, but it looks good on him. He's got a nice muscle daddy vibe going on.

"I remember you," I say. I don't, but watch and learn. "Weren't you on bar last week?"

"Yeah. I remember you, too. You were in here on Thursday. You spilled your cosmo and licked it off the bar."

"Noooo, you're thinking of someone else. I wouldn't do that." God, I absolutely did that.

"I have a good memory for faces," he says. "Especially the cute ones." I grin again and I can tell he likes it. He puts the drink in front of me. "Here you go, one sparkledrank."

Fuck. I wasn't watching, and now I have no idea what's in it.

I stir it and watch the drink swirl with purple mushroom clouds. It tastes delicious.

"Damn, that looks hella good," says someone next to me at the bar. He's got glitter at the corners of his eyes. The lights catch it and sometimes his whole face looks like it's sparkling. Then the lights go dark and I almost lose him in the shadows. He turns to the bartender. "Imma get two o' them sparkledranks."

"Two sparkledranks coming up." The bartender turns to me. "I think you might have started a thing."

A new boy shows up at the bar, no one I'd call cute, but he dresses to make up for it, a blazer and an ascot over a T-shirt. "What the hell's going on?" he says. "Why is everyone drinking my drink?"

I'm about to say something but I don't have to. Glitter boy does all the talking for me. "It's sparkledrank! This shit's tasty as fuck."

"I know it's tasty as fuck, I invented it. It's my drink, and it's called my special."

"I ain't got time for this shit, I'm tryin' to get my drank on."

"What? What are you even saying to me right now?" There is an order at the other end of the bar for more sparkledrank, which makes him freak out even more. "It's not sparkledrank! Why is everyone calling it sparkledrank?" He looks up at the blackboard and sees the bartender has just written "SPARKLEDRANK" on the board in chalk that glows in the black light. He screams, "Oh my God! Take that the fuck down."

Then the ratch grabs glitter boy's drink from right under his nose. As he goes for mine too, he gets distracted by something else. "*And* that's my hat. Who gave that to you? Give that back."

Glitter doesn't care about my hat, though, and tries to grab his drink back from Ascot. "What the fuck, dude? Give it back, thot ass bitch."

Ascot hustles the stolen drink away from Glitter's reach. "What? What did you call me?"

"Oh, you heard. You need to calm your tits."

"Fuck y'all," says Ascot. "Fuck all y'all. You're all a bunch of cunts." He slams Glitterboy's drink back on the bar and stamps off into the crowd.

Shit just got real. Glitter grabs his drink back off the bar and I tell him, "You go, girl. I dunno what the fuck that was all about."

"Bitch try to steal my sparkledrank."

"Check your drink," I say. "She probably tried to slip you a Hot Cosby." I look back and see the neckbeard has left now, probably so he can find someone else to trap with his awful stories, so I decide to go back to find Ashen. "Catch you later." Then I turn to the bartender. "And I *know* I'll be seeing you later."

Glitter cracks a grin. "Ooh, dream on, boy. That man's straight."

"What? Nooooo, we were flirting."

"Uh-huh. And did you tip him?"

I nod but say, "Nah, you dunno what you're talking about." I look back at the bartender. He hasn't overheard us, but he sees me looking at him and winks. God damn it.

I go back over to Ashen and luckily I can get my seat back. I can't figure out how no one else has taken it yet until I sit down and realize there's this rank foot smell in the air. That neckbeard just armpitted the place up.

"You won't believe what just went down at the bar," I say, but Ashen shushes me and points to someone behind him who has just walked into the club. He's an older man with a sculpted white beard and mustache wearing *every* bit of steampunk kitsch he could find: a top hat covered in cogs, circle sunglasses, fingerless gloves, and a cane he looks like he actually needs. He limps to the bar and seems to waft through the crowd. He belongs at Specs' in North Beach, not at Aunty Bob's, and everyone knows it. They're acting like he's not even there. We lose sight of him when he disappears behind the bar.

"Grampaw Death," says Ashen, waving his fingers spookily.
"Try this," I say, handing him my drink.

"Whoo, that is rude. What's *in* it? It feels like pure alcohol."

"Could be. I didn't see him make it."

"*That's* what everyone's been drinking all night. I kept wondering what that strange drink is. It's pretty." He licks his lips. "You know, I might get one of those."

"Oh my God, it's Death!" I say, nodding behind Ashen. He's puttering slowly but determinedly toward us with a pint of dark beer in his free hand.

Ashen looks over his shoulder and then quickly back at me. "Oh my God, it's coming this way."

We watch as Death continues his unstoppable journey toward us. Only at the last minute, he takes a seat at the next table. It's already full of people, but he sits next to them anyway without asking. Like everyone else in the club, they pretend not to notice him. He's just sitting there not talking to anyone. He takes an occasional sip of his beer, but most of the time his head is just hanging down like he's staring into his lap, one hand still clutching the beer on the table.

"Is it…is it dead?" I ask. But then Death's head rolls to the side. He still doesn't look up.

"Are we the only ones who can see him?" asks Ashen. "Is it just us?"

"What are you saying?"

"If we're the only ones who can see him, that means he's here for us! Tonight is the night we die."

"Together? Like, at the same time?"

He shrugs. "Maybe the roof is gonna cave in."

"Then why can't anyone else see him? Aren't they gonna die, too?"

"I dunno, all I know is our number's up!"

I keep my eyes on Death. Suddenly it's like he's the most interesting thing at the club. Fuck the drag act, the real show is going on right here. Ashen's trying to tell me something, but fuck me dead, I just can't think about Ashen with Death right over his shoulder.

"You wouldn't believe the night I've had. Hauling ass all over San Francisco looking for *bees*."

I nod, not really paying attention. "Bees?" I ask, a little too late.

"Don't even worry about it, just don't trust anyone with a suspicious-looking neck injury."

"There aren't any bees in San Francisco."

"Yeah, tell me something I don't know. I had to go all the way to my *lab*—"

"Ooh, ooh!" I interrupt. Something's happening—all the other people at Death's table are getting up to go. They're leaving the club. Now Death's on his own, head still in his lap. They never even looked at him the whole time. "They're gone," I whisper, and Ashen looks over.

"They left a glass of wine on the table."

I look over and realize they've left an untouched glass of white wine on the table right next to Death. Did they even take a sip before they left? Death's head is still down. He looks dead again.

"Weird," I say.

Then Ashen does one of these: "I want it."

"What do you mean, you want it? You can't drink leftover wine. You can't just *find* wine. That's fucking dirty."

"It's fine," he says. "They only just left, and they only took a sip. What's wrong with it? They are gone, right?"

"I guess."

"Right, then it's a waste of wine. If you think about it, this is really an environmental issue. Al Gore would drink it."

"Fine, drink it. But you're gonna have to get it away from Death first."

Ashen looks back, and now he's measuring up the distance.

Death is still looking down and doesn't even seem to know where he is. If I didn't see him move earlier, I'd say he was stuffed.

Ashen gets up and stands between our table and Death's. Death doesn't move. Ashen makes a stupid-ass show of being casual, twisting side to side and putting his hands in the air like he's stretching. Then all of a sudden, he swoops down and snatches that wine. Much smooth. Very wow. Before anyone can see what's gone on, he's hoofed it back to our table.

"Did anyone see me?" He's too scared to look around and see. Death hasn't moved. I shake my head, but that doesn't seem to calm him down. He looks all squirrelly like he's gonna get busted any second.

"Are you gonna relax or what? They're gone, they left ages ago."

"Yeah," he mutters, still checking out the people around him. "Yeah."

"So what happened to your boy-thing, anyway?"

"The bee thing?"

"No, your boy. You never told me what happened."

"He's crazy, that's what happened. I'm going to be single for a while, I swear. I'm deleting all my apps."

Not this again. Ashen deletes his dating apps like once a week. He's always back on the next day. Why pretend? The only person he's fooling is himself. He keeps telling me like he's expecting sympathy, but I only make fun of him.

His phone makes a clonk noise. He's got a new message. I raise an eyebrow at him and take a very judgy sip of my sparkledrank.

"I'm doing it. I'm doing it now," he says. But I can see he's stopped to check the message first. Uh-huh. Didn't even make it as far as deleting the app this time. "Oooh, look at this one."

I take the phone and check out this guy's profile picture. And the next one. And the next one. Fuck, he's gorgeous.

"I bet he's a catfish," I say deviously.

"Noooo, don't say that. Just once I want to hook up with someone with abs. You know that never happens? I don't even need the full set, can I just get one ab? That's all I want."

"One ab? Like one big one?" Ashen grabs the phone back off me, and I go, "Hey wait, I haven't even seen the message yet. What did he say?"

But Ashen doesn't answer me. He's taking a sip of his stolen wine, but he still can't do it without checking around him. He's *still* freaking out about getting caught.

"Oh my God, Ashen, they're gone. They're gone forever. Just show me what he wrote." I grab the phone back off him while he's distracted and check out this message: "*Sup dude. Pics?* Well, answer the man, you gots to send a P if you wants to get the D."

"I'm celibate now." Fuck's sake, I thought we'd got past this already. Before he can figure out what I'm doing, I put my drink down and lift up my shirt. "Dude!" he says, making a grab for the phone, but I lean back out of his reach. And it's too late. The camera snaps, the app whooshes, and I've just sent Mr. Pretty a picture of my nipple ring.

Clonk. Aw yiss. Do I got game or what?

"Great, thanks a fuckton. Now what am I gonna do if we get funky and he sees I don't have a nipple ring?"

"'Get funky'? Did you just say 'get funky'!"

"Shut up, all right!"

"So, get a nipple ring," I tell him. "It'll look good on you."

"And what about my top surgery scars, huh?"

I shrug. "Get some pecs, then he'll never know the difference."

While Ashen takes his phone back and checks the new message, something catches my eye over by the entrance. It can't be—I swear... Oh shit, Ashen is gonna have a baby when he finds out. "Is that them?" I ask.

Ashen looks behind him and sees the exact same thing I do.

The group of people who left their wine didn't actually leave. They're standing by the front door.

"Oh shit oh shit oh shit," he says.

"Come on, they're just hanging out at the door, what were we supposed to think?"

"They're gonna come back. They're gonna know it was me."

"How are they gonna know it's you?"

"I can't drink this now. I can't enjoy it."

A woman breaks away from the group by the door and starts to walk back to Death's table. "Oh shit, they're coming back!"

Ashen grabs the glass of wine and gulps the whole thing down in one go. He winces. "Hide it, hide it!" he says, shoving the glass at me. I put it under my seat where no one can see it. Ashen's keeping his head down.

"She can see me!"

"Here," I go. "This'll disguise you."

ASHEN

12:42 a.m.

1 hour 18 minutes remain

Benny gives me Lawrence's hat. Can I really hide under this? The brim does give me a lot of cover. I try to keep my head down. If I look around now, I'll blow our cover. I keep my eyes on Benny, hand on the brim to keep myself invisible, and try not to think about the pool of cold wine I just drank too quickly. It sits on my stomach like a cat showing me its asshole.

Benny has his hand over his mouth and his eyes are wide open. He's fucking loving this. He's watching it like it's a movie.

"They'll see you!" I hiss at him, but he ignores me. Now the bitch is starting to laugh. "They're going to *see* you!" But nothing can calm him down. I don't know what's going on behind me, but Benny's going to wet himself if he laughs any harder.

Out of the corner of my eye, I can see the woman leave. I wait a second, then risk a quick look over my shoulder. Death is still alone at the table but looking up now. I turn back around quickly. I don't think he saw me. He wasn't looking at me, anyway.

"What happened?" I ask Benny.

"Oh my God, you missed the best thing ever. She looked at the table where her drink was and did one of these." He mimes looking for something. "Then she went up to Death and asked him something, and Death did this." He makes a huge swiping motion, a massive exaggeration of the casual grab I did to get the wine in the first place.

"Are you fucking kidding me? She knows I did it?"

Benny shakes his head. "Death didn't point at you, just swiped. Maybe he didn't see who it was. Or the hat's working after all."

I look over my shoulder again and see the woman has gone back to the bar, probably to order another glass of wine. "She's gonna find out," I moan. "She'll know it was me."

"She won't know!" Benny insists, but I know better. I can feel the white wine burbling in my stomach. My guts feel twisted up in knots. I wish I'd never stolen the stupid drink now.

I get up suddenly. "I have to go."

"Where are you going?"

"I need to leave! I don't care where I go. Toad Hall maybe."

I can hear Benny saying something behind me, but I'm not sticking around to find out what. I take a step toward the door when he grabs my wrist and holds me back. I turn around to tell him off, but that's not Benny's hand. It's gnarled and bony, sticking out of the sleeve of a black coat. I look down. Death's black, circular spectacles look back up at me.

My heart's pounding. He knows I stole that wine.

He pulls me down so my head's level with his. I can feel his stale breath in my ear. Then he lets me go and he's staring into his beer again.

"What did he say?" asks Benny.

"He's looking for someone called Amy. I don't care, all right? I gotta get out of here."

I turn on my heel and make for the door. Just as I'm about to step into the dark corridor leading out, I realize the woman has now returned to her friends and is *standing by the door*. I must have made a noise when I came up short because she turns around and looks at me. My heart palpitates. Suddenly I feel like I'm having a heart attack. Maybe I really am going to die. I'm so sweaty, she must see me. My heart buzzes again. *Buzzes*. And

I realize it's not my heart that's buzzing, it's the test tube I stole from the lab with the wasp inside it. It's in my pocket, and the wasp is getting agitated. Screw it, I'm not carrying this thing around all night. I'm giving it back to Val. But the woman is still staring at me. She's holding her fresh wine in one hand, keeping a tight grip on it. She knows. I know she knows. She knows I know she knows.

I turn away from her without saying anything. That's only made me look more suspicious. As if I'm not already sweating visibly. What the hell's wrong with me. I gotta ditch the hat, it's making me too conspicuous.

I look around, but I don't know what to do. I can't just stick it on someone's head. Can I? What other choice do I have?

A pretty twunk goes by in front of me, and for once my panic about the wine-lady overrules how weird what I'm about to do is.

"Hey!" I say. "You would look *greeeeeat* in a hat."

DEVIN

12:49 p.m.

1 hour 11 minutes remain

"D'you know that guy?" Michael asks.

"No," I say, taking the hat off my head to get a look at it. It's the kind of hat they wear in those old-ass movies. I turn to look at the dude who put it on my head, but he's already gone. Son of a bitch—how did he do that? It only happened a second ago. All I can see is some skanky MILF giving me the stink-eye. She's holding on to a glass of white wine like it's my fault. I push the hat at Michael. "Here, it's yours now."

He pushes my hand away. "No, no, it's yours. You have to wear it now. Those are the rules. Besides, it's kinda cute on you."

I put it back on. What do you know, this is kind of all right. "How do I look?" I ask, though I already know the answer. I look good in everything.

"Perfect," he breathes, and he kisses me. He has full, pink lips, and his breath is sweet from his cocktail. I'm going half-hard, so I grab his waist and pull him in close against me. He grinds against my hips, putting his soft cheek against mine, and whispers, "Let's get out—"

"Hey, Marge!" someone belts into my ear. "I found 'im!" The same someone grabs me by the shoulder and pulls me away from Michael. I can't believe what I'm looking at. It's a fat-ass redneck wearing jeans, a flannel shirt, and *flip-flops*. Fuck no. I try to look away, but I can't. His feet are wide. Wider than human feet should be. Is there even any foot left under there, or is it all crusty skin and diabetes? And tufts of white hair growing out of the toes. Flaky, ragged toenails, inflamed and yellow. Is that a fungus? This dude's got to be over fifty. Seriously, thirty is dead, but *fifty*? That's just necrophilia. He's got a white goatee, which stands out against the ruddy skin on his face. He's so flushed I wonder for a second if this is all a gross-as-fuck drag act, but you can't fake this kind of ugly.

His paw, all fingers and hair, is still on my shoulder.

"Well, there you aaaaaare," says a woman who looks like the man but in a dress. She's not wearing any makeup, which is a mistake. Her lips are large and chapped, and the exact same color as the rest of her skin. Her long blond hair is stringy, like she has never heard of conditioner. Looks like we just found Marge. "Where did you get to?" she hoots. They both have a strong Texas accent. "Me an' Herb have been lookin' all over."

Michael breathes into my ear, "Do you know anyone else here? I want you to spit-roast me."

I cough involuntarily. This kid is a freak and I love it. But I have to get rid of these Texans fast. "You have the wrong person," I shout over the music. "You're looking for someone else."

They look at me for a second with the same large, uncomprehending eyes I've seen in my golden retriever. Then Herb slaps me on the arm and says, "Heyyyy, what a kidder! Can you believe this kidder?"

"Why you always gotta be zingin' us?" says Marge. "Zip-zip-zippity-zing!" She bursts out laughing like she's said something funny.

"No, I mean—" But I don't finish that sentence. I have a sudden suspicion. I look around the club for a second, and there he is. Wes looking at me from across the bar. He shoots a finger gun at me. I shoot daggers at him, but he doesn't care. I didn't even know he was here, but this clusterfuck has his fingerprints all over it. He's just palmed these hicks off on me. It's been years since we did that. Which can only mean one thing. These hillbillies must be so bad, he had to revive the old switcharoo.

"You've made a mistake!" I say. "You weren't talking to me before. You were talking to my twin brother. Look." I point across the bar. What's the point? Wes is already gone.

"Got us again!" hoots Marge. "Zip-zip-zippity—"

"Maybe I should go," says Michael.

"No, wait! I didn't even get your number."

"Catch you next time," he says with a coy wave.

Marge and Herb stand by me as they watch him go. Deep in my pants, I can feel the ghost of my long-dead erection. My underpants are a cemetery, and all the headstones are Texans.

"Aw," says Marge, "that's too bad. Did your friend have to go? Well don't worry, you're too good for him." Then she starts *singing*. "Ohhhh what can you do in a case like that, oh what can you do but sit on your hat? Or your toothbrush, or your mother, or anything else that's helpless."

Herb nods wisely with what little neck he has. "Take it from me, ain't no good chasin' after trouble. I been married three times an' the first two was crazier'n a skunk in a bear trap." *Well they'd have to be, wouldn't they?* I look him over again, taking in the full horror of what's in front of me. He puts his arm around as much of his wife as he can and says, "Third time's the charm. Where you bin all my life, woman? You sure got curves in all the right places."

There's nowhere she *doesn't* have curves. Her curves have curves. "I gotta go," I say, "but it's been great meeting y'all." I clamp my hand over my mouth, but it's too late. I've already said it.

"Wes, you didn't tell us you was a good ol' Southern boy! Where you from?"

"South Carolina," I admit. I've gotten really good at hiding it, but every now and then the accent slips out. It's these two scarecrows. They're frightening it right outta me.

"Herb, we got ourselves a good ol' fashion Southern boy! Well, cheers," she says, going to toast before she realizes I don't have a drink. "What happened to your drink?"

"My brother's probably loving it. What's he having, a cosmo?"

"Sure is," says Herb, taking a sip out of his drink experimentally. He's got a cosmo, too. It's kind of sad. In his own pathetic way, he's trying to blend in. "Whoo, you sure weren't wrong about this thing. Makes a real difference from Bud Light. Folks can say what they like, but you faggits sure know how ta make a tasty drink." He grabs my arm again in a panic. "Am I allowed to say that? I ain't meant no disrespect. I just meant—"

"It's fine," I say, trying to wiggle out of his grip.

"'Cause I got nothin' against it, y'know? Folks can do what they like, is what I say. I'm a Texan, y'know, and we don't see color or religion or faggityness or *nothing*, long as you got the right feelins in your heart. Cause in the end, ain't love all the same?"

"That's beautiful. You should be on the Supreme Court."

Herb nods again. "Always said I coulda been a lawyer." He taps somewhere where his head should be. "I got the best legal mind in San Antonio."

"I can believe that. Not that it's any of my business, but what *do* you do?"

"Roofs, mainly. Sometimes gutters. Only my joints ain't everythin' they used ta be, so these days I let the kids do mosta the roofin' an' I just run the business."

"There's no end to your talents."

Marge elbows him. "Tell 'im, Herb! Tell 'im about how you used ta be on the football team."

"I used ta be on the football team. You like football?" Before I can answer, he's sort of half tackled me, screaming, "Gimme the ball, ya sonuvabitch!" His face is flushed, and he's roaring with laughter. He's also spilled his drink, part of it on himself but mostly on me.

"Herb!" Marge says, "Herb, you spilled it all on you!"

"What's that, woman?"

"You spilled it all on you!" she screeches over the music.

But Herb doesn't seem to mind too much. He brushes at his flannel shirt like he can just shoo the drink away and says, "Never mind. Let the birds get it. Hur-hurr. Didya hear what I said? I said let the birds get it."

"Herrrrrrrb!"

If I have to listen to any more of this Imma cut a bitch. There's got to be some way out. "Let me get you another drink. What are you having?"

But Marge stops me by planting a meaty hand on my chest. "Hell, son, you're nothin' but skin and bones!" Go right ahead, lady. Get a good feel. I work hard for those pecs, and I don't even let boys touch them for free. How the hell is she getting away with this? How am I *letting* her get away with this? "Feel this, Herb." And now Herb is grabbing my chest as well.

I pull away, but Marge is blocking my escape again. "Now son, you're a good Southern boy." Grrrr. "You know how it works, I ain't gonna let you go payin' for our drinks when you been so good to us. *We're* buyin'. What're you drinkin'?"

I look over at the bar and see the blackboard. "Sparkledrank," I sigh. I can't believe my brain can't work fast enough to come up with a way out of this. All I said was "sparkledrank" like some kind of a retard. But then Ian's cocktails pack a hell of a punch. Maybe if I get them hammered, they'll let me alone. Herb said he drinks Bud Light. He's not used to real alcohol. One sparkledrank could kill him, even a man his size.

Marge wanders off to the bar, leaving me alone with Herb.

"So," I say, trying to make this hell pass a little bit faster. "Roofs, huh?"

"Yep. Some folks'll tell ya it don't matter what kinduva roof ya got. But don't. You. Listen," he says, jabbing me in the chest with a finger to emphasize his point. "Now take you, for example. What kinduva roof ya got, son?"

"I dunno."

"And that's your first mistake," he roars. "What are ya gonna do when it hails and your roof caves in on you? What're ya gonna do then, huh?"

"I live in an apartment."

"Ain't make no difference. Roofs is roofs."

Finally Marge gets back and saves me from the roof conversation. Fuck. Is that how bad this night has gotten? I'm actually glad to see Marge. Marge is an *improvement*. Fifteen minutes ago, I was ready to climb up the juiciest ass in the Castro and now I'm grateful just to see Marge. This has got to be a special kind of Stockholm Syndrome. It's definitely a special kind of hell.

She's brought back three sparkledranks. She hands me one and gives another to Herb. I give mine a gentle swirl to watch the clouds burst, but Marge and Herb slam theirs down like it's a shot. I can't even imagine how that tastes, but I'm not complaining. The faster these two get tanked, the faster I can get out of here. Maybe Michael's still here somewhere. The odds aren't great, but there's still a chance.

But the sparkledrank only seems to add fuel to the fire. Herb starts roaring like a Viking, and now Marge is getting all up in my face, too. "Ya know there's some real im-po-lite folks in this city," she says. "When I was orderin' them sparkledranks, some jumped-up piece o' trash started screamin' at me. 'It ain't no sparkledrank, it's called a Andrew's Special' or some such nonsense. Didya ever hear anythin' so rude?"

"No. That's the worst," I say, trying to push her endless blue-cheese boobs off me and maybe lean her up against her husband. And that's when it strikes me. *Rude*. The only reason I'm still with these bumpkins is because they got me a drink. But

I could ditch their sorry asses if I could be *rude* to them, or get someone else to. My friend Amy's always saying she wants to start a business where she says no for people who are too nice to say it themselves. Remember all the bad dates you've been on, all the parties you didn't want to go to and favors you didn't want to do? You'd just call Amy, hand the phone to the other person, and she would cut off their balls with a bread knife.

"Ohhh, oh what's that sound?" I say, pretending to hear my phone ring. "I must be getting a call." I pull my phone out of my pocket and hit Amy's number as fast as possible. It's ringing. Come on, answer the phone. *Damn it, Amy, answer the goddamn phone this is an emergency.*

"Hello?" she says.

"Quit it with the hello stuff, I need you. Remember that thing you always say, where you'll start your own business? Well, I'm your first customer."

"Where are you? You sound like you're at a concert."

"I'm at Aunty Bob's. But listen, I need you to do me a solid here, seriously. You have no idea."

"All right, but you need to give me some background about what's going on. I'm like one of those hit men who have to learn about their victims before they can kill them."

"Never mind that, I just need you to—" I smile at Herb and Marge and turn slightly so they can't hear. "I need you to tell these people to fuck the fuck off. This is an emergency. They're cock-blocking me like you wouldn't believe."

"Can't you ditch them?"

"*If I could ditch them, I wouldn't be calling you.*"

"All right, I guess. Put them on."

I let out a huge sigh of relief. Amy will kill these Texans and leave nothing behind but charred husks. Then it will all be over. I tap Marge on the shoulder and hand her the phone.

"Hellooooo?" she says as if she's never used a phone before. "Who's speaking? Oh, I just loooove your accent!" That can't be good. Amy doesn't have an accent. Unless Marge is talking about her non-Texan accent, but who does that? Why is this taking so long? Just ditch her, don't have a conversation. "Well thaaaank you. We're visiting from Texas, and we're havin' just the most fun. Are you his girlfriend? Well I'm just askin', he's a real cutie!" she says, cupping my chest again. "Okay. Okay. You too, honey."

She hands the phone back to me, and I look at her. She seems happy. Something's gone wrong.

"What did she say?"

"Oh, your little friend there is just darling. She is the sweetest girl. She said you can show us all around the Castro."

Fuck. Shit. Fuckshit. She's thrown me to the wolves. Fucking Amy. "I could have been spit-roasting that twink—" I start before realizing that last bit came out of my actual mouth. "Uh. You don't happen to know what spit-roasting is, do you?"

Marge waves at me dismissively. "Oh honey, I'm from Texas, I know all about spit-roasting."

Oh my God.

But now I see it, and I realize there's a way out. I have just caught sight of Wes. He's still at the bar, and he looks like he's about to head out with Michael. *He's heading out with Michael.* That son of a bitch is stealing my hookup. That's the last straw. The only way out of this is a long shot—the reverse switcharoo. It's never been done. But it could work.

Wes goes to the toilet, probably before he takes Michael home, and I jump. "Oh look, it's my friend again! Let's go say hi!" I scream.

I lead the Texans over to Michael, who seems surprised to see me coming over with Large Marge and Yosemite Sam, but I don't give him a chance to ask any questions. I grab him and shout at the Texans, "You stay right here, and I promise we'll be back in no time."

He tries to say something, but I clamp my mouth over his lips so he can't speak. For just a second, Marge and Herb look really uncomfortable. Isn't it beautiful? I'm about to drag him away when I realize there's just one thing I've forgotten. I'm still wearing that stupid hat.

Easy to fix. I grab the thing off my head and fling it into the air like a Frisbee.

KINGSLEY

1:09 a.m.

51 minutes remain

Son of a bitch. Someone's goddamn hat just hit me in the face. Some punk just threw his *hat* at me. I was so startled I threw my hands up to try and block it and knocked my whiskey all over the bar. I turn around on my stool to try and see who did it, but no one's looking at me. Story of my whole night.

I put the hat on my head and pocket my book so I can wipe up the spill. The super-buff bartender has taken pity on me and has already started pouring me another, which he tells me is on the house. That's where this night has gone. I look so pathetic even the bartender feels sorry for me. He has to listen to drunken sob stories all night, but the sheer force of my misery is so obvious it has made him give me a free drink.

Fuck it. I've earned it. You probably don't know this, but I'm kind of a big deal on the internet. I had to turn off comments on my blog because I was getting more than I could reply to. And they were positive as well, mostly. Sure one or two people reposted my stuff and took a giant piss all over it, but you know what it's like. The internet is full of trolls and circlejerkers. What do I care if someone takes my comics out of context and gets all butthurt.

I haven't done a new comic in a month or two now. For a

while I thought about writing about what I was going through, but the only things I could think of had all been done before, and even then they did fuck all to capture what it actually feels like. A decapitated head, a heart pulled out of a chest, a black empty abyss. Go home and cut yourself, emo kid, we don't serve your kind round here.

One of the great lies about heartbreak is that it has anything to do with your heart, as if you feel like your heart hurts, or your heart is broken, or your heart has been ripped out of your chest. It doesn't. Your heart has nothing to do with it. Heartbreak kills who you are. It flattens your hopes and dreams, and your future telescopes away in front of you into infinite tedium, or collapses to a single burning point where you start to wonder if anyone would miss you at all. If you did it. If you killed yourself now.

And in the meantime, you are a husk. You wake up every morning and your first thoughts are about him. You go to bed every night and your last thoughts are about him. And in that one long night made up of all the nights of your life joined together like folds in the same dark tapestry, you dream about maybe meeting him on the street one day and pretending it was an accident, or you're chasing him around the city and he's not even aware you're there, or the worst one of all where you're telling him everything he's meant to you and he is just so bored with it. Every time you think you've put him out of your mind for a few minutes, those dreams come back to tap you on the shoulder and remind you you can never get over him. You want to cry, to let it all out, but nothing ever comes because there is nothing left inside you.

That's the first lie. Not *one* of the pop songs I ever heard has done justice to the feeling. "Cry Me a River"? Fuck you, Timberlake, you lying piece of shit.

The second lie is that you can drink to forget. Nope. Drinking only makes you forget how you got home last night. It never helps you forget what happened, so you still feel like shit all the time. It doesn't dull the pain, either. That implies the pain is sharp.

It isn't. The pain is a constant throbbing in your skull, and the misery that comes with knowing you've failed at life, failed as a human being, and that your only chance at happiness has gone because he got to know you and discovered that, deep down, you are not worth knowing.

Alcohol doesn't dull that. It expands it, bloats it, engorges it, turning it into an amorphous, all-encompassing pressure on all sides, a swimming pool filled with congealed fat that embraces you, presses itself up against your mouth, forces itself past your lips and into your lungs where it sets and solidifies and stays forever.

Yet here I am, downing another whiskey. No, it won't make me forget, and no, it won't dull the pain, but booze does help the time pass more quickly. You won't be less miserable, but you can hope you have to endure your misery for just a little bit less time. It hasn't done all that much for me yet, but then I never was a cheap drunk.

There's one more lie left, and it's the one all your friends tell you. "You can talk to me. I'm *here* for you." I'm not saying they're lying exactly, but it's still not true. I've had someone break down and cry to me when his girlfriend left him and it was the most awkward experience of my life. I had nothing to say. I comforted him and we talked about his ex and what he was looking for in a woman. Maybe it did help him a little bit after all. All I knew was *I* never wanted to talk to him again in case the sad sack let it all out.

So, what am I supposed to do? Corner all my friends and talk their ears off? Don't forget, this is someone they *met* and probably didn't even like all that much. To tell them how much he meant to me, how I feel now, how my life is going to be spent looking for the second best because I've already met the best and now he's gone—who would spend time with me after that? No one wants to hear that. No one.

"Hey, that hat looks good on you," says some guy who's walked up next to me at the bar.

I look him over: blond stubble, kind of a round face, inoffensive nose, dressed like he doesn't care. After years of sketching, I can usually tell exactly what someone looks like naked right through their clothes.

"No thanks," I say.

"What the fuck?" he says. "All I said was I like your hat. Fuck you, asshole."

I pull my book out of my pocket and take up where I left off.

"Whatcha readin' there, asshole?" It's the guy who can't take a hint. He's needling me now. "You readin' a book? You readin' a book in a club? You got yer little hipster book there?" His voice goes higher and higher. "You readin' your little hipster asshole book at the bar? You must, you must be a real intellectual there, with your book at a club. Whatcha got there, huh? What's the, what's the name of the little book you got there, asshole? Is it an asshole book? Is it a book for assholes? Huh? Yeah, you're a real misunderstood genius."

I look up and make a show of giving him the once-over before I go back to reading. "No thanks."

Out of nowhere he grabs the book out of my hands. I'm so startled I don't know what to do at first. Then I turn to him—calmly, calmly—and say, "You better think about that again." I put my hand out. "Give it back."

"*The Crying of Lot 49* by Thomas Pynchon," he says in a stupid voice. "Hmm, yuss, very smarts. Such wow."

"Give it back. I won't ask again."

He does a Valley Girl now: "Are you like the smartest person evaaaaar? Oh my God, what are you drinkiiiiiing?" He grabs my drink and takes a sip. "*Honey* whiskey?" he sputters. "You're not even drinking real whiskey! This stuff is like for high schoolers. You're drinking whiskey and reading to make a biiiig show of what an intellectual you are and it's not even proper whiskey. Can you even read? Do you even speak English? Are you just one giant, flaccid fucking cock?"

I grab his wrist, the one holding my drink. He tries to squirm out of it, but my grip is too strong. I'm wiry and a lot stronger than most people think.

"Let go!" he mewls.

"Okay."

His arm slips free so suddenly he splashes my drink all over his face. I make a grab for my book while he's still startled, but he's quicker than I thought and yanks it out of my reach.

"Give that *back*," I say.

"Fuck you!"

He ducks away into the crowd and before I know what's going on, he's running. I jump off my stool and run after him. I don't care about the drinks, but *no one* steals my fucking book. My head is pumping with blood. Punk doesn't know what kind of trouble he's got himself into.

First he tries to lose me on the dance floor but I follow him through the dancers, feet pounding to the rhythms of Rihanna, eyes burning like Rome, just keeping him in sight. He hangs a hard left at the door and runs past the booths lining the wall. Then, without hesitating, he runs up the couple of steps and is out into the back garden.

I sprint after him, ducking past human obstacles carrying drinks and chattering, shoving a tray of drinks into a face, displacing bodies by force and slamming through this pissy little garden like a tsunami. Hurricane Kingsley. He's halfway up the stairs to the second floor. I grab the banister and swing around without losing my momentum, barreling up the stairs faster than he could have imagined. He reaches the top and disappears inside. I'm getting close, but the door opens and someone is coming. I shove him out of the way and dive at the door, throwing myself inside. A screaming tries to distract me, a babble of pointless voices. Nothing to say. No point in even existing. Where is he? He's here somewhere.

There's an old Asian lady with a shoebox standing near the door, head craned up. "Come on. Come on, George."

"Get out of the way," I say so ferociously she is startled

backward. But she's still not looking at me. She's looking at something on the ceiling.

I look up. Something falls through the air. A dark shape. Before I know what's happening it's on my face. *IT'S ON MY FACE!* I open my mouth to scream but before I can make a sound I feel something prickly brush up against my lips.

KINGSLEY

1:15 a.m.

45 minutes remain

I don't remember how I got here. It feels like I've always been here. Maybe I always will be here, or I might be carried around Aunty Bob's by some unseen current, who knows? Who cares? For now, I am just content to be.

That's me, down there on the ground, or it's my body at least. He's standing a short way inside the door, and the *thing* has just fallen on his face. Oh! It's a spider. Kind of a cute one, too. I can see myself stuck in a scream, just on the verge of thrashing to try and fling George away. I smile. My face looks funny contorted in terror, half occluded by George's body.

I can't *see* myself exactly—the me that's here in the air—but I am vaguely aware of wearing the same clothes my body is. I can feel the sleeves of my shirt brush against my arms. I can feel the cinch of that red hat around my head. I can even feel George here with me, his prickly body frozen in time as it brushes against my lips and pushes past my tongue on his way into my mouth. Hi, George. You are giving my body one hell of a ride, but from here I think maybe you're not so bad. Hey, boy. Hey.

Maybe I'm dead. But that doesn't seem likely. Maybe I'm *about* to die, and this is the adrenaline kicking in. Seems more likely, but still doesn't make much sense. Nothing is rushing past me. My heart feels still, if it's even beating at all. I realize I haven't even breathed in…minutes? The world just seems stuck for a bit, taking a break while our souls chill out. But then there aren't any other souls here. Are there?

"Hello?" I say, but I don't hear any sound. I didn't even feel my lips move. I wonder why? Or not. I'm not really interested in explanations. There will be enough time for those later. For now, time does not exist.

I can feel a warm sensation I think might be pride. Look at me down there. I am perfectly framed from where I'm looking now—George and I in the foreground, the door in the background, with a suggestion of onlookers around the borders. The scene is skewed at an angle, indicating drama. A world gone out of kilter. I am sketching myself in my head, imagining how this would look as a panel in my comic. I'll have to remember to do that when I get back to my body. *If* I get back to my body. I giggle at the thought that maybe I could bob around like a balloon on the ceiling all night. I hope someone doesn't open the window or I might get sucked out into the sky and float away for ever and ever and ever.

With this sudden calm, I can see how someone might keep a pet like George. I can *almost* understand how someone might keep a dog, and I hate dogs. I think it's the unconditional love. People are always telling me how nice it is to have the constant loyalty and companionship of something that loves you unconditionally. But if it's unconditional, then what's the point? A Tamagotchi can love you unconditionally. I prefer pets whose love you have to earn. Or better yet, cats. Cats are the perfect assholes. I can *respect* that. Maybe that's why I like them so much. They remind me of myself.

I have one cat called Weasel. It's okay, though. I'm not one of those people who turn into Jell-O around their pets. Weasel is an asshole. She will have a freak-out in the middle of the night for no reason and tear up my apartment. She jumps on the kitchen counters while I'm cooking. She prowls around my desk while

I'm working. I spray her with water to keep her in line, but I don't know why. She never seems to learn. It is nice having someone else around, though. I don't need people in my life. Don't want 'em. But Weasel and I understand each other. I wish she were here now. It is lonely here. I feel like I could cry, but whether from sadness or happiness I can't tell.

I don't remember making any movements or thinking myself in any particular direction, but I can feel myself drifting now. There's the Asian lady with the shoebox who was trying to coax George off the ceiling. She is wearing pale blue jeans and a loose-fitting T-shirt, and she has big glasses that she must have bought in the 1970s. Her face is stern, but not unfriendly. Now that I'm looking at her more closely, she appears to have a faint glow. She is luminous like the corona of the sun around the edge of an eclipse. She must be some kind of zany character. Imagine bringing George to a gay club. Maybe George is gay. The thought occurs that if he came here with his boyfriend, there could be another spider on the loose. Maybe more. The club could be lousy with Georges. What a night.

There's the blond punk, the one whose need for other people's approval led him to bother me at the bar. He has a glow too, noticeably brighter than the Asian lady's. I wonder about that. I do not think it is an aura exactly, not in the sense that people say you have a friendly aura or a colorful aura, but it does seem to be a part of him that cannot be considered separate. Blondie is a short distance ahead of my body, but he must have stopped and turned around when he heard me scream. It looks like he was gasping in incredulity, a gasp that is starting to give way to a laugh at my body's misfortune. But for now he is stuck between them. When time starts back up again, his laughter will mix pleasantly with my screams. It will be a strange sound, but I decide now that I will enjoy it.

A man with a mustache is tending the bar here. It is one of those big hipster mustaches in the style of Salvador Dalí but with none of the conviction. If you asked him about Salvador Dalí, he would think it was a tapas restaurant off Valencia. His eyes are troubled. Hey, dude, don't be afraid. What is there to be troubled about? There is no reason to worry. Just be at peace like I am. Let yourself float. You'll find the world is much more pleasant when you float. But he doesn't seem to hear me. Like everyone else, he is frozen in that moment, pressurized by the weight of time all around him, hardening into a cold but beautiful diamond. You are beautiful, bar dude. Never forget it.

There is a pretty Hispanic boy wearing an ascot and a blazer. He is standing, laughing at some unknowable and forgettable joke, cheekbones bursting with life. He is shining so brightly. He is very near the Asian woman and looking up at the ceiling. Everyone has a glow, I notice now, but shining at different strengths. The older people tend to have dimmer glows, but some of the younger people do, too. The tables are packed with these human torches. Their auras brush up against each other, overlapping to shine even more brightly. "Luminous beings are we."

There is a darkness coming from the outside, though. I do not remember directing myself toward it, but I am bobbing in that direction now. I am not afraid. But something inside me feels sad. Not sad—melancholy. It is a happy sad. I float through people and tables until I reach the door, but that won't stop my disembodied consciousness. I pass through it and out over the beer garden where Amy is sitting, alone with people, a gap between her and the rest of the world. Before I even know what is happening, I am next to her, the only person in the whole club who can see her for who she is.

Her glow is so dim that at first it is hard to tell she has one at all. It is almost extinguished, and that makes me sad. Not sad—melancholy. Hey, Amy. Hey. I know we've never been friends, and I ignored you that one time at Kelvin's Halloween party, but just for now, here, I want you to share this melancholy feeling with me. You have an unhappy life. But I am here with you now.

We will always have this moment in which our souls briefly touched. I know that is not much. But it is something.

I am suddenly aware of another aura I had not previously felt because it was so big it envelops everything. It is here at the bench. And it is here in the beer garden. I float up, and the aura is here too. Maybe aura is the right word, because I could not describe this as a glow. It is less than zero, it is like a negative. It is a sickness, an infected tooth, a great weeping abscess. I realize it engulfs the whole club. It is coming from Aunty Bob's. Why can't anyone else feel it? We are all sitting on the deck of the *Titanic* sipping cocktails and making conversation while the ship slips into the icy waters. I am not scared. I am not scared. But I am sad—actually sad now. Something bad is going to happen.

Far below me, I can see the denizens of the bar. They glow fiercely, striking out against the gloom emanating from the club. There is a larger man, a little older than most, who looks like he has inexplicably failed to find love. There is an even older man with a beaky nose and distinguished white hair who looks totally relaxed, in his element. There is a super buff Filipino boy wearing a leather harness, smoking a cigarette by a large outdoor plant. There is someone lying on the ground by the staircase who looks like he is screaming. There is a thirty-something man with a hipster mustache in the style of Salvador Dalí…

I consider the hipster idly. Something is wrong, but I cannot put my finger on it. My thoughts float as aimlessly as my consciousness. Something *is* wrong. But I don't know what.

I descend through the light mist and diffusing curlicues of cigarette smoke. These clouds were only moments ago inside the lungs of the people beneath me, imbued with the warmth of their bodies, kissed by the soft skin of their lips as they exhaled. It feels oddly intimate to be wafting through their exhalations now. I wonder what they would think if they knew.

Now I am inside the ground floor of Aunty Bob's. The sickly aura pervades here too, but for the time being it seems to be held at bay by the vibrant glows coming from most of the customers. My body was here just a moment ago. It seems like a lifetime now. I wonder if time could mean anything in this state. Then I wonder if it ever does. It is all relative. Maybe we will all be back here someday, looking at ourselves and laughing at what small, ephemeral creatures we were.

"Hello?" I ask soundlessly and look around. But I cannot detect the presence of another consciousness here. I am alone.

That is when I see The Ex. I have uncharitably nicknamed him Alabama Hot Pocket. If you don't know what that means, I strongly advise you not to look it up. But here he is nevertheless, sitting against one of the walls with several of his friends who I recognize as Ashen, Kelvin, and Lucien. Hot Pocket has scruffy brown stubble along his chin and jawline, which draws some attention to the light pockmarks on his cheeks. Through his grin, he has bared glistening teeth and his lips are wet and glossy. His eyes spark with a mischievous joy. Although he is frozen now, I can almost hear his laugh and can only imagine what wonderful, colorful thing he is going to say next. He lights rooms with his body. He hasn't changed a bit. I love him still.

I wonder if he saw me sitting at the bar. I hadn't realized he was here tonight, although I had hoped I might run into him accidentally. That's why I chose a seat facing away from the door, so that if he did turn up then I could pretend to be surprised to see him. But from where he is sitting, he has a good view of where I was. My seat at the bar is still empty, and I have to remind myself I only left it about thirty seconds ago. Maybe he has seen me. Maybe that is why he is smiling and laughing.

It is okay. I am glad something is making him happy even though I could not. I wonder if he has found someone else. He is not here with a date as far as I can tell, but I do not think it will be hard for him to find someone better than me.

My attention wanders to another familiar presence somewhere in the room. There, in the back corner where the lights do not reach, is a man with a Dalí-style mustache. The *same* man with a Dalí-style mustache. Now I know something is wrong.

I consider the man placidly. At least, far more placidly than one should consider someone who has defied the laws of physics by being in three places at the same time. But then here I am in two places at the same time, so who am I to judge? Is he, like me, a consciousness free to move in space while time has stopped? Or is he one of triplets? Neither seems likely. And yet here he is, staring out into the club with the same haunted eyes as his other self upstairs. He is up to something. But I don't think I care what. He is not out of place because nothing is out of place. Everything is where it should be, and while the universe still turns, we have nothing we need to worry about.

I wonder if I'll be able to take any thoughts back with me. Will I remember any of this when I wake up? I hope so. I want to keep this feeling of tranquility. I realize that for the entire time I've been floating around Aunty Bob's, I have never once felt the depression that has been clawing chunks out of my soul for the past couple of months. My constant companion, the curse I brought down upon myself for violating the sanctity of the mummy's tomb, has finally gone. I never even noticed. Everything is okay here. Wouldn't it be nice to feel like that all the time? Even for a short time? Or even just one night?

Is that so much to ask?

KINGSLEY

1:15 a.m.

45 minutes remain

I scream. I thrash and throw the thing off me, but I can still feel it on my face. *"Get it off me!"* I scream, batting at my face and whipping my head around in case there are more of them.

The lady with the shoebox shouts. "Shame on you. You're frightening him." She goes running into the corner of the bar, following the shape I've thrown off into the darkness.

I am standing, panting, not knowing what the fuck just happened to me. I'm aware now that someone's laughing. I look up and see Blondie, face contorted in a hysterical laugh. It is a hateful sound. The blood is pounding in my ears.

"You think something's funny, shitbo?"

"I'm done," he gasps. "Oh my God, you're priceless."

I can feel my face is flushed, and my brain has just seized up and I can't think of anything to say. "I'm not finished with you," I tell him through my teeth and storm out the door. As soon as I step out, I realize he still has my book. *Fuck.* I can't go back in now. I can't let him keep it. But I *can't* go back in after I stormed out. I dig my nails into my palms. I'm not looking at them, but I hope I draw blood. I hope I squeeze so hard I crush the bones in my own hands because *that is what I'm going to do to everyone in this goddamn club tonight.*

I run down the stairs. Someone on the concrete below the stairs is shouting something. Maybe it's at me, maybe it's not. I don't give a fuck. At the foot of the stairs, I find some dude with stringy, curly hair smoking a clove cigarette and snickering with a dirty eyeball aimed in my direction. I push past someone's grandpa, and I confront the smoker.

"What's so funny?" I shout.

He shrugs and blows a puff of smoke into my face.

I can feel the smoke that has gripped the sticky interior of his lungs and carried with it some of their phlegm mixed with the sickly sweet stench of cloves.

"Fuck you, asshole! You're smoking a *cigarette*."

I flick the cigarette out of his mouth, and he looks startled for the first time. He's going to protest, but I march back into the club while he is still stunned. There might still be time to get my stool back at the bar and order my drink for the third time. Not that it seems all that important now. I have sobered up so quickly, I've lost my base drunk. I'm going to have to start from scratch.

Fuck. It's Alabama Hot Pocket sitting by the wall behind where I was at the bar. I had never even seen him come in, but he has probably seen everything that just happened. I can tell because he's howling like a hyena.

I storm up to him and shout, "You think that's funny, do you?"

He looks surprised to see me. "Oh! Helloooo," he says with a gentle wave. Twinkly motherfucker.

"Was that a friend of yours, huh? Did you send him to steal my shit?"

"What?" he says, cocking his ear like he can't hear over the music.

I'm suddenly paralyzed by the thought that I might have been wrong about him. Even if I'm right. I can't prove it. I'm automatically going to look like the asshole. There's no way out of it now. Is it too late? I can still leave with my dignity.

I pluck his cocktail out of his hand. He lets me take it. I don't know why. Slowly, without breaking eye contact, I bring it up to my chest. I purse my lips. And very, very slowly I let a huge gob of saliva and phlegm dangle out of my mouth. It stretches and elongates until it lands in his drink. It floats happily and embraces the maraschino cherry in a sticky hug.

I lean in to hand it back to him. As I come closer to his face, he pulls away, but not before I hiss, "I hate you *so* much, and if I ever see you here again I will *break you*." My fingers are clenched so tightly around his glass, I'm worried it might break. They are white and trembling. He takes his drink back without taking his eyes off me.

I straighten up and make to storm off, but as I pass the bathroom there is a loud, dull bang, like someone has set fire to a balloon full of hydrogen. Two people burst out of the bathroom. One black guy is dressed like a jock, and he's going, "What the fuck, man—"

We slam into each other, and I shove him out of the way. "Watch it, frat boy." I look over and see his friend, some hipster with a pointy Dalí mustache. "And you," I shout at him. "I've never seen you before but you've just *gotta* be an asshole." Then I punch him in the goddamn face, and he goes down like a sack of shit.

That's when the bouncer shows up to drag me out. I try to squirm out of his grip, but the man's a giant and his hams are locked around my arms.

"Fuck you, too," I shout, digging my heels into the floor. "Mind your fucking business, Oddjob." Then, right in front of my eyes while I'm helpless to stop him, the frat boy takes the hat off my head.

TOM

1:22 a.m.

38 minutes remain

The bouncer drags away the dude with the attitude. Slayden's still on the floor. I squat down on my haunches and put Andre's hat on my head. I guess I look kind of like a cowboy, only the straight kind, not the YMCA one. I look over Slayden to see if he's really KO'd or just playing possum. Turns out the psycho had a right hook on him. Slayden's out cold.

I look up. Slayden was wrong. We were supposed to reappear in the bathroom only a minute after we left, but everything's changed. We musta been gone a lot longer.

Another dude comes outta the bathroom going, "What the hell?"

"Sorry," I say, a little sheepish. It's not like I meant to see his cock or anything.

"What's the big idea? You bust into the toilets when I'm tryna piss?"

"It was an accident."

I pick up Slayden off the floor. I guess the dude from the bathroom gets a better look at me all of a sudden because he goes real quiet. Now, there's a smile on his face.

"I mean, if you wanted to join me all you hadda do was ask."

I smile. I could get used to being hit on like this. Andre

would kill to get this much attention. Maybe he would, if he'd spend less time twirling his hair and more time at the gym.

"Thanks, but it was an accident."

He doesn't look too happy, but I can't stay. I dunno what I'm gonna do with Slayden. First thing's to put him down somewhere, I guess. I see the back door, and there's the beer garden on the other side. The fresh air will probably bring him round, if the cigarette smoke doesn't. I'm guessing he wouldn't be real used to that.

I carry him up the steps and push through a crowd of people hustling by the stairs to the second floor. I finally get him down on one of the benches against the wall. In the corner of my eye, I see a sudden movement. I turn my head in time to see someone else with the same hipster 'stache disappearing in a panic. Wonder what his deal was. Seriously, man, I dunno what it is tonight, but everyone's in a real funny mood. Though it *is* a gay club. Maybe they're like this all the time. Nah, can't be. Even the gays don't act this weird.

I look back down at Slayden, then look where the man with the hipster 'stache just disappeared to. He had the same ginger hair. He was wearing the same plaid shirt. I swear, exact same colors. Shit, this is doing my brain in. Slayden must be overlapping with himself like I did when I saw myself at the bar. That's why he ran away. What happens if you touch your double? Or get too close? I don't want to find out, and I guess neither does Slayden.

"Hey, Slayden, get back here," I shout after the one that ran back into the club, but he's long gone, leaving me to take care of the other him. The unconscious one looks all right, I guess. He was only punched, and the guy that did it wasn't that strong. You can't die from being punched in the face, can you? I pick up his wrist to make sure his pulse is still there, and it is. You can't die from being punched in the face, even if you are from the future. He looks kinda peaceful now, not like he was earlier. He was all wound up about something. What's so important he would travel back in time to stop it? I shiver. The air's super chilly all of a sudden. I don't like to imagine too much. There's no reason to get carried away.

There's plants growing on the wall behind him. One of the vines is curling around his nose, but he doesn't look like he notices. He's still out cold. Probably he's so used to that 'stache a whole cockroach could crawl up his honker and he'd never know. He looks like a sex offender.

"Hey," says this girl at the next bench over. She's looking at me. I smile. She's cute, too. She looks kinda old-timey, like she's got that really heavy eye makeup girls used to wear in the '60s. For a second I get the crazy thought that maybe she really did come here from the '60s, but then Slayden's right in front of her, and she hasn't recognized him yet. No, she must be normal— well, San Francisco normal, anyway. But she does have a great smile. Her dress is pretty low too, and I can see a lot of titty pressing up against it when she moves. I can tell she's seen me peek. She doesn't seem to mind. She asks, "D'you think they named Mars bars after the planet, or did they name the planet after Mars bars?"

"What?"

"And then they named the Milky Way after the chocolate bar," she says, not waiting for me to catch up. "And Uranus was named after a chocolate starfish. What d'you think Venus was named after?"

I shrug.

She licks her lips. "I think something pink. And sinful." She laughs. "The most pornographic of candies." Then she looks right at Slayden. Maybe she does know him. Fuck, Imma get cock-blocked by a dude in a coma. "Is your friend okay?"

"Thanks," I say. Maybe I can distract her. I scratch the stubble on my chin to give her a good eyeful of the gun show.

"I asked, is your friend okay," she says. She's still smiling. I can bring this around.

"Oh. Yeah, he just drank too much."

"Aw, you're a good friend," she says.

I nod. "Then someone punched him."

"Oh my God, what happened?"

I shrug. "Kinda hard to say. We came outta the bathroom and someone got him right in the kisser. Maybe he really is a sex offender."

She nods wisely. "He does have the mustache."

"I know, right?"

Slayden doesn't look well. He's still unconscious, but his skin is flushed and I can see sweat starting to form on his brow. He almost looks like he has a fever. You can't get a fever from being punched.

"Someone's gotten hurt over there, too," she says, nodding her head toward the stairs that go to the second floor. People are standing around someone who is lying flat on the ground with a broken leg. I'm not a doctor. I just know that legs don't go that way around.

"Fell off the stairs?" I ask.

"Sort of. Some asshole went charging up the steps like the running of the bulls and shoved him right over the edge. He's lucky he didn't land on his head. His brains could have painted the walls. Anyway, about ten seconds later, there's this scream and the same asshole comes running back down the stairs picking a fight with everyone he can find."

"I think I just met him. Look, I got his hat," I say.

"Melody," she says, sticking out her hand.

"Milady," I ask, tipping the hat at her. I stick my tongue between my front teeth.

She grunts. "Oh yes, I just felt my legbeard grow a bit bushier. Whiteknight me again, harder!"

I can't believe this girl. She is cute as fuck, and I can tell she's the kind of girl who knows what she wants. She's direct. Straightforward. And she's called *Melody*.

"Tom," I say, shaking her hand.

She wrinkles her nose. "Don't you have any other names?"

I shake my head, and she says, "Well we can do better than that." She waves her drink around in the air like it's a magic wand. "I hereby dub you...Funyun."

"That is a bad name. You would be a terrible mother."

"All right, all right, it was only a first try, don't get your panties in a twist, Funyun." I give her a look, and she just smiles. "Okay, here we go, this time for real. How about Inigo?"

"*No.*"

"What? Why not? It's a great name, it's super sexy, like Inigo Montoya."

"*It sounds like 'Negro.'*"

"Surely you jest. It's a sexy name, swarthy and Mediterranean—" But she sees me shaking my head, and she doesn't finish the sentence. "All right, have it your way. Third time's the charm...Loras."

I have to stop and think about that for a moment. "Like from *Game of Thrones*? I dunno about the 'ass' bit, but the rest of it's okay."

"You're already called Thom-ass, and you haven't complained about that."

"Maybe that's why I go by Tom."

"Well, we can't just call you Lor, you'll sound like a retard."

I laugh. It's weird, but I guess you don't meet a lot of funny women, you know? Or at least I don't. The gays can't stop telling jokes if they tried. Just look around this place. Everywhere you look they're laughing. And don't tell him I said this, but Andre can make pretty good with the jokes when he wants. But a funny woman? That's a real find.

She looks like she approves of me laughing, and now it's too late to take it back. She says, "Then it's decided, Loras."

"Do you know what time it is?" I ask.

"Don't you?" she asks, nodding at my watch.

"It's stopped," I lie.

She checks her phone. "It's 1:33."

I check my watch—11:51. I look down at Slayden. We

overshot. We've been gone about two hours. I should have never trusted him. I should have just gotten a beer at a bar across the street and waited until we went back in time, then come to Aunty Bob's to take my place like I never left. That woulda tied this up right. But if I've been gone for two hours, what if Andre isn't here anymore? He mighta gone home. But his hat's still here. He woulda taken it with him. He'd never leave his hat behind. I look around, but I can't see him.

"Are you looking for someone?" Melody asks me.

"I came here with my friend Andre, and now I can't find him."

"Oh," she says. Her whole face changes. Suddenly it's like she doesn't even care I'm there.

"I'm straight," I blurt out. I knew it was gonna sound stupid before I even said it, but I couldn't think of a better way to put it. "Andre's just my friend. I'm crashing on his couch."

"Oh!" she says, "That's cool." Suddenly, her face gets back that appreciative glow. That was a close shave. "Where do you live?"

"L.A."

"Aha, that explains why you're so handsome," she says. "Everyone in L.A. looks like a supermodel because they're trying to make it in Hollywood."

"What's your excuse, then?"

"I live in L.A. I'm trying to make it in Hollywood."

"Fo' serious? Where you living at?"

"East Hollywood, with the Armenian gangsters. It's not too bad once you get used to the idea that your car's going to get broken into about once a month. After a while, you stop leaving your best diamonds in the glove compartment, you know? What about you?"

"I keep mine under the seat."

"I haven't tried there. Thanks for the tip."

"Marina Del Rey," I say, answering the question she meant. She raises an eyebrow at me. "Schmancy."

"My roommate works for a tech startup. He pays most of the bills."

"And how do you pay him?"

"I give him the opportunity to soothe his white guilt." She laughs. "It's not a hundred percent ethical, but it's not a bad stepping stone until I can figure things out. I moved there to look for a job."

The girl Melody's sitting next to puts a hand on her arm. "Melody! When do you want to go?"

I can see now Melody is sitting on the near side of a group of girls. She leaned over to talk to me, but I hadn't realized she was with other people. She doesn't look very happy at being interrupted, though.

"Amy! Girl code!" she hisses. Her friends look over at me and realize we've been chatting each other up. Amy...Doesn't Andre know an Amy?

"Oh," she says. "Well, it looks like you won't have any trouble finding a ride tonight."

Melody looks back at me and indicates her friend with a nod of her head. "Unless of course you like Amy, too," she says. Amy has a serious face and looks startled. Still, she hasn't said no. And she is kind of cute. "What do you think, Loras? Is three company or a crowd?"

My throat goes tight. Is it a trick question? She can't mean it. But Amy didn't know about this and she still hasn't said no. In fact, she looks like she's coming round to the idea. I say, "You're both very pretty, but Melody and me have a special connection." Sah-mooooth.

"Oh, I didn't say anything about fucking Amy. She's a lesbian. You'd both be doing me. What do you think? Are you the type that can share?"

Amy and I glance at each other. We see the panic in each other's eyes, but at the same time there's something else in her face. I know that look. She wants Melody, too.

"Maybe another time," I say. That's playing it safe, right?

She winks at me. "Pity. It's been a while since I went down on a woman."

I choke and struggle to swallow, and Melody bursts out laughing. I still can't tell if she's playing with me or not. It's a joke, it has to be a joke. I think I passed the test.

"So what's 'girl code' mean?" I ask. There, that should get the ball back in my court. Amy crosses her eyebrows at me and turns back to the other girls.

Melody says, "Girl code is how you warn someone they might be clam-jamming you." I don't say anything for a second, but I can tell she's got something planned. "Aren't you going to—"

"What's clam-jamming?" I ask, taking the bait.

"It's the lady version of cock-blocking." I'm laughing before I've even wrapped my head around it. The more I think about it, the more disgusting it gets. I love it. She says, "I like your hat. Can I try it on?"

Like I'm gonna say no.

MELODY

1:46 a.m.

14 minutes remain

I like this. I pull the edge down over one eye I so I can smolder at Loras with the other one. He looks gorgeous in bad light. He has beautiful dark skin, some of which disappears into the night, but his shoulders and arms catch the light so sharply they look like they're shining with their own glow. As I follow the line of his arms down to his hands, I notice his friend again. He's still unconscious on the bench behind him. I try to ignore him. Maybe if I ignore him, he'll go away. Problems usually do. Or they don't.

"Now it's your turn," I tell him. "I let you in on the secrets of the girl code. I broke an *oath* to tell you that. If the sisterhood ever finds out, my life will be worth nothing. So, to even this up, you gotta tell me the secrets of the man code."

He shrugs. "There is no man code."

I laugh in his face. "Is that the cover story? You can do better than that."

"Well, maybe there's a little bit of a man code. Like, a few weeks ago it was my bud's birthday, but at the last minute I wind up with a date with this chick."

"Which app?"

"How d'you know I was on an app?"

"I didn't, but I do now. Come on, which one?"

"Tinder," he says, like I'm going to believe that. I raise an eyebrow at him until he caves and says, "FetLife."

"Boy, we are gonna have us a time." He smiles, but I can tell he's not sure how to react, so I say, "So, you took her to the party on a first date? It might be coming on strong, but a bold move can pay off."

"I skipped the party. I just went out with the girl."

I suck air through my teeth. "You abandoned your friend on his birthday? That's cold."

"No, that's the man code," he says. "If there's any chance you might get to fuck, it beats any plans you already have. You gotta support your bros."

"Man code..." I say thoughtfully. "See, if it was me and a dude, I'd have brought him to the party so my friends could see him."

"Yeah, like arm candy?"

"No, so my friends can ask him questions and make sure he's all right. Friends always want to vet your dates, make sure you're not dating an asshole who's gonna hurt you."

"Not my friends," he says. "It sounds like you're planning to marry this guy."

"If he's good in bed," I say, and he smiles again. I go to take another sip of my martini and realize I've hit rock bottom. "Oh no! I'm dry."

"I'll make a beer run," he says.

Smart man. He'll go far. "Gin martini with a twist," I say, handing him the glass.

He crosses the garden to the bar on the other side. Now that he's not right next to me, I can see how tall he is. He's just short of brushing against the lights strung across the open sky. He's filling out those running shorts nicely too.

Amy nudges me. "How does he measure up?"

"Cute, funny...a little bit slow..."

"Sounds like a real keeper," she says. No expression in her voice.

I know what I'm doing, and I know when I'm on to a good thing. This one's got real potential.

Loras comes back from the bar holding the drinks. He hands me my martini, and we clink our glasses before taking a sip. He's got himself a nice gender-normative beer, but who am I to complain? Just because it's a stereotype doesn't mean it's bad.

"What's that?" I ask as a silver chain around his neck catches the light. He pulls it out from under his tank top where it's been nestling between his chest. Aaaand it's a crucifix. "Oh," I say. It's okay, there's lots of reasons someone might wear a crucifix. Maybe it was his grandmother's. Maybe it reminds him of someone. Yeah, someone like Jesus. "Why are you wearing that?" I blurt out. I could have phrased that better. I just can't think how.

"Because I've accepted the path of our savior," he says. Shit. Was that a joke? I can't tell. It sounded like a joke, but that's how those people actually talk. They don't even realize how stupid they sound. He asks, "What church do you go to?"

"I'm an atheist," I say, trying not to make that sound like an accusation of stupidity. Though it always does.

"It's okay, it doesn't matter to me," he says. Okay, I can work with this. "We're all God's children."

"No," I say, shaking my head. "We're really not. You can't just appropriate people who disagree with you, like it's just a matter of time before they realize they're wrong. That's so patronizing. I'm allowed to have my own opinion."

"Calm down, it's no biggie."

"Don't tell me to calm down."

"I don't understand what the big deal is."

"Listen, you're a nice guy, but being religious means a big part of your brain just ignores rational logic. And if one part of your brain's insane, who knows what other parts are insane? You could be a 9/11 conspiracy nut or an anti-vaxxer."

"I *am* an anti-vaxxer."

"What the *fuck*, dude? Seriously?"

"Lots of black folks are. The government did experiments on us for decades. They let people think they were getting vaccines, but they only wanted to watch them die of syphilis."

"Oh, so you're going to endanger your children today because of something that happened in the 1950s."

"How do you know it stopped in the 1950s? That's the thing about conspiracies. You don't find out if they're real until it's too late."

"Right, well let's just ask all the polio and smallpox victims what *they* have to say." I make a big show of looking around for people who aren't there. "Oh. Will you look at that. There aren't any."

"Lord give me strength," he says, and actually means it. I think I scoffed. Yeah, I definitely just scoffed, because now he's looking at me and says, "It's just a book to you, isn't it."

That hits me harder than I expected. For a second I don't know what to say. And then I say: "There's no such thing as just a book."

There's an awkward silence. In the middle of it, I hear something coming from my right. When I look over, the man with the mustache is waking up. Why he was asleep in the first place? Do I buy the story about getting punched in the face? He's sweating so hard. Maybe the heat and the noise inside were too much for him. I've seen it happen before. But then maybe he's on a bad trip. I don't want to get stuck with a psycho for the rest of the evening.

His eyes are bulging out of his head like they're about to explode. He grabs on to the bench, and his hand is a relief map of veins threatening to tear right out of his skin and thrash around like live cables. He checks his watch, then dismisses what he sees with a groan.

"What time is it?" he gasps at me.

I check my phone. Again. "1:57."

"*Oh my God!*" he screams, jumping to his feet. He gazes up at Aunty Bob's, and when he looks at it like that the club really does look ominous. Like the big black rectangle in *2001: A Space Odyssey*. "It's too late," he moans in his fever-dream.

Tom tries to calm his friend down, but the man in the mustache pushes him away. "There's no time! You have no idea what happens…" Now he's looking at me strangely. "That's the hat," he says. "Give it to me."

"Hey, back off!" I say, batting him away. Tom is already in the fray trying to hold his friend back, but he's going berserk. I can see his pulse through his skin.

He slips out of Tom's grip and swipes the hat off my head.

SLAYDEN

1:59 a.m.

1 minute remains

I HAVE IT. But I can't stop now. Only one minute left. They're chasing me already. Tom and the woman. I'm running. Pushing people out of the way. The sweat is blinding me. I'm so hot. Why am I wearing so many clothes? It prickles, the skin at my neck. My shirt is strangling me. I ignore it. I pull great buckets of air into my lungs. It doesn't help. They're not big enough to hold all the air I need. Makes me feel worse. Short of breath. Drowning in fire. I need to find…I need to find…Tom catches me. Grabs my arm. I slip through. But his hand catches mine. My bare hand. He is so cold. He screams. Pulls away. The smell of burning skin. His or mine? I get away. Find a door. Get inside. The noise subsides. My lungs are collapsing. But the pounding in my head won't stop. Why won't it stop? Why won't it ever stop? The hat's not destroyed yet. But now I have it. Stinging at the corner of my eyes. All the colors of white wash over me. Burning cold in my veins. Too fast for me to stop it.

There are no dreams here now.

Did I save us?

I don't know.

But I tried.

VAY

"Here, just because you're dying doesn't mean you can't look fabulous."

One of them puts the hat on my head and leaves the office. It's quieter now, but I can still feel the beat from the club music in my stomach. I don't know where they've gone, but they've shut the door behind them and left me alone in here. Probably they're going to wait for the ambulance. I told them an ambulance would take too long and one of them should drive me to the hospital, but the older one snorted and mumbled something about liability insurance. I believe I launched into a scathing rejoinder about how high their premiums would get if I died on their property, but I don't remember if I actually said anything.

It's hard to remember what happened after I fell off the stairs. My skin is whiter than it should be. I know that. And I'm shaking and I can't stop. Everything is happening now. There is only the present. There is no past. I realize my heart is racing in my chest. Maybe that's not good. Should it be doing that? Am I bleeding? I don't think I'm bleeding, but maybe I am and can't feel it. I can't feel anything in my left leg.

No, wait, I remember. I didn't fall. I was *pushed*.

I'm going to sue that idiot for everything he's got. He looked poor, so everything he's got probably only adds up to lunch money, but the legal expenses will cripple him for life, just like he's done to me. I might never walk again.

I shiver. They've been telling me I look white ever since they picked me up from under the staircase, but now is the first time I've felt cold. I look at my hand again. I'm normally pale, but now I look like a corpse. I touch my face. I can't feel it.

What if I never *play* again?

I put the thought out of my head. It's just a leg. I don't care if I have to strap a *table leg* to my stump, it is not going to stop me playing. But will I ever be as good? Fuck.

Just wait till my parents tell their lawyer.

I reach into my front pocket. I have to be careful of the leg, but I can't feel anything at all. My pants are on so tight and I can't seem to work my fingers, but I manage to get my phone out and text Bailey.

Vay: *someone broke my leg*
Bailey: *not the one who got me*
Vay: *no havent seen him since he peed on you*
Bailey: *who then*
Vay: *how the fuck should i know where r u i need help*
Bailey: *i went HOME*
Vay: *well what am i supposed to do*
Bailey: *call an ambulance*

He follows this with a GIF of that *Simpsons* episode where Homer gets airlifted into an ambulance and bumps his head against the cliff all the way up.

Great. The advantages of knowing someone with a medical degree. I've never actually seen him *use* it, and now I'm wondering if it's just for decoration. For his next birthday, I'm going to cut it up and use it for wrapping paper. Call an ambulance…That's what the others said when they brought me in here, but I haven't seen a stretcher party yet. What if they've left me here? Or dialed the wrong number? Fuck them. Fuck everyone. I can do it myself.

I flip back to the home screen and fumble the phone. It falls on the ground next to the stretcher. I reach over the edge and grab it, but there's something else there, too. The phone's fallen in a big pile of crap. Looks like ashes. This is where they picked the hat off the floor. It was just sitting in the middle of a pile of dust like someone had knocked over an ashtray. It's in the outline of a person. Did someone spontaneously fucking combust in here or what? What the hell is going on in this club? All I know is I'm lying in a big pile of gray shit. The hat is covered in ash, too. Fucking *hell*, it must be all over me by now. These are three hundred dollar jeans and now they're probably ruined. I'll add that to the damages.

I wipe off the screen and dial 9-1-1.

"9-1-1, where is your emergency?" a woman answers.

"Aunty Bob's."

There's a kind of heavy sigh on the line and I can tell already she's going to make trouble. "Sir, this is 9-1-1. Do you *have* an emergency?"

"You're damn right I have an emergency. I'm lying on the floor covered in shit, and my friend who's a doctor told me to call…"

"Sir, please put the doctor on the line."

"I can't. He got peed on by a Romanticist in a red hat. Wait, is this the hat? Oh my God, I'm wearing a *pee*-hat."

"You're covered in feces, and your friend is covered in urine. Does this emergency pose a risk to public health? Has there been a leak at the sewage containment plant?"

"What? What are you gibbering about? I broke my leg."

"Why did you break your leg?"

"I didn't do it on purpose, you demented virago, it was this maniac at Aunty Bob's. Who the hell do you think would break their own leg? Are you congenitally stupid? Who do they get to answer these calls anyway? Do you even have a degree? Oh my God, you're probably getting minimum wage. Whatever it is, it's too much. My life is in the hands of a high school graduate."

"Sir, please describe the nature of the emergency."

"That's what I'm trying to tell you. He was on some kind of a rampage. He pushed me off a staircase."

"Was the suspect armed?"

"He will be when I get hold of him. Wait, did you say 'harmed' or 'armed'?"

"We are dispatching officers to your location now. Please remain calm and stay out of sight. If you see the suspect again, please do not approach him."

"Will you shut up and listen to me? It's not officers I need, it's—"

"Sir, you need to keep your voice down. Whatever you do, do not attract the gunman's attention. You need to hang up this phone right now."

"No, I—"

"*We are not allowed to hang up first. I need you to hang up the phone now!*"

"I pay your salary and—"

"*Hang up the phone!*"

"*Son of a bitch!*" I scream, and I throw the phone across the room in frustration. I see the screen go black. At least it's hung up now. I guess that means "help" is on its way. Our nation's emergency response system at work. What a crack squad. What an elite force. No wonder half the country is underwater and the other half is on fire.

I let my head fall back on the stretcher so quickly it spins. It feels like there's no blood in my whole body. Judging by how clammy my shirt feels, there's not much water, either.

"Hey," I say in the direction of the door. "*Hey!* Someone get me a bottle of water." But all I can hear is the thump of the music coming from inside the club. Great.

Then the office door opens. *Finally! The ambulance is here at last.* But my hopes fall when I see it's only what's-his-name I was grinding against on the dance floor. Darren. Darryl. Whatever, it started with a *D*.

"Oh my God!" says D. "They told me you were in here. What happened to you?"

"I was playing leapfrog on the edge of a cliff."

D nods sympathetically. "You gotta be careful, boo-bear. You could have really hurt yourself."

I pause to admire him for a second. D's big, stupid face is filled with nothing except happiness and generosity. He might be the single dumbest person I have ever met. Stupidity on that kind of a scale is a wonder of the natural world. It would be sheer folly to go correcting him and shatter the perfectly smooth, unwrinkled surface of his cerebral cortex.

"Right," I say. "I'll be careful next time I jump out of an airplane without a parachute."

D clicks his tongue. "You shouldn't do that. You're gonna get yourself killed. Here," he says, pulling off his tank top and using it to prop up my head. He kicks the outline of ash into an unrecognizable mess. I don't suppose anyone will believe me now. *It was in the shape of a person.*

"Does that feel better?"

It does. And the view doesn't hurt, either. D is built like a gymnast, and I thought he looked good *in* the top. Now that he's out of it and leaning over me, I can see a trickle of sweat drip down the valley of his chest past the fine brown hairs around his nipple. I am going to find the guy who pushed me and rip his dick off. I was five minutes away from fucking D tonight, and now I can't even stand up.

I nod faintly. "I don't suppose you could prop my head up a bit higher?" I ask with a weak cough. As D leans over me again, I catch that perfect view and smell the deodorant mingling with the sweat under his arms.

"Where does it hurt?" he asks. "Maybe I can help. I am a fully qualified homeopath."

I may choke to death on my own scorn. If the broken leg and the high school graduate don't kill me, then this mountebank might finish me off.

"Can your magic water fix a broken leg? Because I have a broken leg."

"It's not magic. It's an ancient, proven system of medicine."

"You're damn right it's proven, it's proven to be a big pile of horse shit."

"That's just the pain talking. You're filling up with negative emotions because of your injury, and it's clouding your world view. You'll never get better with an attitude like that. The placebo effect has shown the power of positive thinking."

"Oh woooow, you're an expert on placebos. I would never have guessed."

"Shhh," he says, putting a finger to my lips. I briefly get a taste of something sweet and sticky and salty all at once, sweat and cocktail and the flavor of human skin. "Don't worry, I'll get you out of here and get you the help you need."

"Wait, what? What does that mean? There's an ambulance already on its way, I really don't think—"

But I don't get to finish before he hauls me up off the floor. I screech in pain. I thought I couldn't feel anything. I was wrong. My legs are dangling over his right arm, and it feels like knives lacerating me from the inside. I look down at the impossible jumble of limbs. I can't tell which leg is my left and which one is my right. Now there's three of them. Now there's four. I try to lie back and clear my head, but I feel so dizzy. How long have I been in his arms?

"Don't worry," D says, "my friend has an aromatherapy clinic in the Haight. She'll make sure you're comfortable."

"Aromatherapy? For a *broken leg*?"

"She's just installed some of those sensory deprivation chambers, only instead of using Epsom salts, she's using mineral water infused with hydrogen sulfide." He sees I'm about to ask something and all of a sudden the idiot becomes conveniently savant. "Yeah, it totally stinks, but you get used to the smell of rotten eggs after fifteen or twenty minutes. And then you just soak your way to peace of mind."

"My mind's already fucking peaceful," I snarl, trying to keep him in focus.

"How can you expect to fix your body if you haven't fixed your *mind*," D says pseudo-meaningfully.

I lie back again. "Noooo," I hear myself groan. "I don't want to smell like farts."

Balancing my weight across his arms, he grabs the door handle with one hand and eases it open enough to push the rest of the way with his foot. Now we're out in the club again, music pounding in my ears, and the room is swirling around my head.

"Help," I mumble. "This is a kidnapping." But I can't make myself heard over the music. No one notices me. A few people even give me pitying looks, and I realize they think I've had too much to drink. Help isn't coming. And the gravity of the situation begins to set in. If I don't get medical help, I could die. My leg is going to go septic and I'll get gangrene and I'll be dead forever. We're getting close to the exit. If D gets me out on the street I'm done for. I try to call for help again, but the effort makes my vision go cloudy. I slump in his arms and hope some blood will flow back to my head. I have to stay conscious.

Wait! I can see a familiar shape in the distance. At least I think it's him. My eyes roll sideways in my head, desperate to attract his attention. It is! It's that black guy I talked to after Bailey got pissed on. By some miracle I catch his eye. He recognizes me.

"Dude, you wearin' that piss-hat? You nasty."

"Help," I moan, brushing his arm with my hand.

For an amazing second, D stops his death march to the exit. I think he recognizes him. "Hey, Marquis!" he calls out. "Great to see you again."

"Hey, what up? What you doin' carryin' Frasier round like that?" Frasier? *Frasier?* I am not fucking *Frasier*. Marquis looks me over and realizes I look like I'm about to die. "Shiiit, what happen to yo' leg?"

"I'm being kidnapped," I mumble. "I need to wait for the ambulance."

"Uh-huh," he says in that way that means he doesn't believe me.

D doesn't do much to set him straight. "I think he hurt his leg. I'm taking him to get help. My friend Sarah has this aromatherapy clinic..."

"Aromatherapy?" Marquis leans over my face, and I can feel myself go even paler. My stomach is churning. He is even more hideous up close. "You gonna get you some aromatherapy fo' yo' leg? Is that what you want?"

"Help me!" I gasp.

He leans in closer, and now I realize he is enjoying making me uncomfortable. He is doing this on purpose. "Lemme see. What did you say to me when I was sittin' at the bar havin' a conversation wit' my friend? Was it, 'Git yo' ghetto ass outta my face, I'm tryna get me a drink'? Yeah, that sure sounds like it, but I don't remember so good."

"I'm sorry, I didn't mean it."

"Now, what excuse does a nice white boy like you got to be so ignorant?"

"I don't know. I'm sorry. Please, just help me." I can feel his breath on my ear. It's like a dog is breathing in my face. I flinch, hoping he won't touch me. For a second I get an image of those fat lips mashing themselves on mine, his thick pink tongue like an animal's forcing its way past his tombstone teeth and down my throat.

Marquis stands back up and says to D, "You better get him to that aromatherapy emergency room real quick. He startin' to get delirious. An' you know they say eighty percent of all permanent injuries coulda been prevented wit' early aromatherapy." D nods wisely and starts back to the exit.

We're just about to hit the doors when Marquis says, "Wait up, wait up. I can't let this happen." Thank God. He was just playing with me. He's coming back to save me after all.

Then he grabs the hat off my head and leaves.

MARQUIS

I brush the hat on my arm. There's some shit comes off the edge but it looks clean, specially fo' a piss-hat. It's prob'ly safe, but I reckon I can't miss an opportunity like this. I put it on an' wave back at that racist piece of shit. "See ya nex' time, Frasier. Disabled entrance is round the side, yo."

Daniel takes him out front, and as they goin' out two police come in. They ain't wavin' they guns around, but they look real wound up about somethin' an' I ain't takin' no chances. I know what the police do to black folks in this city, and that's jus' the straight ones. Ain't nobody want a cap bust in they ass when they tryin' to dance. I was comin' back to the bar when I got sidetrack by Frasier, but if the cops see me they might try to hassle me. I take a detour through the dance floor an' get lost in all the dancers until the cops move along. Through all the bodies I see 'em walk past the bathrooms an' in a unlabeled door. I guess that's where the manager office at.

I go back to the bar an' sit down nex' to Amy. I'll tell her later about what happen to Frasier. She got a dark sense o' humor an' a strong sense o' justice, so she'll get a kick outta that. Right now, she still talkin' to Benny an' I don't wanna interrup'.

I wave at Ian an' order another IPA. The good thing about bein' a beer drinker at Aunty Bob's is the beer never runs out, so I get to drink what I want. A lot o' this weird-ass drink goin' aroun' that I ain't seen before but when I met Benny, he called it a sparkledrank. They tasty as fuck, but it was hella sweet. I swear I could feel that thing dissolvin' my teeth. My grandma used to have one dead tooth—not one o' the front ones, but jus' a little bit on one side so you could see it when she smiled. It shined in the light. Now when I drink somethin' too sugary, I can jus' feel my teeth dyin' an' turnin' gray. Same reason I'm tryin' to quit smokin'. The menthol makes my teeth tingle.

I keep my eyes on the door nex' to the bathrooms, an' sure enough in a couple minutes the two police come back out, this time with Mr. Robinson. I keep my head down at the bar below the level o' the other drinkers but not so low I look shady. But they not lookin' this way. Mr. Robinson takes 'em out inta the beer garden an' they disappear. Somethin' goin' on, but I ain't about to find out what.

"You feeling all right, Marquis?" says Benny.

I'm sweatin' somethin' fierce for some reason. Guess I didn' realize how nervous I was. Get a grip. What do I think is gonna happen? I wipe my forehead on my arm. My hair don't look too long, but if you grab it an' stretch it out it comes down to my chin. It trappin' the heat in the club an' makin' me sweat—prob'ly time to get it cut, but I been puttin' it off 'cause I can't find a good stylis'. I take off the hat fo' a minute an' fan myself with it. That don't help.

"Yeah, I'm fine," I say. "I'm jus' sweatin'. It hot as hell in here tonight." Right after I say it, I realize Amy an' Benny ain't sweatin' a drop. It makes their skin look col' an' white an' smooth, like a albino snake.

Benny says, "No, I mean you've got something on your shirt."

I put the hat back on an' try an' look what's on my shirt. "What? Where?"

"Back right shoulder."

I twis' an' try to get a better look at it in the club lights. Then I see some bird gone an' shit on me. Prob'ly when I stepped out fo' a cigarette, but maybe it happen when I lef' the house. Shit, I coulda been walkin' round with bird shit on me *all night*.

"Looks like bird shit," Amy says, helpful.

"It *is* bird shit," I say.

"Is this a new thing?" she asks. "Is everyone wearing bird shit now?"

"No, it musta happen before I come in. Shiiiit," I moan, dabbin' at the bird poop with a cocktail napkin. I can't tell if it's workin' or I'm jus' spreadin' it aroun'.

Benny nods all wise an' all-knowin'. "Well, that's it. You've got bird AIDS now."

"What? What you talkin' about bird AIDS?"

"That's how it happens. Bird AIDS gets in through the poop. All you need to do is get crapped on once and *bam*, bird AIDS."

"Shut up, I ain't got bird AIDS."

He smiles sadly. "Denial is the first symptom of bird AIDS."

"No it ain't."

He quiet for a second before he adds, "Bird AIDS."

"Stop sayin' bird AIDS!"

He looks at me with a huge smirk all over his face like he holdin' it in.

"Bird AIDS," says Amy, an' Benny starts crackin' up. I try not to smile, but I can't help it, an' in a second I'm laughin', too.

"Still," Benny says, "it would explain why you're sweating so much. The fever that accompanies bird AIDS has been well documented by the world's most expert brainiologists and scienticians."

"An' you a expert scientician now, are you?"

"Marquis, 'scientician' isn't a real word," he says. "Are you hallucinating words? What year do you think it is? Who's the president?" Then he turns to Amy an' says, "That bird AIDS is worse than I thought. Much worse. We gotta get him to a hospital."

"Or maybe an aviary."

"If we don't get your wings clipped right away, it could spread to us."

I say, "Everybody freakin' hilarious today. Must be somethin' in the water."

"There is something in the water," Benny nods solemnly. "Bird AIDS."

An' now he crackin' up again. Even Amy got a tired smile on her face. But I feel like the heat ain't goin' away. A drop o' sweat drips down the side o' my face, but I'm holdin' bird crap napkins in my hands and can't wipe it off. It rolls down my neck an' disappears on the hem o' my shirt. I'm sweatin' so much, I'm glad I wore a white T-shirt. At leas' this way I can look sexy while I'm dyin'. I throw the napkins on the floor an' take a long drink o' my beer. It cools me down some. Not much, though.

"But—" I say, but Benny cut me off.

"Did you say, 'buck'?"

"Buck?"

"Buck-buck buck-awwwwk," he says. Fucker makin' chicken noises.

"I always knew you a cock." There. That'll fix his wagon.

"It's okay, I forgive you. I know it's just the bird AIDS talking."

God damn it, I ain't never gonna get rid of this damn bird AIDS. I grab my beer to take another cold sip—nipple buzz bomb! A blast o' pure diabetes hits me in the face like bein' turkey-slapped by Willy Wonka. I'm so surprised it goes down the wrong tube an' I cough it up inta the glass. Aw man, it's that sparkledrank. I musta picked up someone else's drink.

"Hey, what's the idea?" someone barks at me. I turn to my lef' an' see this old white dude wit' perfec'ly chisel gray hair, black pants, an' a borin'-ass business shirt. He looks sorta like a less shady Dickie Nixon, but fo' some reason he lickin' his lips all the time like they covered in tits. I dunno what '50s dad doin' here, but he be gettin' his drank on 'cause he good an' liquored up.

"Sorry, man, I thought it was mine."

" 's all right," he mumbles. "Tastes like shit anyway."

"Here, lemme buy you another one," I say, reachin' for my wallet.

"Naw, I got it. Keep your money." He turns to Ian an' shouts, "*Hey!*" An' now he slammin' his hand on the bar like Ian his bitch. "What do I have to do to get a decent drink around here?"

Ian got other customers firs', but he knows it's easier to get the asshole outta the way instead o' makin' him wait. "What do you want, sir?"

Uh-oh. Now he bustin' out the "sir." That the rudes' thing you can call someone without callin' them a fuck-shit-stack to they face. I know, I used ta wait tables in college.

"I thought you fags're s'posed to make good drinks," says Nixon. I turn to Amy an' Benny. Benny givin' me a face wit' his mouth wide open like this the funnies' thing that happen all night. Amy still got her poker face on, but she got that one eyebrow that goes up when somethin' funny goin' on. Nixon tells Ian, "Gimme a double Scotch."

"On the rocks?" he says.

"You do an' I'll shit in your ice."

Leas', I think he said "ice." It mighta been "eyes," but I don't wanna think about that too hard. So Ian goes an' pours Nixon the meanes' Scotch I ever seen. If Ian likes you, you be gettin' generous pours o' liquor all night, but if he givin' you the col' shoulder you ain't even get enough liquor to get a buzz on. Nixon looks like he too fucked up to even notice.

"Did I tell you," he tells me, "I make five hundred thousand a year and I have a twenty-five-year-old girlfriend. Or I did, until this week. Her parents found out about me and made her end it. What do I care anyway? I can get pussy like that any time I like. I can pick up any chick in this bar."

"Lotta them chicks lesbians," I say wit' a nod at Amy. "But show us what you got, maybe you got good game. Let's say you meet Amy here. What's your openin' line?" But Nixon don't take no notice o' me. Guess my attemp' to drop Amy in it didn't work. I'm stuck in this conversation and ain't nothin' I can say to stop it. I might as well be a ghost. I'm sure startin' to feel like one.

Nixon goin' on. "Man she was great, though. She used to walk around the house in a real short skirt with her cunt hanging right out."

My eyes go wide. I ain't heard that one in a while. Not at Aunty Bob's, anyhow. Ain't nobody got time to listen to this bullshit. I try to get up but Amy an' Benny push me back onta the stool. "You've gotta keep this old creeper talking," says Benny. "He's the worst. Make him say something else."

"I don't want to," I beg him. "Please, guys. I wanna get some air."

But they push me back again an' I don't even have to try to keep Nixon goin'. He talkin' an' talkin' like he the mos' interestin' man in the universe. "You're young," he says, grabbin' my arm. His hand feels cold. "Jesus, you're burnin' up," he says. "If you're on something, you ought to share. 't's only polite."

I shake my head. "I jus' need a haircut."

"What's a kid like you doing in a club like this?" he asks, an' outta the corner o' my eye I can see Amy's jus' figure out what Nixon gettin' at. I gotta get outta here. I don't wanna be here for this conversation. What am I gonna say? But before I can say anythin', he slammin' his hand on the bar again an' shoutin', "Hey! Get him another one of what he's having."

Ian raises his eyebrow at me but pours the beer anyway.

"No, thanks, but I—"

"Take it," says Nixon, pushin' the glass at me. "What do I care. D'you have a boyfriend?"

Fuuuuuuuuck.

"Yeah, I—"

But Benny jumps in. "Noooo, he really doesn't!" Imma kill that wiseass. He leanin' across me now to talk to Nixon, an' he look so hot in them lights. The firs' button open on his shirt, an' when he leans across, I can see down to his chest. I dunno if it's the fever talkin', but suddenly I'm in the mood. Maybe that's what it is, this heat buildin' up inside me that I can't get rid of. Maybe I jus' realize how to get rid of it. I could tear Benny's shirt off wit' my bare teeth right now.

Nixon nods. "You guys are cute friends. You ever have sex with each other? Like just for fun?"

"No," Benny says. "But every time I see him I just wanna jump his bones." Fuck. I gotta hol' myself back. "Check out those pecs, man. He is wearing the hell out of that T-shirt. Flex for the nice man, Marquis." I give him a stare like I'm gonna rip his head off. That don't stop him. "See? Look at those come-to-bed eyes. Blue Steel's got nothing on Marquis here. But he's not interested in me." No! I am! "Between you and me, I think he likes older men."

Fucking Benny!

Nixon says, "You know I always wanted to try it with a dude, like once. You know, like I might be bi, but I need someone to show me..."

Oh, hell no. I ain't nobody's experimen'. I stand up so fast I knock over the beer Dickie Nixon bought me. It splashes on my shirt, makin' me even wetter than I already was.

"Hey," he says, "I just paid for that."

"What do you care, you make five hunnert thousand a year," I tell him.

He looks surprised. "Who told you that? Look, your shirt's all wet. You oughta take that off or you'll catch pneumonia." Now he grabbin' at my shirt an' tryin' ta lift it up.

I pull away from him an' mumble, "I gotta go. I ain't feelin' well. I think I need a little air."

"D'you wanna go out with me sometime?" But I ain't even lookin' back. As I'm pushin' away, I see Benny nod at Amy.

"Yup, that's bird AIDS all right."

Son of a bitch friends. I'm sweatin' fit to bust an' they jus' talkin' shit an' fishin' for ol' creepers. I'm startin' to wonder if I am catchin' somethin'. I mean, yeah, it's hot as fuck in here, but it ain't *that* hot. Not bird AIDS, but somethin' else maybe. I wipe my hand on my shirt. Shit, what if some o' that bird shit really did get inta my drink or I touched my mouth or somethin'. I really coulda caught somethin'. *Is* there a bird AIDS? There can't be. But I think I heard somethin' once about a cat AIDS. Or was that made up, too? 'Cause if that was real, then ain't nobody can say bird AIDS ain't real either.

My drink…That ol' creeper was hangin' round my drink. An' when I grab the wrong one, wasn't it where my beer was suppose to be? My hand moves down my chest until it reaches my stomach. I feel somethin' weird movin' inside. Somethin' ain't sittin' right. I think Nixon maybe tryin' ta pull a Hot Cosby on me.

I stagger away from the bar to try an' get away from all the noise an' the lights. There's people dancin' all aroun' me an' for a secon', I can't even see where I'm goin'. There gotta be a quiet place somewhere in this club. If I can jus' get outside an' breathe some fresh air. Maybe a cigarette'll quiet me down some.

I step out inta the beer garden an' breathe in deep. The air feels cool on my skin, an' I'm startin' to feel like a goddamn human bein' again. I fan myself with the hat an' feel the air on my forehead. I slump down onto one o' the picnic tables an' let my ass touch the cold wood seat through my jeans. I light up a Pall Mall an' slip the pack back in my pocket.

"You've been dancing too hard," someone says. "You ought to take a break."

There's a boy sittin' on the other side o' the table. He pretty, too—brown hair, kinda plump skin, little bit o' scruff on his cheeks too, patchy like he don't know how to grow it. I can work with that. He on his own, an' he looks happy I sat down. I smile, too. Maybe I ain't goin' home wit' that creeper after all.

"Yeah, I guess so. I'm Marquis." He says his name is Ashen, an' I'm like, "That a weird name."

"You're right. Boy do I feel stupid, Maaaaaarquis."

The boy got a mouth on him. I like that, too. I'm jus' about to say somethin' when a hand gets up in my face. It's gone by the time I figure out jus' what the hell goin' on. Some woman came up to us an' put her empty glass on our table an' didn't even look at us. Now she talkin' to her friends an' makin' for the door. She a real SF money type, a manager at a tech company who thinks it's edgy an' outrageous to spen' her night in a gay club.

"Oh hey, ain't nobody here. Jus' leave yo' shit wherever you want. Bootsy-ass bitch." She ain't lookin', but she already half gone. I pick up her nasty-ass glass an' stan' up to try ta throw it after her, but it slips in my hand an' nex' thing I know, the melty ice an' slush spilled all over me. God fuckin' *damn it*. I can't even pick up a glass right. I feel my head gettin' dizzy again, but Ashen gigglin' to himself, so maybe it ain't all bad. "D'you believe that shit?" I ask.

"*Bootsy?*" he asks with a kind of amazed look.

"Oh you know. She trashy, she bootsy, she jus' whack."

"I'm glad I asked. You really let her have it."

There's a lump in my throat. Ain't nothin' workin' wit' me tonight. "Damn straight. Bitch needs to learn her some manners. Treatin' people like that jus' rude."

I go to sit back down, but nex' thing I know, I miss the seat an' fall agains' the concrete groun'. My leg hurts. I musta stepped on a piece o' ice an' slipped. I eff'd up. But before I know it, Ashen is over me an' he supportin' my head wit his hand.

"What's wrong? Are you okay?"

"Yeah, I think so." Like hell I am. "I don't think I can walk." The world spinnin' aroun' me. Who was that woman? Was she with the ol' creeper? They in on this together.

I pull myself up to look around an' try to find where Benny at, but the movement's too fast, an' I can feel my legs givin' out again.

"Put your weight on me," Ashen says. I feel his other hand on my chest. Maybe this ain't all bad.

I get up an' have to hold on to Ashen right away. I can't seem to keep my balance. He guides me back into the club, an' we stop outside the door where I saw those police earlier, an' I realize he takin' me to the office. He knocks on the door, but nobody answers, so we go in on our own. Just a empty desk in here an' a floor that no one clean in forever. Everythin' covered in dust an' grit.

I collapse inta the owner's chair an' before I know it, Ashen standin' over me lookin' down. My hand holdin' his. The chair's one o' those fancy-ass padded ones, an' it reclines when I lean back. The movemen' pulls Ashen toward me. Our lips touch—his breath hot an' sticky, an' he been smokin'. I don't min'. His lips are so small an' tight. At firs' it like I don't even know what I'm kissin', but then his mouth opens a li'l wider an' my tongue touches his.

"Take off your shirt," he says.

I rip open my shirt from the neck down. The air on my skin feels so cold, but I can still feel myself burnin' up. I can't hardly see nothin' right in front o' me. Ashen puts his hands on my sweaty, beer-soaked chest an' sits on my lap.

Maybe I'm still nauseous from the bird AIDS or the fall but somethin' feels weird. My stomach all churn up. My head poundin'. I reach his jeans an' pull open the top button. They so low slung, the fly practic'ly pops open on its own. An' I grab his crotch.

Ain't nothin' there. Ain't nothin' in his underpants but… What is that? He a man, I know it, but—my head swimmin'—the world stop makin' sense a long time ago.

He open his mouth to say somethin', but I'm already sayin', "This is shady as fuck, dude. What the hell's goin' on here. Did you put somethin' in my drink?"

"No!" he says, an' now I can tell he's super pissed at me. "*Someone* did."

Five hunnert thou a year. Cunt hangin' out. He jumps off an' pulls his jeans back up. He shoutin' somethin', but I don't know what. Shit in your ice, man. I know he right. I felt bad ever since before I met Ashen. I'll shit in your eyes. Did ol' man Nixon slip me a mickey? Or maybe Benny was right. Maybe I *do* have the bird AIDS. I look at my hands to find where the contamination at, but I have twelve fingers an' they won't stop movin' around. Eleven. Thirteen. I rub my eyes, but if I have touched the bird AIDS, then now it's all up in my eyes, in my blood, in my brain.

"Who are you?" I ask Ashen, but I know I can't hear the answer.

I lick my lips. I didn't realize how hard I'm sweatin'. At firs' I taste nothin' excep' salt an' my tongue is flooded with sweat. Then I taste the sparkledrank that was on Ashen's lips. An' cigarettes. Nasty ones, all chemicals. It all chemicals.

I make for the door o' the office an' catch a look at myself in the vanity mirror. I look like somebody else. I can't even recognize myself no more. I'm shirtless an' sweatin' hard. I'm pullin' a face. An' wearin' a red hat that makes me look like a pimp. What if that *is* somebody else? What if I changed? I move, an' the dude in the mirror moves wit' me. It's a trick. It's gotta be a trick.

I punch it an' it breaks. I can't hear Ashen scream. I open the door an' run out inta the club. I can't even hear the music. The me that ain't me looks like hell, but ain't nobody pay attention.

Shit. The two cops standin' on the other side o' the bar. They got ahold o' Nixon an' they pullin' him away from his mean Scotch. I turn aroun'. I can't let 'em see me. I know what they'll do. I know what they do to folks with the bird AIDS.

An' now I'm surrounded. There's birds on every side. They come for me, the birds have. Long beaks. Bulgin' black eyes. No expression in they faces.

"In there," I try to explain. "It's a cuntboy."

But without even lookin', I know he's gone. I wouldn't stay either. An' now I'm on my own, an' the birds have come to take me, an' I can't hear them squawkin'. But I know they are.

An' I let 'em take me.

LUCIEN

"*Vive la 'Pataphysique! Vive Dada!*"

"Lucien Lefevre, criminologist," I say to the people in fancy dress, flashing the ID card they gave me for my Criminologist costume. They're standing around chanting at the guy who just passed out on the floor while I'm trying to fan him with his hat. "Stand back, give him some air," I shout over the music and the chanting. "Can't you see he's hurt?"

I don't know if they heard me, but they're moving away. There are about half a dozen of them, all wearing long purple coats covered in little comets and lightning bolts and spirals and question marks. It's not Halloween, but they're wearing those scary old-timey plague doctor masks with the long noses. They look like a flock of evil birds.

"I can't believe it," says Kelvin. "It's the Royal College of 'Pataphysicians. I saw their exhibit at Maker Faire last year." I put the hat down on my head and take the guy's pulse. His heart's all right, as far as I can tell. As long as it's beating I don't know if I can do anything else to help him. "How do you do that? You actually look like you know what you're doing," says Kelvin.

"Oh my God, rude. I am a dancer. I know first aid, you know." I lift the unconscious man's head gently and try to look him in the face. "Are you high?" I ask loudly and clearly. "What did you take?" But he's not coming around. I lift his eyelids and examine his pupils.

"Is he all right?" asks Kelvin.

"I think so. His pupils aren't dilated. Probably just drunk." Kelvin's still looking at the receding cloaks of the 'Pataphysicians. As they disappear into the crowd, the last one swirls the cape around him like Dracula. "What are they doing *here*?" I ask him.

"Same as us, probably—following the yellow dick road."

"I didn't know you were into Asians."

"Yes, Asian men with enormous fake tits. Why don't men get breast implants? It's a crime, I tell you."

"You don't like tits," I say. "You never even lost your gold star."

"Did so. I dated Jenny Alencar for a week in the fifth grade."

"You didn't have sex in the fifth grade, I'd know about that. You have to have sex to lose your gold star."

"Can't you see what I'm trying to tell you, Lucien? I love you."

"No, you don't," I say. I can't even deal with Kelvin sometimes. But then I guess he's like this all the time, so what are you going to do?

"All I ever wanted to be was the albatross around your neck," he says.

"I don't know anything about that."

"'It is an ancient Mariner, and he stoppeth one of three...'" he says. "You've shot me with your bow, and now we are inextricably intertwined, a beautiful miscegenating Gordian knot, a sparkledrank mixed to such perfection that its component parts could never be extracted by any fractional distillation or alchemical witchery."

"What? What the skaboopy are you saying?"

"Shush, my cursed sailor, we are one."

"Will you stop it with all that hoodoo and gimme a hand with this guy?" I say, pointing at the man who *is still unconscious on the ground*. Can you believe Kelvin sometimes?

Kelvin picks him up by the legs while I take him by the shoulders. I'm sure he'll be all right if we can get him some air. It's not far to the beer garden, but he's heavier than he looks. I'm used to lifting people, but I can tell Kelvin is having trouble holding on.

"I need a break," he gasps.

"No, you don't. It'll be good for you to lift something heavier than a piece of chalk."

I bump the guy's head on the door when we try to get him out to the beer garden, which just gives Kelvin an excuse to go, "Easy there, cowboy. Not laughing at my math degree now, are you? See, if you knew about rotational symmetry, this guy would still be able to remember his Social Security number. But because you scorned the numerical sciences, he's probably got a concussion and a fractured skull and, yep, I definitely saw part of his brain fall out—fuck!" He's just dropped the man's legs, but it's okay. I drag him the last few feet until we can sit him down on one of the wooden benches along the walls. I check his pupils again now the light's not strobing. I send Kelvin for a glass of water. He should be able to lift that.

As soon as Kelvin moves over to the bar, two people step out from the club and walk up to me. One is a pretty blond boy wearing a fancy button-up T-shirt. The other is a short girl with close-cropped hair. Amy, right? She was someone's plus-one at a party I can't remember. She doesn't look too happy with me.

"What in the hell did you do to Marquis?" she says.

"We think he fainted."

"Marquis?" she asks, putting her hand on his shoulder and shaking him gently. The boy starts miming Amy grabbing Marquis's chest. She turns to see what he's doing, and he stops and looks innocent all of a sudden. She goes, "Are you going to stand there being stupid or are you going to help?"

"He'll be fine," says the boy. "You heard, he only fainted."

"Yeah? And what if it's serious?"

"Like the bird AIDS?" he says, making a derpy face.

"Like that moldy old sexist at the bar slipping something in his drink."

"Oh shit," says the boy. Suddenly, he's paying a lot more attention. Then two cops and an older man with some nice daddy vibes come running in from outside. Seriously now, a bit of gray hair, and a neat little goatee. Ooof. Yes please.

"What's going on here?" says one of the cops. "Your friend have too much to drink?"

"They're dropping like flies," says the older man. "I knew it. Where the hell's Andre?"

"Andre's here?" both me and Amy say at the same time. We look at each other. I'm just curious, but it looks like she's sizing me up.

"You know Andre?" I ask.

"What's it to you?" I can't tell if it's good or bad that Andre's here tonight, but she was all confident before and now her shoulders are tensed up and she's moving awkwardly.

"Ma'am, is your friend all right?" asks the cop more forcefully.

The other one bends down to take his pulse. He looks up to the first one and nods. "He's alive."

Kelvin nudges me. "Willya look at that? You guessed right."

I go to smack him on his arm, but it comes out more like a kind of doggy-paddle. "I know when someone's alive!"

He shakes his head sadly. "Well, there was that one time…" He's never going to let me forget that. You mistake one mannequin for a saleslady and you have to hear about it for the rest of your life. I turned to ask her if Macy's had a sexy underpants section, and when she didn't say anything, I just thought she was being rude, so I grabbed her arm and the whole dummy fell over. And I might have screamed a little. A lot.

The girl is talking to the officers. "You call the ambulance. We'll get him out front to wait for it." She and the man's other friend drag him toward the exit the best they can.

"The ambulance is on its way," says one of the cops.

"Thank God," says the manager. "It's getting harder and harder to hide them."

"Is something wrong?" I ask. "I know first aid."

No one's been paying attention to Kelvin for more than five minutes, so he butts in. "And I'm a mathematician."

They start leading us to the manager's office, but I can tell Kelvin is still antsy. I think I've got him. I've been saving this. "He is a pretty great mathematician," I nod.

Kelvin starts giving me some wicked side-eye. "How do you know? You don't know anything about it."

"I left you a review online," I say like it's nothing. Hehe. "'Best mathematician. Would come again.'"

"You're lying," he says, swiping like crazy on his phone. "Oh my God, you're not lying. How long has this been here?" He checks the date on the review. "Six months? You did this six months ago and didn't tell me? Kids kept calling me at night to do their trig homework. I had to change my phone number and lost all my contacts. I missed my brother's *wedding*."

"Maybe you should be a less good mathematician."

"In here," says the manager, bundling us into the office. This was where the man ran out before he fainted.

It's quieter in here. The office isn't big, but we can hear each other without shouting. The whole room still shakes with the beat of the music. The floor is dusty AF. Looks pretty recent too, so maybe some construction work's been going on. I look up, but I can't see any fresh plaster on the ceiling. Just chipped, off-white paint. Mold and cigarette smoke. In the middle of the office is an ancient desk from like the '70s made of MDF. The drawer handles are rusted and paperwork is scattered everywhere. I get closer to see some of the words, but I can't read any of the letters. Despite what Kelvin will tell you, I can actually read—just not this, whatever it is.

The owner hurries over to the other side of the room where

there's a safe in the wall. Only it's not a safe. He pulls open the door and inside there's some kind of ventilation shaft. He leans in and looks up.

"All right!" he calls up. "Send it down!"

The sound of squeaky pulleys comes from the shaft, and I realize it's not for ventilation. There's a little shelf inside that's being lowered down from the second floor. It's one of those old-timey elevator things. I've seen them in old-ass movies.

"It's a dumbwaiter!" goes Kelvin. I nod. I knew that. "Aunty Bob's must have been here for ages, probably built right after the earthquake."

The dumbwaiter doesn't take long to reach us. Whatever they're sending, it must be heavy.

The bottom of the dumbwaiter appears at the top of the window. Followed by a shoe. And a leg. And a shoulder. There's just about enough room for a person to fit inside if you really jam yourself in there. I know some contortionists who could do it, but not many other people. But this guy doesn't look like comfort was his first priority.

"Jesus!" says Kelvin, and I don't blame him. He steps back in shock, but then he's only a mathematician. What can you expect? I rush up to take his pulse.

"Don't bother," says one of the cops. "He's deader than shit."

"What the skaboopy is he doing in the wall?" I ask.

"He died upstairs," says the owner like it happens every day. "In the toilet. Tweakers and speed freaks are always taking something up there. Normally we find the overdoses quickly enough to get them to a hospital, but not this one. Anyway, whenever we need to move something between the top floor and the bottom floor without taking it through the club, we use the dumbwaiter. Not that it's usually bodies," he adds quickly for the benefit of the cops. "But I'm not marching a dead man through a nightclub. That can give a place a reputation."

"But what do you need me for? I know first aid, but I can't to bring people back to life."

"We don't need you," says a cop. "What we need is a mathematician. Ideally someone who understands rotational symmetry."

What? I can't believe what I'm hearing.

"You see, we got him in there, but now we can't get him out."

Kelvin pushes his way to the front like Superman. "Gentlemen. Help is at hand."

He nudges me aside and gets right up close to the body. What's happening? When did we step into the *Twilight Zone*? We walked into this club and the world's been topsy-turvy ever since. Bird-people. Bodies. *Mathematicians.*

No one is even aware I'm here any more. I feel like I'm invisible. I look around the office, but I'm as useful as a condom machine in the Vatican. I spot the papers again, and this time I pick them up. At least it will look like I'm doing something while Kelvin is humming and hawing over the body. The words don't make any sense. It's all scribbles. Something's wrong. I can't even make out any of the individual letters. Everything seems like it's blurring together, like it's not even real.

"Kelvin, check this out," I say, but he can't hear me. "What language is this?" I say to the owner. No one can hear me. No one reacts. Am I invisible now? What is going *on*? They have to be able to see me. I'm wearing a bright red hat bigger than Margaret Thatcher's.

Kelvin is tugging on the body's arm, which has flopped half out of the little window in the wall. But the body doesn't seem to be getting any less stuck. The owner and the two cops all grab hold of each other and the cop at the head of the line grabs Kelvin. Together they all pull on the arm in a disgusting tug-of-war. There's a noise. I haven't heard a noise like this since Marjorie launched into a pirouette and collapsed on the ground with a broken leg, and we realized her bones had turned to glass. A crunch. A tear. And four screams drowning in silence.

They have pulled the arm clean off the body. Kelvin is

standing a little way back where he and the others tumbled after the arm came free. He's holding it, looking at it in horror. He can't believe what he's done, but he's too shocked to let it go. At least I thought it was horror. But then he turns to the others and he has a huge grin on his face. He waves the arm like he's waving hello. And they *laugh*.

"Whoops!" he says. "I didn't mean any *'arm!*"

One of the cops says, "Look out, he's *armed* and dangerous!"

And they laugh like it's the funniest thing in the world.

"We only wanted to lend a hand!"

"Hey, look at me, I'm the *long arm* of the law!"

I back away. I don't know what's going on, but that is not the Kelvin I know. He's a mathematician, and a royal smart-ass. The most violent thing he ever did was play *Call of Duty*. But not now. Not waving around the torn off arm of a dead guy we found in a dumbwaiter at Aunty Bob's. I turn and grab the handle of the door, but my hand slips right off, slick, no grip. Am I sweating? Not that hard. But suddenly I can't get a grip on anything. I try again. It's like the handle doesn't want to be grabbed, but if I concentrate hard enough I can force my hand around it. Come on, *grip!* It starts to move. My knuckles are spasming, but the handle is starting to move.

The latch comes free, and I'm in the club again. The door to the office swings shut behind me, leaving Kelvin and the others inside, still slapping each other's backs with the dead man's hand. It's a different world out here. A different planet maybe. The lights are strobing and catching everyone's faces in ugly freeze-frames. Lips sticky. Shirts sweaty. Wild, animal expressions. No one I know. Maybe it's the lights that are doing this to me. Maybe I'm having a seizure or something. That would explain why I can't seem to move right. Why I couldn't hold on to the door handle. Maybe even why no one could hear me when I spoke. If I spoke. But I can't be having a seizure. It didn't start in the club, it started in the office. If I was in the office.

I force myself to turn and look at the door behind me. The

lights have sped up, flashing so fast they look slow. The world is swimming through syrup. It all falls away around me—the people, the lights, the thumping sounds and sour smells, it all disappears, because I'm staring at the door in front of me. And the door is staring back. Humming. Pulsing. It's going to open. I know it is. I can hear my heartbeat, filling my head, pounding in my blood like the skin of a drum. On the other side of that door, another heartbeat rumbles in the distance. And it's getting closer. It's taking its time, but with every second that stretches out for another hour, for another year, with every second that heartbeat takes another step toward me. Beat—another slow step. Beat—and another.

It senses me like I sense it, and it's reaching out for me. In the darkness of the club, nothing stands between it and me except this flimsy wooden door. It's going to open, and when it does… How long have I been standing here? How long has it waited? The time has only made it hungrier. It *knows* me. This is personal. And it's coming to kill me. I know it is. Don't ask me how, but I know. I know it with the same certainty I know heat is hot and sleep is just another kind of death. A shadow falls across the thin sliver of light coming from the gap under the door. The heartbeat is standing on the other side. And slowly the handle begins to move.

The sliver of light grows, stretches out along the frame of the door. It's opening. What's inside? Why won't anyone stop it? It can't be allowed to get out. If it gets out, I know for sure the world will end. It isn't human. It's a screaming animal, tearing limbs out of sockets and shattering eardrums with its howls, face contorted with passions too violent to be human. And then it's standing there, a silhouette in the light streaming from the office, haloing its head. The shadow is huge and hunchbacked, the outline of a silverback in Kelvin's body. Gross, ugly hand-feet and powerful shoulders tensed. His head is bowed low. His eyes stare into mine through his lids, gleaming in the dark. He is smiling.

I run. I have to force my legs to move and every second is impossible, but the alternative is worse. I have to get away from this place. I'm in the crowd now, pushing past anyone in the way. I don't dare look back to see if Kelvin is still behind me. I know he is. Looking will only make it worse.

A face jumps out at me from the sea of strangers. It's Amy again. She's not with her friends anymore. She's pushing through the crowd in the opposite direction and before I know it we are face-to-face with each other. At first she doesn't seem to recognize me. She just tries to get past. But then she sees my face, and the light in her eyes is magic to me.

"You can see me," I say.

"Of course I can see you. I have to get to the manager's office."

I block her way, and at first she looks at me with outrage until I tell her, "You can't go back there. I was just there and…" I can't get the rest of the sentence out, but she can see in my face that whatever it is, I mean it. I can't ask. I have to ask. But I don't know the words. But I'll try. I have to try anyway, because if I don't, it's going to stay trapped here inside me and never get out and then I might burst with the tears that are all backed up behind my eyes. My throat tenses up, trying to stop me. "Amy. Have you ever known—like, *known*—that you're about to die?"

She pauses for a moment, meeting my gaze. Then she lowers her head and she's staring somewhere in the distance. Somewhere that's not real. And in the strobing of the lights, I think I can make out a tear in the corner of her eye.

"All the time."

"I have to go," I say. "But here, take this."

And I give her back her friend's hat.

AMY

This *is* Andre's hat. I thought it looked familiar when I saw it on Marquis, but then there was no way to tell. It's not as if Goorin Bros. ever made just one of every hat; only this one happens to have the scorch mark on the underside of the brim where Andre nearly set himself on fire trying to blow out the birthday candles on a banana/walnut stack at an all-night pancake restaurant in Oakland two years ago. I sigh. He's probably going to want this back.

I have the sneaking suspicion this hat's been on every head in Aunty Bob's. I've been seeing bits and pieces of it all night—on Marquis and on that man who managed to bomb with Melody. It's probably full of lice and scabies by now. Fuck it, who cares? I put the hat on.

My phone stopped working, so I don't even know what time it is. I check it again. The screen comes on, but there's no reception in here tonight, and the clock seems stuck at two a.m., maybe because it can't sync with the time servers. But the good news is Sudoku is working right, so at least I won't get bored while I wait out the end of the world.

I scan the club for Andre. I know that guy said he's here tonight. To be honest, I've been trying to avoid him. He saved me last time, but this time I don't want to be saved. He's probably the only person I really want to say goodbye to. I just don't know how.

My first thought is to check the stage to see if I could get up there and get a better view of the club, but a drag act's up there and I know better than to get too close. It looks like Lucinda Fanny, the alter ego of one of the bartenders, and if she recognizes a regular patron, she'll give you a lipstick smear across your face that will take days of acetone scrubs to remove. Better keep a low profile.

I stand on my toes to get a better view of the crowd. Maybe I'll catch him on the dance floor, but even on my toes I can't see far enough. Short people problems. But there's Melody's paramour coming in from the beer garden. Did I overhear him mention Andre? I flag him down and ask if he's seen him anywhere. Instead he tells me he's just got into a huge argument with Melody, then they made out, then they argued again. I don't say anything, but I swear under my breath. I'd been hoping that first argument would be the end of it, but they sound like they have some fiery passion that's going to torture them but keep drawing them back together. How boring.

I shrug my shoulders like I'm trying to get rid of something. It's the thought that I've never been that much in love with anyone in my life; at least, not when I was loved back. It would have been nice to feel that just once, but I don't even know if I have the energy left in me. I'm tired all the time. For a second, it felt like maybe I had a chance with Melody. But like all the best crushes, it was one-sided. She's probably straight. But isn't it worth trying?

I catch myself hoping. I didn't think I'd hope for anything again. But that's how they get you. There's always one last hope to nurture, one more goal to shoot for, one more reason to stay alive. Then when that doesn't pan out, you start hoping for another MacGuffin, and another one, and another until you're dead. I won't let myself fall for that old trick again. There's a lump in my throat. This time I really will kill myself. It can't be that hard. Everyone dies. I'm just getting out early.

If Andre's not on the ground floor, then he must be outside or upstairs. I leave Melody's himbo to whatever the hell he's doing and go out to the beer garden. I can't feel the San Francisco chill on my skin. It's cold, but a dead, airless cold, like the vacuum of space. I look up and see the stars. They are very beautiful tonight, but they do not twinkle. I don't know why, but I don't know a lot about astronomy anyway. I have always lived in the city, so I've never seen very many of them, not like you see in movies where the enormous expanse of the Milky Way stretches on and on forever across the whole sky. And definitely not like tonight. The stars are a great, dead blanket bearing down upon us and smothering the life out of me bit by bit. Where is the moon, anyway? I can't see it anywhere.

I sidestep a couple three people smoking at the foot of the wooden staircase. I can hear them hacking up smoke behind me, and for a minute I'm envious of them. It must be so much easier to go slowly. But who has the patience to live themselves to death?

I start up the stairs to the second floor. It feels a bit rickety, but it isn't until I get to the top that I notice part of the wooden guardrail is splintered and is allowing the staircase to shake with every footstep. I stop for a second and peer over the side. There are some potted plants down there, and one of them has been shattered. I realize this is where that poor drunk took a nosedive. Or was pushed. The gays don't normally get violent, just bitchy, but every now and then one of them experiences a surge of testosterone and someone loses a tooth. It's not a short fall. I hope a tooth is all he lost.

I open the door and step inside. An older woman is cooing to something on her arm that I can't quite make out in the darkness. Someone appears to be trying to climb down the dumbwaiter shaft behind the bar. He has one leg inside the shaft, another outside it, and his shoulder jammed up against the top of the opening. He's got himself this far but doesn't seem to know which direction to approach this from next. Whenever the bartender's eyes are turned, the man grabs a nip of something from the bottles on the shelf. Unfortunately, he seems to be stranded on the absinthe, grappa, and fernet side of the bar. All the bottles are encrusted with dust, except for where he's just grabbed them and left streaky handprints. I can't tell if the scowl on his face is because of his conundrum or because he's just taken a mouthful of fernet and can still taste the weasel.

I go to the bar and order an Andre's special. It's a shocking drink, but at least it has a flavor. Beer has just started to taste like bile at the back of my throat. The bartender with the Dalí mustache was here before, but his shift must have ended because now someone else is tending the bar. The tendrils of his dreadlocks undulate like tentacles in the air, searching and grasping for something unknowable. He places the drink beside the head of a man who has been tied to the bar with some sturdy-looking rope. He is gagged and struggling hard. The sweat is standing out from his otherwise smooth forehead. He has pretty, dusky skin.

It's Andre.

For a second I consider just going. I've spent so long avoiding him, but it's harder to ignore someone in real life than it is to ghost on a text message. He's eyeballing me, pop-eyed with the strain, and trying to shout something through the gag. I pull it out of his mouth, and he says, "Thank fuck for that. Where have you *been*?"

I shrug.

"I was *worried* about you," he says. "I thought you were dead."

Well, the jury's still out. Still, I don't think I've ever heard him care about anyone else before. I wonder if I've been too harsh on Andre, but it's hard to look my friends in the face these days. I'm trying to avoid the idea that if I did look them in the face, one of them might look back. And then I don't know what might happen. I shiver. I still haven't replied to Andre, and I don't intend to, so I deflect and tell him we need to stop meeting like this. This isn't the first time I've caught him struggling across the bar at Aunty Bob's. I still don't know what he was so worked up about that night we met when he was drunkenly trying to launch himself over the bar to punch the bartender. With Andre, it could be anything.

"Someone tied me to the bar," he shouts, still struggling to get free. "I don't just go get liquored up on weekends and climb over bars."

I shrug. "I thought you were into being tied up." It seems like the kind of thing he'd be into.

"No, I'm not. And if I was, there's no way you'd know about it."

But you never have to know anything with Andre. You can usually take an educated guess and then confirm the truth of it by seeing how hard he denies it. This is definitely one of his things.

"What? What are you saying? I don't even know what you're talking about."

I tell him I got his hat back and hold it out. This seems right. For a second, the cloud that's hovered over my mind for the last three and a half years seems to lift. My head feels light after being free of the weight it's carried around for so long. Can depression leave so quickly? Can everything suddenly be made right? God knows it came fast enough. Why shouldn't it go just as swiftly? The night looks happy. Almost promising. Melody is still here somewhere, I know she is. I can almost smell her perfume. It will be something cheap, I know, but she'll wear it like it's classy, and it will stick in my brain forever, a part of her becoming a part of me.

Andre struggles against the ropes; he can't move his arms. "Nice. Well done. You can give it back right after you untie me from this bar..." He trails off and starts eyeballing my drink as well as he can from that angle. "Wait, is that an Andre's special?"

I know just how much it will aggravate him, so I tell him it's a sparkledrank.

"No, it's not, you've seen me order those a hundred times. That's an Andre's special!"

I tell him that can't be true; the sparkledrank tastes way better.

He sputters and curses—definitely a few made-up words in there. He's forgotten all about the hat, so I put it back on for now. The happiness starts to wash away from me like a wave that's crashed on the beach and is rushing back out to sea. Terrifying in its swiftness. Chilling in its absence.

See? Nothing lasts. It's better just to accept it.

Wes comes over and says hello, so I replace the gag in Andre's mouth and turn my attention to him. Where is Devin? They're not exactly joined at the hip, but ever since I found out they were twins, it's been hard to look at one without thinking of the other. I think he must be unhappy in his life, the way he jumps from date to date. No boyfriend hops like that if they're happy. I'm really starting to run out of fake enthusiasm for every new boyfriend he shows me, like each one is The One. He always says, "It's different this time," or "There's something special about him." Right on cue, he decides to introduce me to the latest The One.

I notice a presence beside me, and I roll my eyes in search of patience. The large, looming, poorly shaven shape is Lawrence, insinuating himself awkwardly into conversations like he does. I thought I'd done a good job of avoiding him the last couple of months, but the man is a bad penny. The smell of inappropriate sweat washes over me, too late to act as a warning of impending Lawrence.

Wes introduces his boy-thing to Lawrence, who jams his finger meaningfully at the boy and launches into that awful cis male bullshit where he says, "If you hurt him, I will kill you."

"Oh fuck off," I blurt out. Interesting. Turns out you don't have much patience when you've decided you want to die. "How small does your dick have to be? You just met your friend's new boyfriend and instead of being happy for him, the first thing you do is threaten him? Fuck you, Lawrence."

He mumbles something about how it was only a joke.

"Is that why everyone's laughing?" I ask, leaning against Andre's struggling body on the counter. "And now what am *I* supposed to do? Do I treat you as someone who's not as funny as he thinks he is, or as an insecure, petty little softcock who can only make himself feel better by making other people unwelcome?" He doesn't seem to have a reply on hand and looks like he's hoping everyone will forget it and move on, but I'm not letting him get away with this. It's like with children. If you don't teach them, they'll never learn. "Well? Which one are you?"

He mumbles something about not being as funny as he thinks he is.

I slap him on the back and tell him I'm glad to hear it. I turn to the bar to order him a sparkledrank and show him there's no hard feelings. The bartender places an empty highball glass on the bar and pours the cocktail shaker into it from a great height. We clink glasses and both take grateful sips.

Wes is telling Lawrence a story about a bee sting. At first I'm not paying too close attention, but it gets stranger and stranger as it goes along until I realize I haven't taken a sip of my drink in almost five minutes.

"Val calls me this evening, and she's shitting herself because her girlfriend has been out of town for a week and she's coming back tonight."

"'So what?' I go, and she goes, 'So, I got a hickey and I can't get rid of it.'

"Turns out she's been having some crazy ex-sex behind her girl's back. Have you ever had ex-sex?" he asks Lawrence, and then me. We both say no, Lawrence because he doesn't have any exes and me because I'm not insane. "Oh man, you're missing out. Hooking up with your ex is one of the worst ideas since the Berlin Art College wrote a letter saying, 'Sorry, Mr. Hitler, but we must decline your application at this time.' But man, do you get some crazy battling-wizard jungle-monkey sex out of it. All that resentment and unfulfilled desire bottled up for so long, and then it all comes out in one night of passion so violent you feel like you just fucked a live alligator.

"Well, Val knows how that feels right about now. So she's got this massive hickey, and her girl's coming home in a couple of hours, so she's freaking the fuck out. So I go, 'Did you try putting foundation over it?' and she goes, 'I'm a lesbian, I don't have foundation.'"

I nod. It's a fair cop.

"So I go, 'I know how we can get rid of this hickey, but this is only going to work once.' So she comes around to my place and when I open the door this woman has the biggest hickey you ever saw. It's like she's had a lamprey sucking on her neck."

I look slightly uncomfortably over to where that older woman is still playing with her pet.

"Now she doesn't tell me how good that ex-sex was, but she doesn't need to, you know? Judging by the hickey-meter, she must have cum so hard they felt it in *China*. Alaska Thunderfuck doesn't have enough Estée Lauder to cover up this scorch mark. For that matter, neither does Estée Lauder. Now the only thing is, we're going to need a bee."

Everyone groans apprehensively as they realize where this story is going.

"But where do you find a bee at five p.m. in San Francisco? I've got this friend Ashen who's a biologist who's studying newts or axolotls or something. If anyone can hook us up with a bee at this hour, it's him. So we're all over at Dolores Park picking through grass and swing sets and all we're getting is used condoms and cigarette butts. It's getting darker and Val's starting to freak the fuck out, but Ashen's like, 'Calm your tits—we're not beat yet.' Turns out his lab does have some wasps, and I'm like right, let's MacGyver the shit out of this and use a wasp instead. It's not like Val's lady-girl's gonna know the difference.

Twenty minutes later, Ashen's at my place with a wasp in a test tube.

"Now, I don't know if you know the difference between a bee and a wasp."

I know, but I like hearing Wes tell it.

"A bee can only sting you once before it loses its sting and dies. But a wasp can sting you from now till Christmas and feel just fine. So we open the lid of the test-tube and hold it up to Val's neck, and that wasp starts fucking her neck with its sting. The whole area swells up and gets so inflamed you can't even see the hickey any more.

"Mission accomplished, or so you'd think. While Ashen and me have gone to open a couple of beers, Val's in the bathroom checking out the damage. She comes back like ten minutes later and we're like, 'What the fuck happened?' The swelling is *gone* and the hickey is back. Turns out it was hurting so much that she put some ice on it and all the swelling went down. But we still have the wasp in the test-tube. So we put it back on her neck again and start tapping the glass to get it good and angry, and it's drilling away at Val's neck like it's fracking for oil. Before you know it, swelling is back, problem is solved. Her neck is full of holes and weeping more pus than Rosemary's baby, but you gotta admit, her girlfriend never saw it coming."

Someone slams a drink on the counter behind Wes and stomps away. I can't get a good look at her face, but it's definitely a woman.

I say, "You're such an asshole, Wes."

He takes a little bow. "I am but a humble asshole putting my superpowers to use for the good of others."

"Yeah," his boy tells me. "You should be talking to Val. She's the one that cheated."

They're not wrong. Just assholes.

Lawrence's drink slips out of his sweaty hand. The glass doesn't break, but the drink spills all over the floor and splashes onto Wes's shoes.

"Oh gross, man. What's wrong with you?"

Lawrence says he's not feeling well. He's not looking well, either. His sweat smell is washing over me in waves, and it's taken on a feverish odor like his body has started to break down. His skin is yellowish, except for the purple blotches I can see on his arms. They weren't there before. If I didn't know better, I'd have said he had the plague.

"That's a great hat," says the boy, and I wonder if I should give it to him out of spite for Andre. I ought to give this hat back to him or I'll never hear the end of his bitching and moaning. If being a prissy little princess was an Olympic sport, he'd get the gold, silver, *and* bronze. But then maybe he should learn to cope with loss. Sooner or later we all have to learn that we're going to die. It might as well be sooner.

I feel someone tap me on the shoulder, and I turn around to see Melody.

"Have you guys seen Tom anywhere?" she asks us.

I shake my head. "He's probably left," I say.

She smiles. "Not if I'm any judge of men." She has such a beautiful smile. I get an image of her in gaudy Technicolor wearing a miniskirt and a T-shirt with a big stylized circle in the middle riding a moped through a narrow Italian street. This is the wrong club for her. She should be in movies.

That flirty "judge of men" thing irks me a little, but all I need to do is get enough time alone with her to start chatting her up myself.

"I love your hair," I say. I hate the words as they come out of my mouth, but, hey, I know my audience. She's already smiling again and thanking me. Her finger has strayed up to one of her strands of hair and is playing with it. "You must be a performer."

She tells me she's a musician. I ask what kind, a little apprehensively, but when she says French horn, I almost kiss her on the spot. You know what a French horn means. Great lung capacity. *Great* lip control.

"What are you drinking?" I ask. "It's my round."

She says, "Thanks, but I should find Tom. You know what men are like."

Not really. Before I can think of anything to say, Melody has already turned around to go find her missing frat boy. As she steps away, I catch sight of someone behind her—an old man with a scruffy white beard, a top hat, and circular dark glasses. It's hard to tell, but I think he's looking at *me*.

"Hey, you look great in that hat," someone says from the bar.

I thank him without looking at him and take a step toward Melody, but before I know it, he's standing in my way.

Melody is getting farther away.

He asks where I got it, and I tell him I don't know.

The man in dark glasses hasn't moved.

Melody is almost at the door.

I call out her name, but she's too far away now. I try to push past this idiot at the bar, but he's so dense, he can't seem to take a hint. Now he's asking who made it.

"How the hell should I know?" I say. "Here, have it. It's yours." Because fuck Andre why not.

I shove the hat at him and go to catch Melody before she hits the stairs.

BAILEY

I knew it. It's the hat that guy was wearing when he pissed all over me. I didn't go all the way home to change only to come back and put on a piss hat. I give it an experimental sniff, but I can't smell anything wrong with it, even though it's obviously just been on a sweaty dyke's head for half the night. How did she get it? What *happened* after I left, anyway? I've been all over Aunty Bob's and I can't find Vay anywhere. He texted me that someone broke his leg, but I can't tell whether or not he meant that literally. Maybe someone just stepped on his toe. Or maybe he really did get hurt. Even a minor injury could affect his career. There aren't too many organists with one leg shorter than the other.

But Vay isn't here, and no one seems to know what's happened to him. Everything just looks normal. I lean up against the body tied down on the bar and sip my beer. He struggles to speak through his gag, but all that comes out are muffled screams. Something's up tonight. I just wish I could put my finger on what.

I look around the room and recognize at least half a dozen people. Lucien is on the other side of the room attempting to do a handstand on the table and take a sip out of everyone's drink upside down. There, on the opposite end of the bar, I can see someone jimmying the window from outside, and suddenly Kingsley comes tumbling in, landing on a table and sending the drinks flying. I've seen this maneuver before. He's gotten kicked out, and he's sneaked back in by climbing the wall. I glance back to the bar, but I can still hear him swearing at the people whose table he just wrecked. Then he goes quiet. I look back and see he's glowering across the room at that aggravating moron Benny, who doesn't seem to realize Kingsley is staring at him so balefully. I sip my beer and wait, but no one has invited me to join them.

Benny gets up to cross the room. The only words in Aunty Bob's are in his pocket. I can't believe it, but the sign of the Trystero is unmistakable. Benny the idiot has a copy of *The Crying of Lot 49*. He must be *reading* it. Of course it would be Pynchon's shortest novel, but I never even knew he could read. I wave hello, and Benny takes a hard left and makes for the door. That was weird. Maybe he didn't see me. The one time I almost wanted to talk to him, and here I am sitting on my own.

I'm feeling more and more alone these days. Maybe it's because I spend most of my free time with Sylvanus. Maybe it's time to cut him loose. Whenever we're out, everyone just thinks we're a couple. But I can remember life before I met him, and it wasn't any better then. The reason we became so close was because we were the only people we could find who weren't completely puerile. It seems so long ago now. Maybe it's this city. Silicon Valley tends to attract overgrown children—the grown men who spend all their money on video games and lap dances, the college graduates who think books are for homework and music is only for listening to, the millionaire CEOs who dream the dreams of ten-year-old boys. Who could be happy with *that* lot? San Francisco just doesn't have the right people in it.

I hear a voice next to me and realize there's a boy ordering a drink. He's beautiful, with those perfect model good looks, hair buzzed close all over in a way that only accentuates his beauty, and honey skin you just want to sink your teeth into and leave a bite to mark out your territory. The bartender places his drink down, and I slide a twenty across the bar. "Let me get that for you."

The boy slides the twenty back toward me and says, "I don't think so." Then he hands the bartender his credit card.

"Take it," I insist. "I can pay for one little drink, can't I?"

He slides the money back toward me without another word. I take the bill and push it into his back pocket, reveling in the warmth of his body and the curvature of his right ass cheek.

"What's your name?"

He takes the twenty out of his pocket and shoves it in the tip jar.

"Hey!" I shout. "That was for you." He doesn't respond. "Nah, you're all right, I forgive you," I say. He's signing his receipt and still not looking in my direction. I look over his arm and spot his name on the receipt. "Wes—that's a cool name. So, Wes, do you live in the city?"

"Fuck off, Bailey," he says. "No one wants to sit with you."

He turns around and goes. I don't think he looked at me once the whole time. How did he know my *name*?

An older Asian lady comes up to the bar, not the kind of person you normally see in the Castro, but maybe she's someone's mom. That's cute, I guess, though it's hard to imagine what kind of a loser brings their mom to a club on a Saturday night. I don't care how much the Scissor Sisters say it's okay, it still means you have no friends. She orders a dry white wine and grabs a dish of the spiced popcorn they use as bar snacks. I tried it once. It's all right if you want to shit orange for the next two days.

She has something on her arm. Something is alive. I stare at something. Something stares back at me. I want to move. There's somewhere else I have to be, something else I have to be doing. But I can't move. All I can do is stare back at this monstrous spider, not even sure I'm making eye contact, but knowing all the while that it is staring into me hungrily. It feels right. Part of my brain is screaming at me in a panic like a frightened horse tearing at its bridle and snapping its reins in wild-eyed desperation. But another part of me feels like I'm coming home.

I realize the old woman is gazing at me kindly. She doesn't

look like someone's mom anymore. More like someone's grandmother. Kindly. Old. Benevolent. She can see into me like the archaic torso of Apollo—all the parts of me that no one else understands, but *she* does, and she approves. I am all right. I am a *good* person. She speaks, and her words are soothing, though I couldn't tell you what she said. The words themselves have no meaning. It's more like the shapes they make in my mind. The colors. She is painting for me in words, a stunning, breathtaking landscape looking down from a jagged outcrop of rock into a valley filled with mist from which protrude the ruins of a shattered antiquity no one can remember. And I am there, a lone traveler, allowing the purple and orange sunset to wash over me.

While she was talking, her spider crawled off her arm and crossed the bar between us. I can feel it brushing my fingers where my hand is resting on the counter. It pings the hairs on the back of my hand like the sensitive spines on the leaf of a Venus flytrap. It is crawling up my arm now, and I am not moving. Why would I move? Everything is right here. Everything is as it should be. I feel it reach the sleeve of my T-shirt and for a second I think it might crawl up inside and make a nest, brushing against my nipples and tickling the hairs in the valley of my chest. But it continues up the outside of my shirt, mounting my shoulder and climbing up my neck in slow, deliberate movements. It finds purchase on the cusp of my ear, making its way along the outer edge, following an arcane map not made by human hands, but a path laid out centuries ago by a forgotten god.

And now I understand. I lift the hat, and the spider comes to rest on the crown of my head. I place the hat back, carefully covering the spider as it brings its warmth to the skin on my scalp. Part of my brain is screaming something I can't hear. I can feel the spider snuggling into the nest it is making on my head, parting the hairs and gently prying at the skin on my crown, burrowing now, pushing away skin and gnawing through bone, picking its way into the soft meat of my brain. An anemic shiver makes its way from the top of my head down to my toes as if

I'm standing under a cold shower. Then my brain goes numb, and suddenly I can no longer feel my skin. I can see like I have always been able to see, but I can't feel anything. I can't even move.

I set my drink down on the bar, but it isn't me. It's George. I know him now, as if I've known him my entire life, this friendly master who has come to inhabit me, to steer me while he sits in the center of my head pulling the levers that operate my body.

The old lady smiles. "How are you feeling now, George?"

"Perfectly calm, thank you, Madeleine," I say. *He* says.

"This has been a very exciting adventure for you," she says. I nod. "But I think you'll be quite happy in your new home."

And it's true, I can feel it. I am happy. *George* is happy. I...I don't know what I am. Something's not right. The part of me that's still screaming. What is it trying to tell me? I need to clear my head. I need to focus. Why can't I focus? Where is Vay? He'd know what to do. He always gets his way. The only person getting his way now is George, nestled inside me like a tapeworm. A parasite. That's what he is, I realize, a filthy parasite that has infected my brain, operating me like Cusack operated Malkovich.

George smiles. He can share my thoughts, knows what I know, realize what I realize. I want him to let me out. He does not. I want him to set me free. He does not. That is the end of that conversation.

An alarming sloshing noise emanates from somewhere to my left. I turn around to see someone approaching me. It is the former wearer of the hat—the little one with social anxiety and an overfilled bladder who pissed on me, made me go all the way home to shower and come all the way back to try and find out what happened to Vay. Here he is again, but he seems scarcely like he did before. The last time I saw him, he was almost painfully thin. Now, his bladder has filled back up far beyond its maximum capacity. It has inflated inside him like a balloon, distending his belly and forcing him to waddle slowly under the enormous weight of the water stored inside him. His previously loose T-shirt is now stretched over his bloated midsection.

He sits at the bar on the other side of me from Madeleine, groaning with evident relief at being able to take the weight off his feet of all those gallons of sloshing water. His belly rests in his lap like a basketball. When he moves his thighs apart, his stomach slips between his thighs and plops on the edge of the stool.

He rests one hand on his belly, catching his breath for a moment before motioning to the bartender. "Beer."

The bartender hands him the hose from a keg, which he inserts into his mouth as the bartender turns the tap. I don't see him pause for breath. He doesn't even swallow. He's just piping beer directly from the keg into his stomach, swelling his already dangerously overtaxed bladder. His bladder continues to expand, slowly at first, but before I know it the thing has attained a monstrous size like an engorged tick ready to pop. But he does not pop, just continues to cram more and more into his trembling bladder. It must be stretched almost to transparency. A thin balloon skin is all that's protecting us from the atom bomb ready to detonate in his guts.

His grotesque stomach slips out from under the hem of his shirt, revealing first a half-moon of skin on the lower part of his belly, and then his navel, now stretched so tight it is completely flat and featureless, making him look like a malevolent alien hatched from an egg, coated in sticky protoplasmic slime and fragments of membrane. Finally his shirt slips all the way up to the top of his stomach, covering only his chest and arms. The monstrous belly is free, stands boldly in the open, challenging the world by its very existence. His face is purple with the strain of holding the deluge inside him, but he is refusing to budge. His urinary sphincter must be knotted tight. It is cemented shut by his iron will.

His bladder has expanded to the size of a beach ball. Instead of allowing it to push him away from the bar, he simply lifts it up and rests the enormous piss-balloon against the bar itself. The bomb looks ready to detonate and shower everyone in the club with his urine fallout, and I'm sitting here at ground zero waiting to have the blast wash over me, strip the skin from my skull, and melt my screaming skeleton into the void.

I'm howling inside my own head, thrashing and hurling myself against the walls of the world. I have to get out of this hell. But George's control is unflinching. I'm staring at the swollen bladder as the man spits out the hose. He has exhausted the entire keg.

Some vague consternation crosses his face. "I think..." he says. "I think I need to use the bathroom."

He lifts his belly off the bar and carefully slides off his stool. He is so big his stomach is visible from behind him. If he were to get on all fours, I doubt his hands could even touch the ground. I follow him to the restroom at the near end of the bar. He lumbers with difficulty. When he gets to the door, I step ahead of him and open it to let him in. He pushes his gut against the door frame, struggling to squeeze it through, face empurpling again with the effort of holding back the explosion waiting to erupt inside him. His belly pushes against me, forcing me into the restroom ahead of him and cornering me in the tiny space.

The door closes behind him, leaving us jammed up against each other. His gut is pushing up against the sink on one side, and the cold tiles of the wall on the other. Only I stand between him and the toilet, but he's no longer looking at the toilet. He's looking at me. And I'm looking at him. And I have no choice. We slowly lean toward each other. I feel his skin push up against me. It is taut and warm. Smooth. It does not give easily, but George is determined to reach his mouth and slowly I feel myself compressing the piss-balloon by pushing myself against it. The man pushes back, reaching for me with his quivering lips.

Our mouths meet. I want to hurl but can't. I want to scream but can't. The only indication I'm in here at all are the tears rolling down my face as I embrace the rubbery balloon of warm piss and kiss him. It is not even his own will holding in the apocalypse now. The only thing preventing the escape of all those endless gallons is a piss hard-on as epic as the ocean it restrains. I hear an ominous creaking noise that can only mean one thing.

"I gotta go," he chokes out.

"I know," I say, and rest my hand on the trembling surface of his stomach.

He takes the red hat off my head and flings it out the window.

BENNY

It's cold as tits out tonight, and the hat's all I have to keep my head warm, even though it's probably giving me a nightmare of hat-hair. I don't know *how* it wound up flying out of the second-floor bathroom window. I thought Ashen was going to give it back to me, but he didn't keep it for long. He said that woman was starting to suspect him after he stole her wine, so he got rid of the hat as fast as he could. Then a few minutes later, I saw it on that pretentious hipster at the bar, but *he* only held on to that thing for a hot second. Didn't keep his book long, either. I pat my jacket, feel the corners of the pages getting bent out of shape in my pocket, and smile to myself.

I lost track of the hat until I saw that *asshole* Bailey at the bar trying to catch my eye. I only avoided him by ducking outside for a cigarette, so I don't know what's going on upstairs. All I know is the party must be going *off the hook* because the next thing I know, there's a huuuuge thud, like someone drove their car over a fire hydrant, and something is splattering all over the bathroom window.

As a rule, I don't French inhale outside. It doesn't matter how calm you think it is, there's always some cunty breeze that comes along and ruins it. But tonight it's so calm out, I can't feel any wind at all. The air's just still. I push the smoke out of my mouth and breathe in through my nose. The trick is making it look like you're not trying too hard. I am one sexy bitch.

I blow out the smoke and realize the hand holding the cigarette is shaking. Why is it shaking? Weird. Like I'm cold and hot at the same time. I look up at the sky, but there's nothing above me. I mean *us*—the garden is full of people. I don't know why I said "me." It's just...I don't know. I suddenly feel like I'm standing here on my own. I've got a club full of friends and I never have a problem landing a man, and yet here I am. No one to talk to, even.

"That's awesome," says a woman on my left.

I smile. She caught my fantastic French inhale. I push the thoughts out of my head and the smoke out of my mouth and say, "You know how it is, babe, you just put your lips together and blow. What am I talking about? I practiced for years to get that right."

She laughs. "It can't have taken you that long."

"Oh, long before you were born. I'm practically ancient. Did you know I'm nearly twenty-five?"

"There is *no* way you look twenty-five," she says.

"Aren't you sweet! Flattery will get you everywhere."

"You've got to be forty at least."

"Oof, you are a bitch," I say, only half laughing. If that was supposed to be a joke, I don't get it.

"Can I try?" she asks. "I haven't smoked in years. It's just tonight..."

I hold up my hand. "Don't say another word. Light up and let Grandma Benny hear all about it." She introduces herself as Regan, and I offer her my cigarette case and lighter.

"Sir, you have so many fancy things! Are these Parliaments?" I nod, and she says, "That was my brand."

I raise my cigarette in a toast: "Next year in Jerusalem."

"Mazel tov," she replies, and lights up. She stifles a choke on her first inhale before breathing out the smoke in a slow, smooth cloud. "God, I forgot how nice this is. I can't remember why I ever quit." I decide to wait and let her talk on her own, so it's quiet for a second before she says, "I found out my girlfriend's cheating on me tonight."

"Just now?"

She nods.

"How did you find out?"

"I was at the bar upstairs, and I overheard someone talking about it. Apparently, everyone in the world knows except me. And she did it in the worst way possible."

I nod sympathetically. "With someone you know?"

She shakes her head. "No. She did it *funny*. When she steps out on me, she makes it sound like, 'Oh what a lovable scamp. There goes Val and her wacky hijinks.' No one ever stops to think on the other side of a wacky hijink is someone getting hurt. Because it doesn't make a good story. It doesn't make you laugh. Not funny now, is it?"

I shake my head.

She says, "Come on, let's get back inside. You must be getting tired."

She's right, I am. How did she know?

We stub out our cigarettes and head back in. I take it slowly as I cross the wooden boards under the staircase and take each step back to the club one at a time. She's nice enough to lend me her hand, and I find myself leaning on her more than usual for balance. That sparkledrank must be like a hundred and fifty proof. I can hold my liquor, but I feel *wasted*. My whole body feels like it's been through a tumble dryer.

The lights inside the club have slowed down a lot now. They're throbbing and pulsating, and I remember it's time for the amateur strip show. Lucinda Fanny is still on the stage, and it looks like it's already started. They're two contestants in, and she is announcing the third. We all give a big hand to welcome him to the stage.

I start clapping. Regan says, "Easy there. Let's get you sitting down."

She guides me to the bar, where all the stools are swiveled around to face the stage. We're lucky to find a couple of free seats, but then it seems like the club is so full of dancers that no one has time to sit down. They're running around and screaming so loud, it makes it hard for me to concentrate.

I lower myself onto the barstool and groan as my knee joints click and my feet tingle with relief at no longer having to carry my weight. I reposition myself slightly, and Regan takes the seat next to me.

"I'll get us some drinks," she says.

"That's very kind of you. I'll have a Brandy Alexander." I can hear how strange the words are even as they're coming out of my mouth. A Brandy Alexander? What am I, like a million years old?

The third contestant has taken his position now. He's a pretty one. Looks like a college student, maybe, in jeans, sneakers, and a shapeless gray T-shirt. He has a confused straight boy look, which means he's doing this for the money and he's not used to being in a gay bar. Let's face it, no one who knew what they were doing would enter a strip contest wearing a shirt that *hides* everything. He's got kind of chubby cheeks, which means he could be a bit chunky, but I bet he's secretly buff under the clothes.

Regan wrinkles her nose. "He's a bit fat."

"Those are pecs, ducky," I say, putting my hand on her arm.

She double-checks. "Maybe you're right."

"I know I am. You don't get to my age without learning a thing or two."

The contestants give the DJ their music ahead of time, but there's a delay getting his track to play, so for a second he's just standing there on the stage in his starting position. Someone wolf whistles, which makes him look nervous. See? First-timer. If someone wolf whistled at me on a stage, I'd give 'em a show they'd never forget.

The lights dim and the music fades in. Girl, you won't believe it, it's that "She's Lump" song, the one no one's listened to since 1997, the last time those jeans were in style. Are we really doing this? Magic Mike couldn't dance to this number, I don't know why Lump is going to try. He's starting to gyrate, but it's not doing him any favors. Did he even practice this before he came in? He knew he was getting up on a stage, right?

Oh, fuck me sideways. Lump's got the cuff of his pants stuck on his heel. Nooooo, stop! He's stepping on the cuff of his pants with his other foot to try and pull his leg out. This is just darling. Which means when he finally gets the jeans off—yep, there it is. He's wearing his underpants and socks at the same time. Rookie mistake. And come on, seriously? They're big baggy tighty-whiteys. This is just sad.

By the time the song ends he's finally got rid of the socks and the shirt, but he's *still* wearing the sad dad undies. Lucinda Fanny comes out and coos over him, "Honey, these people are millennials, they've been desensitized by *years* of internet porn. You're gonna have to lose those tighty-whiteys if you wanna raise any eyebrows around here."

So, he turns shyly away from the crowd and slides out of his underpants like a gay boy in a locker room. Everyone cheers, but we all know this duck is dead in the water.

He scuttles offstage, leaving Lucinda Fanny to introduce the next contestant. And *this* one looks much more promising. He's not as good looking as Dad Pants, but he has a fuckton more swagger. He strikes a pose on the stage and waits for his cue like it's waiting for him.

The harmonies start up, making this sound like those stupid songs from the '50s where teenagers are the first people who ever fell in love. The singer starts to tell this story about her high school homecoming, and our contestant is strutting up and down doing his best impression of a Valley girl. The kid's milking this for all it's worth, miming the pink dress and the tiara, waving to the crowd from the top of his imaginary float. This song is so damn extra! How have I not heard it before? Every drag queen in the country should be dancing to this.

Suddenly the song takes a turn. The music hots up as the homecoming queen goes on a shooting spree, picking off cheerleaders with pure '80s glee. The stripper whips off his shirt and the crowd is going nuts. I turn to Regan and raise an eyebrow. She's got the same expression on her face as me. We just can't believe what we're seeing.

Our stripper continues. The socks come off next—smart move. He's avoided the socks-and-undies trap the last guy fell into. Then off come the pants—and yes, he's done it! He's over the heel and home safe. Now he's down to his undies, and *hello*. He has padded the hell out of those bikini briefs. Who's he trying to fool? He knows he's going to have to take that off, right?

The kid turns to face the audience, pointing his package in our direction. He tells us the only reason he's shooting up his high school is because he's having a really bad period. Right on cue, a firecracker goes off in his crotch and a big red patch starts soaking through the briefs. He reaches into the front of his undies, takes out a menstrual pad, and throws it away with a shrug. Girl, this stripper is a *star*.

Now he's teasing us with the waistband. A dribble of fake blood snakes its way down his broad, smooth thigh. He's egging the crowd on, and we're all shouting for him to take it off. He mimes not being able to hear us, so everyone shouts twice as hard, "Take it off!" He shrugs, like all he's doing is following instructions, and reaches out a hand to a spot behind his opposite shoulder. For a second, we can't see what he's doing. Then the hand comes back into sight, dragging with it a hidden zipper. Slowly he pulls the zipper from behind his shoulder across the front of his chest. Like one of those jackets that unzips diagonally, he is removing his skin, peeling back the open flaps on his chest to reveal the muscle underneath, crisscrossed with red and blue veins, pockmarked with deposits of fat, peeling away and glistening in the club lights.

The crowd starts cheering even harder. This is the best show they've ever seen.

Still working the beat of the music, he steps out of his own skin like a wetsuit. The only part of him that's still covered is his head, which still has a mischievous grin on its face. He reaches up and starts rolling back the skin around his neck, up over his face, until he finally flays the last bit of skin from his scalp. His face looks exactly like one of those Ronald Reagan Halloween masks when you turn it inside out. He throws it into the crowd like a thong, and the people push each other out of the way to try and catch it. The lucky audience member holds it up to his face to smell it, then gives a flirty wave to the stripper on the stage. When he smiles, I can see traces of the stripper's gore on his face. You know whoever catches a stripper's flayed face is going to get married next.

Now the stripper is stepping into the audience, grinding up against people while they cheer him on, straddling people with his thighs and miming a lasso like he's riding a bull. The people in the crowd grin from ear to ear, and anyone lucky enough to get a lap dance grabs on to the kid's meaty ass.

I nudge Regan. "There's no way this kid's an amateur. Did you see that act? He's got to be a pro."

She nods wisely. "It's not bad. Maybe a little overdone."

She reminds me a bit of a mortician I'm friends with online. She says morticians are the most racist people she ever met. Which is totally weird, right? You think that if you saw everyone dead and naked, you'd realize we're all the same underneath. Underneath makeup. Underneath clothes. Underneath skin.

The flayed man's making his way through the crowd as the song winds down, but it's clear he's got one more lap dance left in him. Suddenly he's meeting my eye, and he's coming toward me.

He presses his glistening, twitching internal organs against me. I can feel his whole digestive system slowly churn and pulsate. I hold out a shaking hand to touch his beautiful hip and see, with shame, how old I am compared to him. I'm in Aunty Bob's, the club where nothing ever changes, and I've grown old.

My hand is liver-spotted and wrinkled, the joints all crooked and bent with arthritis. Fingers aren't supposed to bend that way.

Regan takes a photo of us on her phone. She's grinning like crazy and giving me a thumbs up. I know what the picture looks like without seeing it—a sad old man with a beautiful stripper wrapped around him. His thighs are straddling mine. His are thick and firm, and I can see the arteries standing out strong against the straining muscle tissue. Mine are thin and weak. I can almost feel them withering away to nothing.

He feels something in my pocket and pulls it out. It's the book I took off that asshole at the bar. *The Crying of Lot 49.*

"*There's* my book," someone says, and grabs it out of the stripper's hands. He wipes the stripper's gunk off it disdainfully.

The stripper backs off me. "All right. I was only looking." The song is over now, anyway, and he goes back to the stage.

I look up to see who took the book, and sure enough it's the asshole again. Someone's left an angry red mark on his cheek about the size of a fist. *Quelle surprise.* He's probably been charming his way round the club all night.

"What the hell happened to you?" he asks. "You look like shit."

"I was about to say the same thing," I croak, and realize how difficult it is to speak. I try to remember how long it's been like this. Did I ache this much when I came out this evening? I don't remember. It was decades ago now. Who can remember that long?

He asks something, but it's hard to hear him over the music. He shouts, "Here, let me give you a hand." I hold on to his arm and he guides me out to the beer garden step by painful step. I have to shuffle slowly, but he is patient with me.

He helps lower me on to one of the small benches along the wall.

"Here," says the asshole, and takes the hat off my head.

KINGSLEY

Fuck. I mean *fuck*. He's so withered and shrunken that he's swimming in his clothes. His hair is wispy, and some stray strands are sticking out from his skull at odd angles where the brim of the hat was. I use the hat to fan his face, and it looks like it's working. He looks more relaxed. Or maybe he's just dying. This is clearly an eighty-year-old man I'm sitting with, and he's the same blond club kid who stole my book off me earlier. I look up at the wall of Aunty Bob's and get a brief impression of something like déjà vu. A devil's halo looming over the club. Aunty Bob's suddenly seems to reach off into space, all grasping spires and flying buttresses like Grace Cathedral. I don't even know where that image came from. Aunty Bob's looks like it always has. Nothing has changed. Everything is normal.

Someone's tapping me on the shoulder. It's a boy. I'm surprised they let him in here, there's no way he's twenty-one. He's got some wispy scruff on his chin, but that's not fooling anyone.

He says, "Excuse me, is that Marquis's hat?"

"What? I don't know. Probably. Here, take it."

ASHEN

I take the hat and try to find Marquis again. Probably he's gone home. I think he wasn't feeling well. But maybe I can find one of his friends and give his hat back. I sigh and tell myself to stop it. I'm lying to myself again. I don't care about Marquis's friends or his hat. I'm hoping we might be able to save what we had, even if we only had it for a few minutes. It's hard to form any kind of meaningful connection with people, and I felt like we had a spark. You have to hold on to the good ones when you can find them.

But is he one of the good ones? Fuck him. I don't need him. And that's true. I don't *need* him. But I want him. He can't handle me being trans, and that's all right, but then I didn't give him much warning. I kept meaning to, but the opportunity never came up, and I got swept up in the moment. The next thing I knew, he was gone. He *wasn't* feeling well. I know he wasn't, so maybe everything's all right after all. The only thing I really need to do is get his hat back. We can sort the rest out after.

I go upstairs to see if I can find him there. I pull the door open and yes! There he is—tall black guy at the bar, standing with his back to me. I was up here before, but I must have missed him in the crowd. He must be feeling better. He looks a lot stronger on his feet than before, though he has changed his clothes. When did that happen? Did he go and come back? I circle around him, trying to catch his eye.

"Oh. Sorry," I say. Crap. It's not him. Did I really think he was Marquis because they're both black? Crap.

"What's up?" he asks.

"I thought you were someone else," I say.

"Are you looking for Andre? Is that his hat?"

"No, it belongs to my…my friend, Marquis." I hate how I hesitated before I called him my friend, but it's too late to go back and change it now. Stupid. Stupid thing to say. This guy noticed and nods with a grin, like he knows what's up, like I go around gay clubs hooking up with every stranger I can find.

"No, it's not like that," I say, even though I really am just looking for the guy I hooked up with for five minutes. But he doesn't seem to care any more. I follow his gaze, and he's fixated on this crazy pretty guy who looks like he stepped out of an Abercrombie & Fitch catalog. Not exactly my type, but damn, I'm not dead. I can't think of a single person who'd kick him out of bed, though you'd want to make him work for it a bit first. You let someone like that have their way, and they'll treat you like trash. He knows people are looking at him. He's making a big show of not caring. It's more annoying that the guy I'm actually talking to isn't even trying to hide how much he's checking him out.

He lunges for the model and grabs him by the shoulders. I hadn't realized, but the guy I mistook for Marquis is tall. He's easily got a head on the model.

"You've traveled in time," he gasps. "Where's Slayden?"

"Who?"

"Slayden," he says. "The dude with the hipster mustache."

"The doorman?" the model asks like the guy's an idiot. "He's probably watching the door."

"He was, he was, but that was all before. There's been half a dozen of him. Every time he got to two o'clock he went back to try again. But you know how many of them are left now? *None.*

They're all gone. Which means I don't know *what's* going down, but whatever it is, we're too late to stop it."

"I don't know what you're talking about."

"You gotta. I just saw you go out that door two minutes ago but here you are again. Unless…" He backs off for a second. "Unless you're the earlier you, and you haven't crossed over yourself yet. But then how would you get a time machine without Slayden? You gotta be from the future."

"I'm a *twin*, you moron," he says. The tall guy doesn't look like he understands, so the model puts his fingers in his mouth and whistles hard. The other twin walks back in from the beer garden, and sure enough there's two of them and they look identical. I don't even know where to look. I'm seeing pretty in stereo.

"Twins?" mumbles the tall guy.

"You're *high*," responds the first twin. The disdain makes the tall guy look like he just got punched in the stomach.

"If you're twins, then you can touch each other. I've seen movies. Time travelers can't touch each other or you'll rip a hole in the universe."

They suddenly look less sure of themselves. "I don't think that's a good idea," says the second one, but before he can step away the tall guy has grabbed him by the wrist. The twin struggles to pull out of his grip, but those nice arms are all for show. The tall guy is way more athletic, and he's not letting the twin get away that easily. He grabs the first twin with the other hand.

"Tell me where the time machine is," he grunts, struggling to hold on to the twins, inching them closer together.

"*Don't*," screeches the first twin. My blood runs cold. He's not kidding. He's terrified. The tall guy lets go of the twins' hands in surprise. But something is happening. The twins' hands are pulling toward each other in the air like two magnets. They are struggling to pull away, but the force that's dragging them together is too strong. They dig in their heels and throw their weight in the other direction, but their hands are still inching closer together. Their faces flush, suddenly ugly now, all teeth and sweat and squinting eyes lost in their faces like the dead eyes of sharks.

The magnetic force reaches a tipping point, and their strength gives out. They fall together and their mirrored hands meet, the first twin's left hand and the second twin's right, stuck together like glue.

"Look what you've done," sobs the second one.

The twins grit their teeth in agony. For a second, no one can tell what has happened. But then I hear a crackling, sizzling noise. The pressure their hands are exerting on each other is *melting their skin*. Slowly the twins start to fuse together. First the palms of their hands start to melt. Then the process continues up their wrists and arms. As they melt together up past their elbows they start to look more and more like Siamese twins in a circus act.

Now their shoulders are pressing together. The only grip they can get to try and pull away is by pushing up against each other. Their other hands meet before anyone can stop them, and now they are fusing even faster than before. Their heads are pressing up against each other, filling the bar with the smell of burning skin and hair. They start screaming.

The tall guy puts his arm around me and turns me away from the sight of the twins' faces burning into each other. Their screams peter out to an anguished howl that sounds like the sobbing of a wounded dog. Then it fades to nothing.

"What happened?" I ask. I'm trying to hold my voice steady, but I don't get far before it wavers.

The tall guy turns and looks over his shoulder. And suddenly he barfs all over the floor by the bar. The smell hits me in a great wave. I'm used to the smell of piss and vomit in the streets of San Francisco, but the smell is overwhelming. It's making my head spin. I breathe in but can't get enough air into my lungs, only more lungfuls of the pungent vomit. My eyes go blurry and it's suddenly hard to see anything. Two people at the bar. Now four. Now eight.

"We're Johnny," says half of them.

"And we're Will," says the other half. The Wills have an English accent.

"And we are a multitude," they all say together. "We flock and we swarm and we devour all that is in our path. We make it like us."

"Like you?" I gasp.

They are multiplying all around me. I don't know how or when it happened, but it seems like the bar is suddenly full of Johnnys and Wills.

"We've been watching you," they say. "We've had our eye on you for years. When you're at home. When you're on the street. When you're at work. We've been with you this whole time. Don't you recognize us?"

I shake my head.

"We recognize you. We only want to be your friend. Why don't you join us?" They offer out their hands, and I can feel myself want to grab on to one and feel like I'm finally a part of something. I've never even had a relationship longer than three months, but I want it. I want it so badly. It would be so easy just to accept. But another part of me recoils. Who *are* they, really? "We have so much to offer. And we like you for who you are. We know your flaws. We know your weaknesses. And we still like you. In the end, isn't that more important than anything else? What else have you ever wanted?"

I feel myself shaking my head, though inside I can feel my heart nearly bursting to say yes. Yes! Finally. Isn't this what I've always wanted?

"Leave him alone," comes another voice from within the multitude. A single voice, not Johnny's or Will's. And here he comes through the multitude, standing out from the sea of white and blond. It's Marquis.

I push him away. "I don't need your help," I tell him, but he stays. Secretly I like that, even if I also resent him butting in.

He tries to use his body to shield me from the multitude, but they are all around us. They creep closer up behind me. He realizes he's fighting a losing battle, and turns to face me. "I'm sorry," he says. I hug him and he hugs me. I hold Marquis close to me and try to shield my eyes from the multitude. It's toying with us like bullies in a playground. I've *been* bullied in playgrounds, and that bullying never stops just because you get to be an adult. "It gets better" has always been a lie. The only reason anything gets better is because *you* get better. You can't wait for the rest of the world. It's up to you. If the rest of the world had its way, it would sit around all day jacking off to the apocalypse because it's easier than trying to do anything about it. Then what's left? They worship the insipid and the bland. They surround themselves with more and more of the same, self-selecting to reproduce and recreate the asshole-gazing technocratic dystopia San Francisco has become.

Their hypnotic urging gets more intense. Sometimes they are my friends. Sometimes they bait me with loneliness and paranoia. Inside I feel like they're *laughing* at me, like they laugh at everything. Nothing means anything to these people.

Marquis lurches forward and takes a swing at the nearest one, but I grab him and pull him back before he reaches them. His swing goes astray and he falls into me, and we fall on the ground. My head hits the floor and my hearing goes white. My head feels like it's full of bees. The room won't stay steady above me. My stomach hurts. No, I mean it *really* hurts. Like when I had my hysterectomy and felt this vacuum inside me, knives stabbing away at something that was no longer there. I had to be taken away in an ambulance because the doctor had screwed up the operation and I was bleeding internally, dying and I didn't even know it. My organs are swimming around in the space left over, rubbery gelatinous masses sliding past each other in a disgusting ballet. The blood is pulsing under my skin. I feel flushed all over. And I'm *warm*, down there, my clitoris is throbbing too. I can't be turned on. I've never felt less aroused in my life. But the blood is boiling in my veins, and my skin starts to split and crack, my insides are turning into outsides, and there is a pain somewhere. I think my body is screaming.

I shut my mouth. My jaw is sore, like it's been wedged open for hours. I'm soaked with sweat, more sweat than I knew I had in me, like I've been standing under a shower head. Marquis looks into my eyes. He's holding my hand.

"You doin' okay, babe?" he asks.

"'Babe'?" I mumble, but the word doesn't come out right. Fuck "babe." If I wanted to be called stupid pet names, I'd have never transitioned.

I put my hand on my stomach. I know that old wound can't just pop right open and start bleeding again. But it wouldn't be the first time I've woken up with that nightmare. Everything feels fine.

"Dude, what you doin'?" He puts his hand on mine to try and calm me down, but I don't want to be calmed down. No one calms me down.

"I gotta go," I say, leaning heavily on Marquis to get up on my feet. The multitude hasn't gone, but it's not here any more. Don't care. I have to sit down. I take the hat off my head as I go and I can feel the heat escape. The air feels cool and perfect on my head as the heat flows out of me. I run my hand through my hair and feel it come back clammy with old sweat.

"Ashen!" Marquis calls after me.

I turn back to him for a second and say, "Marquis! Your hat." I fling it back at him.

Tom

"Gotcha," I say, grabbing the hat out of the air before it gets to Marquis. He doesn't seem to care. He just runs after his boy, but then we both know it's not his hat. It's Andre's. Is this what Slayden was talking about all the time? Did he come back in time to stop Andre from losing his hat? I gotta force myself to swallow, and I can feel the vomit trying to force its way up my throat but never making it all the way. It doesn't make sense. But Slayden mighta known what he was talking about, and he's not here anymore, which means it's all up to me. Only I can stop whatever's coming, only I can prevent it happening. Whatever it is. Motherfucking Slayden. If he only would have told me what to look for, I could set all this straight.

A girl's coming my way, so I try to step to one side but she tackles me. For a second I think she's gonna take me down, but then I start pushing back and get my balance. She's not tackling me after all. I think she's *hugging* me.

"You all right?" I ask.

"Hey," she says into my armpit.

"Hello?" I try to push her off me a little. She's resisting, but then she lets go and pulls back long enough for me to see she's got this *thing* growing out the other side of her neck. Did you ever see those pictures of people in third world countries with huge goiters? But this isn't just big, it's bruised, it's angry and purple, like something is fighting its way out of her neck. She looks up at me and opens her eyes. Then the goiter opens *its* eyes—soft, sad, and mushy.

What the *fuck*, man? What the actual *fuck*?

"You're Andre's friend, aren't you?" she asks. "Val. We met when you got here."

I nod slowly. Could this actually be the same girl from the start of the night?

"What happened?" I ask. I have to force the words out of my mouth. My tongue feels dry like the moisture has just been sucked out of my whole body.

She rubs her neck slowly where the second head is bulging out of her skin. "I don't feel well," she mumbles. As her mouth moves, so does the goiter's. It's lipless, so thin I didn't even know it was there until it started mouthing something too quiet to hear. Does it have vocal cords in there? Does it have a brain? What am I even looking at?

"I got a bee sting," she says.

"Woman, that ain't no bee sting like I ever saw."

"Regan dumped me. She said I was ugly. I'm not *ugly*, am I?" she asks. "You find me attractive." She rushes to add, "I'm not making things weird, it's not weird. But objectively, I'm attractive aren't I?" The mewling, pleading eyes of the *thing* are staring up at me.

I nod, trying to hold back the vomit. "Sure. Sure, you're very attractive."

"If we were both single, would you go on a date with me?"

"If the timing seemed right…" I stammer.

"If the timing was right? And we were both into it? You'd go out on a date with me?"

She's stepping closer to me. I don't like where this is going. I try to step back, but people are blocking my retreat.

"Yeah. I'd go on a date with you."

"This might sound weird, Tom." I can't take my eyes off the

goiter. It's like it's trying to tell me something, trying to hypnotize me. "But right now, right in this moment, I think I love you."

What is she saying? She looks disgusted by me. Bitch, I'm not the one with a mutant head growing out of my neck. I thought she was a lesbian. Why is she making herself do this? "You love me?" I ask.

She nods. "I think I do. Isn't that all we need? The here and the now, this moment right now where nothing else matters in the world and you and me can be together?"

I don't care about the people behind me. I back up through their conversation until I hit the wall, but Val is unstoppable. She's bearing down on me and doesn't even notice how far she's chasing me. She presses her hips against mine. My heart is pounding like I just got back from a five-mile run. Time is slowing down, getting lost in the soft, mushy eyes of the abomination. I can feel myself getting hard against my will. *Noooo. Stop it. Go down.*

I'm begging myself to be turned off, but the hormones are raging inside me and Val is grinding against my crotch. She leans in to hug me, but this time I'm on the mutant goiter side of her neck. No, it's not a hug. It's a *kiss.* The goiter looms bigger and bigger in front of me, its wet mouth opening like a surgical wound, mushy eyes gazing adoringly, lidlessly into mine, until our lips meet. It tastes like raw meat on my tongue. I try to push Val away, but my hand lands on her breast and makes the goiter coo with pleasure.

I finally shove her away from me and all she can do is look up at me, both of them looking up at me, hurt.

"You don't think I'm attractive," she says as she starts crying uncontrollably. "You think I'm ugly."

I can't respond. All I can taste is the metallic tang of raw meat on my lips and the vomit still lapping at the back of my throat threatening to come spewing out of me again. I push Val out of the way so I can get to the bathroom. I don't care if I have to lock myself in there.

Val falls into the arms of the drag queen who was performing downstairs. "That's no way to treat a lady," he screams. "You don't have to be straight to kiss a woman, you know."

"I am straight," I say without thinking.

"You aaaaaare? Well, we better get a proper look at you. C'mere, sweetie." He grabs my arm with his claw. He digs his fingers into my bicep the same way you pick the meat off a chicken bone. I flex my arm to try and push back, but that only encourages him more. "Don't you just hate it when you get a bite on the line, but he puts up a struggle when you reel him in? You little prick tease. You didn't think you could hide away up here, did you? Now I know where all the fresh meat's been hiding all night. I wondered why the only morsels downstairs were the gristly chicken nuggets. Ooooh, we got us a big ol' slab of beefcake here, don't we?" The lights are shining in my eyes. I'm in the show. He's doing his routine right here for everyone around us. "Now, why don't you calm down a minute there, honey, and tell us your name."

"Tom," I mumble against the light.

"Whaaaaa?" he cackles. "Dumb?" The makeup is caked around his nose and the corners of his mouth. He looks like a talentless hooker.

"*Tom*," I say.

"Dong?"

Yeah. He's on a fucking roll. "My name's not fucking Dong, all right?"

"Ooooh, you're this sensitive about your name, are you sensitive anywhere else, Dong?"

I try to wrestle myself out of his grip, but he's stronger than he looks under all the women's clothes. What the hell does he look like out of drag? He must have muscles like a horse.

"Now, Dong, I'm gonna let you go on one condition." He reaches out, and the bartender hands him a shot glass of something nasty-looking. It spills over the lip of the glass a bit and coats his disgusting fingers. The thought of everything he's touched mixing with the drink makes my stomach flip. Does he wash his hands? He probably touched his dick with those fingers. "You gotta do a shot," he continues, strategically placing the shot glass between his boobs. Her boobs. Whatever. They look real. But they can't be, can they? If it's just padding, then what's the difference. But I'm staring down at his cleavage and I see *skin*, warm, disgusting skin mushing around the edges of the glass and holding it in place. His grip is like iron.

I dive in and grab the glass between my lips and knock the thing back. It burns and I shudder, but at least it's gone. The drag queen is cackling again.

"Dong, you just got a taste of Lucinda Fanny. I make all my drinks with a little bit of love, if you know what I mean."

I fall on my knees and heave, but nothing's coming out. My throat has sealed up. I can't make myself vomit.

"Awwww," he coos. Then he leans in and whispers to me in his man voice, "Don't worry, Dong, there's nothing you gotta worry about."

"What? There's nothing…?"

"Nah," he says, "just a little something to help you have a good time. By the end of the night, you're gonna be *anyone's*."

Now I *have* to throw it up. How long has it been in me? *What's* been in me? It feels like hours. It's probably already half absorbed into my system. That motherfucking drag queen *roofied* me.

I finally pull out of that bastard's grip and make a run for it. I'm heading for the bar to try and wash the taste out of my mouth or throw up in a sink or something. The counter has been flipped up and there's no one manning the bar, so I just run in, but then I stumble and fall. My legs are weak. My coordination is going. Oh my God, I'm losing control over my own body. I'm gonna get gang-banged on a pool table, and I can't even fight back. Before I get pick myself up I hear something. It's a nasal voice, and it's *complaining*. I don't believe it.

I look behind me. Maybe I'm not losing control of my body

after all. I didn't fall on my own, I tripped—on Andre. He's tied up on the floor and he's going off at me.

"What the fuck! What'd you do that for?" says Andre, like I did something stupid.

"What are you doing on the floor?"

"Quit being a smart-ass and help me out of these knots. I got off the bar but I can't undo my hands and legs."

I grab his hands and turn him face down on the floor.

"No, not like this! The floor is covered in shit."

I kneel on his back to keep him in place while I pull at the cords holding his ankles together. My hands are sweaty and shaking. Andre is struggling. Whoever did this to him wasn't fucking around. Slowly the knots start to come undone and I move on to his wrists.

As soon as Andre's hands come loose, I lift up my knee and he gets up. I stand up slowly. The bar is turning around me. I can't seem to keep my head straight. Everything is going so slowly. Time is inching along, second by long, endless second. Is this something to do with Slayden? Is this his temporal paradox dooming us all to get stuck in time? Or have I really been drugged? It almost doesn't seem to matter now. But Slayden wanted something. My fingers reach up like they've got a mind of their own and toy with the brim of the hat. I realize I'm still wearing it.

Andre says, "I hope you're not expecting a thank you." After a second's consideration, he adds, "But I'm going to thank you anyway and there's nothing you can do about it. So there. Hey, is that my hat?"

"Yeah," I say, absently taking it off my head and holding it out. This is it. This is what Slayden was trying to do the whole time. I can feel my head clearing. Time is resuming its normal clip. Maybe all the horror of tonight can be undone if the paradox can just be resolved. If the time streams can be brought back into alignment. If Andre can get his hat back.

"*There's* my hat," says a voice, and we both look over to see a dude on the other side of the bar. "I've been looking everywhere for that."

"Who the hell are you?" Andre asks.

"I'm Lawrence," he says like Andre should already know. "We met—"

"Well, fuck off, Lawrence. That's my hat. I lost it to a mad lesbian at the start of the night."

"My hat…" moans Val, who's followed me to the bar. Her second head mouths something incoherent along with her, faint bubbles of spittle popping at the sides of its repulsive gash.

"That is not your hat, and you know it," insists Andre.

What's the matter with him? Can't he see what's wrong with her? Can't she see it herself? Has everyone gone *nuts*?

"I think you'll find it's mine," says Lawrence. "The boy who lost control of his bladder also abandoned it on the dance floor."

"So you didn't buy it," crows Andre. "How convenient."

"My hat…" sobs Val, grabbing on to the brim like a zombie looking for brains.

"And *you* got it from *me*!" screams Andre, rapidly losing his shit. "Don't act like you didn't. I have witnesses."

He grabs the hat and pulls, but Val has a firm grip on it.

"Give it back," says Lawrence, grabbing on while there's still room.

I tighten my grip on the hat and shout, "Give it back to Andre. You don't know what you're doing."

"All right, let's break it up," says Amy, entering the fray. She's the last thing we need. Where did she even come from? She tries to push us apart, but it only makes us bunch together more. There's a man at the end of the bar wearing a top hat and watching us intently. He takes off his dark glasses. He's got tattooed eyeballs, and he's staring at Amy.

We're pressed up against each other. Val's goiter gazes up at me adoringly. I can feel the vomit rising at the back of my throat again, but it's not enough to make me let go. Lawrence tugs so hard he pulls both me and Andre into the shelf of bottles behind the bar, and I can hear one roll off the shelf and smash. Our stumbling footsteps crunch on a floor of broken glass. Val looks unfazed. Andre doesn't have the upper-body strength to pull back against Lawrence's weight, but I do. I yank it back toward us, and in that second the hat comes free all at once. I fall backward, clutching the crumpled hat in my hands, and my elbow slams Amy in the chin. She falls, catching her head on the side of the bar.

She's not moving.

Andre stamps his foot like a kid. "Well, great. Thanks a fucking lot, Tom. You've killed Amy."

She doesn't have a pulse.

"Tom, stop fiddling with my lesbian and let's get out of here."

"She's dead," I say.

"Shut up. No, she isn't."

I gently turn her head to one side and suddenly everyone can see the head wound. I wince and put the hat over Amy's head to cover it up.

For once Andre doesn't know what to say. After a second's pause, he checks his watch.

It's still two a.m.

AMY

A ghost once told me the last moments of your life would seem to last forever. Because your brain's electrochemical impulses are slowing and fading, your perception of time telescopes and you remain conscious forever. What a cruel joke that would be. Just when you think you've gotten away, you get trapped in an eternal limbo with nothing but your own consciousness to keep you company for a hundred years. A thousand. A million. How long can your brain make a second feel? When it comes down to it, nothing and everything are much the same thing. Neither can be measured. One is infinitely small and one is infinitely big. Both are meaningless by that point and are, therefore, equivalent. By being vanishingly small and getting smaller all the time, your consciousness might actually expand to encompass everything in the universe.

I told her she was talking complete crap. Your mental processes can't keep slowing down forever and ever. Your perception of time might telescope, but in the end it would be more like how you're never aware of the moment you fall asleep. When the final moment of death really comes, you would simply never notice it.

She frowned at me judgmentally, and we talked all night.

It was college, at a party held by someone I'd gone on a date with once. She was just being nice to me when she said we'd still be friends, but I'd never gone to many parties before, so I went anyway. She didn't look happy to see me. God, I think I showed up with a bottle of crème de menthe, because I thought that's what people did at parties. Everyone else was drinking vodka mixed with anything that's not vodka. No one wanted to tip radioactive green mouthwash into their drinks. A room full of media studies students and history majors playing "E-Pro" on *Guitar Hero*, trying to sing Beck's monotone and failing. Who knew it was so hard to sound so flat? That medievalist on vocals with all the swagger in his step is going to think twice next time before he takes the mic.

She, standing in front of me with a stoop in her shoulders and a vodka-and-Coke in her hand. Red Solo cup—the proper round kind, not the ones with the squared-off sides so they're harder to knock over and easier to tessellate. Fuck. When did cups get *sides*? Someone somewhere made a lot of money from that. All I want is a goddamn circular cup. There must be a hidden cache of them somewhere, a box or a bag from ten years ago being sold on eBay for an exorbitant price. I could get that and hoard them. No, you can't drink from my Solo cups. You don't *understand* my Solo cups, you inauthentic piece of shit.

Her name was Lianna and she hated old movies but loved astronomy. I don't even know where to start with her. But when I think about her now, the first thing I remember is her supercilious Ignatius J. Reilly eyes, watery blue and yellow in a way that highlighted their striations and the cutting edge of her pupils. Eyes that laughed and judged, eyes from another world that saw everything our world had to offer and disapproved.

She lived on a higher plane than the rest of humanity. And yet she saw many things a lot more narrowly, too. Parts of the world just didn't register with her. Others she had no patience with: telephones or the wrong kind of toilet paper. But for some reason she had patience for me. I fell in love easily in those days when my feelings were still undercooked. I'd come away from one small conversation filled with fantasies of the rest of my life. I think Lianna was the only person I talked to at the whole party.

I'd run into her at the café on campus, and we'd sit outside next to that one guy in the whole university who still insisted on chain-smoking hand-rolled cigarettes and talking socialism like a bad parody of himself. She had plastered the university with posters advertising Baron Happyplap's Kindly Brainwashing Corporation to spite the rigged student council elections. The stifling heat made us sweat into our shirts and baked the ground bone dry, but it also drew a thick, earthy smell from the eucalyptus trees. Their leaves dangled in the half-hearted breeze, very far from home now, but if you shut your eyes and breathe deeply, you could have imagined you were in the Australian bush.

There was one perfect night, too hot for sleep and too humid for anything else, when we went down to the beach to perch on huge stone steps made for giants to walk but perfect for people to sit looking like children swinging their legs in the air on adult furniture. We ate Spanish olives and cheap brie, and drank a bottle of Midori that we hated but kept drinking because it was hilarious. No one else was in sight, even on the streets behind us in the ethereal bubbles of light that surrounded the street lamps. The rest of the human race had gone, and the night belonged to us. The moon shone over the ocean and left a great, long trail reflected in the water. Lianna said it looked like a snail had crawled over the ocean and up into the sky and left this silvery wake behind it.

Davey's Book Arcade was about a twenty-minute walk from the university, so Lianna and I used to hang out there when neither of us had classes, waist-deep in scratched vinyl and tangled cassette tapes, giggling at the shelf of 1950s sex manuals. We didn't have enough money to buy anything, so we picked one thing we really wanted and walked around the whole shop with it, putting it back when we found something we wanted more, changing our minds and then trying to find the book we'd lost in the great towering stacks. A review in a newspaper described it as "not so much a good place to buy secondhand books as to hide a body." They weren't wrong. Lianna and I got trapped in an annex that smelled like cat pee when an avalanche of books cut off the narrow path that had led us there. It hadn't been cleaned in about forty years.

Davey's shut down the summer after I graduated. Couldn't make the rent, apparently. No one's buying books and records and tapes anymore, and the rents just keep going up and up. The owner would never have let it go, but he died. And the shop's cat got run over. And the family tried to keep it going for as long as they could. And then before I knew it, they were gone.

There's no afterlife, but I like to think at the end of every life we might be judged not by the kind of life we lived. Instead you would be presented with everyone in your life who ever caused you pain, and you would be given a choice to suffer that pain again or to make them suffer it instead. Compassionate and selfless people would own their suffering, but people who were selfish and cruel and spiteful would make someone else suffer for them. When I think about some of the absolute assholes I've met, I go back and forth about whether or not I'd take my suffering out on them. But I don't know about Lianna. There's so much we never said. Will she be there after I die? And will I be there when she dies? The only thing I know is that I would gladly suffer everything again.

I miss her. I still don't know what happened. We graduated and grew apart. Which one happened first? It's hard to remember now. I just remember seeing her from time to time and feeling wells of frustration and resentment inside me at the person she was becoming. Had everything we'd done together meant nothing to her? She wasn't just cruelly strangling herself. It felt like she was strangling me, and leaving me all alone. Every now and then, I go on the internet to try and find her again, but she's a ghost. She left fewer and fewer traces in the world until finally she disappeared completely. I wonder if maybe she decided to end her life the way I decided to end mine, so I check the obituaries. But no, it's not like her to be found out. She vanished, like all proper ghosts do.

I think, maybe, it is time for me to go home. My head is full of dreams now. Dreams of, if not happy, then at least happier times; blazing hot, starry nights that pull you into the sky to join them; terrible music on the stereo because the host joked that it was a Mexican death metal party and had to follow through on it; somehow, the drinks buoying us into the early hours of three or even four o'clock; back aching from carrying heavy books around all day; the bags of store-brand chips; and cups, so many cups, red and round like cups should be. I hope that wherever she is, Lianna thinks about me from time to time. But she probably doesn't.

ANDRE

I'm starting to think this night is taking a turn for the worse.

I lift the hat off Amy's face and stare at her. She's not dead. She can't be. I put my hand on the top of her head and feel her scratchy hair under my fingers. Too late for conditioner now. Too late for anything. I couldn't stop her. She didn't do this to herself, but I know how much pain she was in. She wanted this. But I didn't want it for her. Shit, I'm going to cry. I stand up and turn away, trying to stop Tom seeing.

"Andre…" he says.

"What'd you go and do that for, Tom?" He's heard my voice cracking. He knows I'm crying.

"I didn't kill her," says Tom. "I mean, I didn't mean to kill her. She was just there." Tom's holding his head in his hands. I kneel down and put my arm around him, but he doesn't look up.

"It was an accident," I say. "We all saw what happened." He doesn't seem to hear me.

"This can't be real," he sniffs. Then the sniffing stops. "It's not real," he says. "What time do you have?"

"Two," I say.

"Two…It's always two o'clock. That has to mean something."

"Yes, it means my phone doesn't work."

"No, it means none of this is really happening. It's not too late. If we can go back, we can undo all of this."

"Undo killing Amy? You can't unfuck a tranny, Tom, You've fucked the tranny, and now we're both tranny fuckers."

"Slayden, the dude with the hipster mustache, was a time traveler. He came here from the future or something. I know, I traveled back in time with him because he had this kind of a watch…"

He's really lost it now. "Come on, Tom. Should we…like, call an ambulance? Or what?"

"Shut up and listen to me. She's not really dead. We can still save her. It started when we got here. Do you remember when I didn't get you that drink?"

I sniff. The tears have stopped, but my nose is still wet. "You're not getting me a drink right now. That doesn't mean you can travel through time. I'll show you. We just need to find that hipster piece of shit, and he'll tell you you're retarded."

"No, we can't. He couldn't come this far. They all jumped back in time before two."

"Who's they?"

"Him and his other selves. He overlapped. He lived through the night once, but he couldn't fix it so he went back in time again. Didn't you see him more than once? In more than one place at the same time? It was all the different versions of the same Slayden."

"So, how does this work, then? Is it *Back to the Future* rules or what?"

"I don't know! Wait, we can figure this out. What happened to the last Slayden? If we can find what happened to him, we can find his time machine. He had your hat. He took it off me in the courtyard."

"So?"

Tom grabs me by the shoulders. "So, if we can figure out how your hat got from him back to us, we can figure out the last time anyone saw him. Where's that guy I got it from? He was throwing the hat around when I caught it."

I know who he's talking about. It was right before I escaped from being tied to the bar. It was Ashen. Urgh. I hate that guy. He needs to lay off the cheese or something because he's always shitting farts so hard I'm surprised he doesn't blow out the back of his pants.

"I don't wanna talk to Ashen. Not without a gas mask anyway. That guy's ass is a nuclear disaster."

But Tom's not listening. He's already running back from behind the bar and calling out, "Ashen! Ashen!"

A chorus of birds replies, "Ashen! Ashen!" I follow Tom around the bar and see a flock of purple and gold birds perched around the booth at the corner table. Ashen is sitting at the table making out with some black guy like he's trying to tongue-fuck his throat. Gross.

Tom tries to get his attention, but the bird people are protecting them. They caw and start pecking at Tom, who tries to bat them away. But there's more of them than him.

"I just need to talk to Ashen," says Tom.

Ashen pulls his tongue out of his boy's mouth and makes a soothing sound to calm the bird people down. "What's up?" he says.

"Where did you get this hat?" Tom asks, sticking his finger in my face to show them my hat. "Who did you get it from?"

"It's Marquis's," says Ashen, pointing at his boy.

I blurt out, "It's not his, it's mine!" I turn to the boy, who's sitting there with a happy, goofy grin on his stupid face. "Where did you get it from?"

"I got it from Frasier," he says.

"You got it from *Frasier*? What are you, from the '90s?"

"*Are* you from the '90s?" Tom asks, wide-eyed. "Do you have a time machine?"

"I mean some racist-ass white boy got carried outta here wit' a broke leg."

"Outta where?"

The other guy just shrugs, but I know where Frasier was. I've seen more than one person get carried out of Aunty Bob's, and Willie always takes them to his office while they wait for the ambulance. The door to the beer garden is hanging off its hinges, and the stairs look like they're about to give way, but I try not to think about that. Tom runs ahead of me, making the whole staircase shake, and it feels like an earthquake is hitting the city. When I get to the ground, I'm still dizzy and it's hard to get my footing. The ground's still shaking under me.

We run into the ground floor of the club and turn toward the office.

The door is closed. Tom grabs the handle, and it seems jammed until finally it gives way and Tom falls into the room. Somebody is already in here. He's on the desk squatting on his legs with his arms out wide. The man lashes out at a body with a dismembered arm, beating it even in death. I hardly recognize him. I can't believe it, but I think it used to be Kelvin.

"Are you Frasier? Where did you get this?" Tom demands. He's pointing at the hat as if the animal's going to know what the hell he's talking about. But fuck, maybe it's working. The gorilla looks like he recognizes it. He jumps down off the desk and saunters toward Tom with a lopsided gait.

"Tom!" I hiss. "This is a bad idea. You know you're not an alpha male. You're an alfalfa male."

"Oh, I ain't doing shit," he says. "You're the one with the hat."

"What? Are you serious right now?"

Fuck. Fuck fuck fuck. He's right. The gorilla isn't going up to him, he's coming up to *me*. I back away until I'm against the wall. The gorilla's matching my steps, and now he's right in front of me. He seems so huge with his hunched shoulders and crooked yellow teeth and big, meaty hands still holding the dead man's arm. He's the only thing I can see in the whole room. I look into his eyes, and he's not happy to see me. I hold out the hat, and the animal sniffs it carefully, brushing my hand with his bristly monkey lips. It leaves behind a streak of saliva.

He roars, and I can smell the stink of his breath from here. I press myself against the wall. Even Tom's shaking and trying badly to hide it.

Then the gorilla growls, "Marquis," and slinks away. He grabs the body and drags it behind the desk. I open the door behind me without taking my eyes away from the gorilla. Then we duck back out and slam that fucking door right behind us.

"Jesus Christ!" I say. "What the hell was that?" I take the hat off my head and start whipping him with it. "Don't you ever do that to me again, d'you hear me?"

Tom smiles a big, toothy smile. "How do you walk around with balls that big swinging between your legs?"

I put the hat back on. "All right, I half forgive you. But keep talking."

"Marquis," he says from between gritted teeth. "Back upstairs."

We run back to the second floor where Ashen and Marquis are still in the booth. I'm panting, and my feet hurt. This is Tom's thing. I'm too pretty to run.

"What is it this time?" demands Ashen. "I'm trying to get the D here."

Tom ignores him and says to Marquis, "You dickin' me around? Frasier says he got this from you. You can't have got it from each other."

"Frasier gone, bro, I tol' you that already. It always the same with straight boys. You gotta listen."

Tom slams his hand on their table and shouts, "Fuck you, buddy, and fuck your green-eyed granny." Whoa, what the fuck? I never heard *that* one before. Tom looks like he's about to have a nervous breakdown. "I got the hat from Ashen," he mumbles to himself. "Ashen got it from Marquis. Marquis got it from Frasier."

"I didn't get it from Marquis," Ashen interrupts. "I got it from some guy in the beer garden who was here with his dad. Or his daddy, if you know what I mean."

"Fuck you too, Ashen," Tom shouts, and before I can make a devastatingly shady crack about Ashen King of Farts, we're pushing through the crowd of people and making for the stairs again. We were fucking lucky to make it up and down that death trap twice, but Tom doesn't seem to care and slams his full weight on each step as he goes. I bite my lip and follow him carefully.

We can't miss the couple Ashen was talking about. They're shouting at each other so loud, they're even drowning out the music from inside the club. And that ain't easy.

"What's that supposed to mean?" shouts the younger one. I don't recognize him, but the old man looks familiar. Is that…? It's the cunt from the bar who got everyone saying "sparkledrank." I *hate* that guy.

He's shouting back at the other one, even though he doesn't have half the strength of his friend. His voice is old and raspy, and he's having trouble holding himself up in his seat. "Don't act like you don't know. I *hate* it when you do that. Who the fuck goes to a bar with a book? I'm not saying it's a bad thing. I'm just saying you were gagging for the attention." He trails off here and starts coughing a nasty cough the way smokers do after a lifetime of tar. He looks up and sees me there.

"Oh look," he says, "it's Scooby-Doo."

"*Benny?*" says Tom.

I turn to Tom. "You know this asshole?"

"Shut up, Andre," hisses Tom, but that doesn't seem to placate his friend.

"Hey, fuck you, fucko. Mind your own business."

"We're really sorry," says Tom.

"*I'm* not," I mumble.

Tom continues. "But we really need to know where you got this hat."

Benny nods. "I was over there," he says, pointing to the other side of the courtyard. "And it came flying out of the bathroom window."

"That's it? You didn't see who had it before you?"

Benny shakes his head sadly. "But I saw what they did to the inside of that bathroom. They were having some dynamite pee party in there."

Tom looks at me expectantly. Oh, hell no, I am not gonna let this fly. "Like I'm supposed to know every pee pervert in the Bay Area," I say. "Who do you think I am? Some kinda giant pee whore?"

"*Do* you know who it was?" he asks.

"Well, yeah. I do. But it's the way you asked that I object to. I was tied up on the bar and I saw him coming out." I shudder. "Gross. I think I saw him in here one or two times before. And *he* got it from Amy," I say, suddenly remembering. And suddenly remembering where Amy is now—dead on the floor behind the bar upstairs. Do I really believe there's a time machine? That's insane. I'm just running from the problem. I push the thought out of my head. I know I'll have to face the music sooner or later. But just for a while longer, I can pretend like everything's going to be okay.

"And I saw Amy with it downstairs," Tom suddenly remembers.

We go to run back into the club, but two people are standing in the way. I say people loosely. They are the fattest people I have ever seen. Like, I'm not even joking. They are disgustingly fat. I'm surprised they're even still alive. I didn't know you could be that big without all your organs getting clogged and exploding. And it's not the kind of muscle-fat some people get, either, where it's like they're fat but can also punch a whale. Their stomachs hang off them like plastic bags filled with water, sloshing back and forth every time they take a step, swinging in front of them in huge folds. Their tits are so big I can't even tell if they're women or men.

They're paused in front of us. One of them looks like it's

looking at me, but it's hard to tell when its eyes and lips and nose are so compressed by its face. Its cheeks are rising up over the rest of its features like the top of a muffin. "Heyyyyy," he booms at me. "What happened to that hat that belonged to that nice Carolina boy?" His voice sounds like it's drowning in his face. He turns the best he can toward his friend and says, "Hey, Maaaaaarge. Whatever happened to that nice Carolina boy?"

"Whaaaa?" she gurgles back at him.

"You remember the nice boy we was talking to earlier. These folks got his hat."

They seem to be talking more and more slowly all the time. I can see them getting fatter and fatter even while we're standing here talking. A fucking disgusting gurgle comes out of the woman's stomach, and she opens her mouth and lets out the *longest* burp I ever heard. I clamp my hands over my nose and mouth, but it's too fucking late. I can already smell it. Fuck! I can even *taste* it on my tongue. Particles of her half-digested pizza have bubbled up out of her guts, floated through the air, and landed in my mouth. Pepperoni.

I start yakking violently on the cement. I've never been so grateful to taste my own stomach acid. Anything's better than tasting the blob-monster's dinner.

"Well, lookit that," says the man. "You can't let that all go to waste."

He kneels his huge ass down on the ground, and as his ass cheeks hit the cement I could swear I felt the ground shake under my feet. Then he rolls over on his front and puts his face in my vomit and starts licking it up off the ground.

"Herrrrrb," says the woman. "You're terrible!"

Herb is smacking his lips. I can see long threads of vomit and spit stretch between them. One of them breaks and what's left drips down his chin. "These big city folks sure do eat fancy," he says between chews.

There's no other way to get past them. I can do this. I can

jump. And I'm going to do it in these shoes and yes, you are correct, I will look *fabulous*.

I take a step back and then run toward them. I land on Herb and climb over, trying not to think about where I'm putting my hands and feet. I grab on to huge folds of skin to pull myself up. Herb doesn't complain except for a couple of grunts. I wonder if he even knows I'm up here. It's awful. He's sweated through all his clothes and everything I touch is soft and damp and clammy.

I reach his soggy, shapeless ass cheeks and for a second, I think I'm about to fall into the crack between them and throw up again and stay trapped forever between that moist sticky fat pressing up against me and mashing my own vomit into my face. But when I tumble, I miss the crack. Before I know it I'm on the other side, though the smell of sweaty ass crack is still up my nose. I turn and suck in the fresh air. Gotta try and clear my lungs.

Tom's still on the other side, but it doesn't take him long to figure out what I've done. He vaults over them and lands next to me.

"I touched that thing's back-fat!" I start shouting at Tom, wiping my hands on him in a panic. It's still on me. I can still feel its gross clammy skin.

"Quit being so fussy."

"*It's on my hands*," I say, slapping him now, but he ignores me and makes for the club. "Don't run away while I'm complaining at you!" But before I get any further, something soft and moist and fatty slams against my face. Not more fat people. Oh my God, anything but more fat people. I'm picking myself off the ground from the tangle of arms that's me and the chunky steampunk. Oh god, it was her tits. I accidentally touched her tits. Her skin is so pale, I can see those disgusting blue veins stretch across her epic boobage.

Something tickles my neck for a second, and I slap it. I look at my hand and—oh my God, is that a wasp?

"It's a wasp!" I shriek, waving my hand in the air, not

knowing how to get this thing's mashed body off me. "What the hell's a wasp doing in here?"

"There's more," whispers Tom, putting his hand on my arm.

"What, now you're psychic?"

"No, listen," he says.

There's a humming noise. No, not a humming. A buzzing.

A big, dark shape steps forward from behind Regan. I can't make it out in the club lights. It's just a shadow—a shadow that's *moving*.

The shape says, "Oh, hi, Andre."

"*Val?*" I say. It is, it's Val. And she's fucking *covered* in wasps. "What happened to you?"

She lifts a hand to look at it, though I can't see her hand and I can't see her eyes. Just that carpet of wasps crawling all over her.

"Will you look at that," she mumbles. "My wasp must have got out."

"*Wasp?* That's not a wasp, that's a million wasps."

"It's okay," says Regan. "They're not that bad once you get used to them…" Before I can stop her, the wasps have spread onto her hands. In just a couple of seconds, she's covered in wasps, crawling in her hair and ears and down her corset. I can't see her face anymore. I get a sudden image of her, not a person anymore, just colonies of wasps walking around in human shape.

They take a step toward us.

Tom and I try to take a step back, but the wasps fly off her and circle around us. They've got us trapped. And they're narrowing the circle. I can't hear the music anymore. I can't hear voices. Just the buzzing all around us and in my head and on my *skin*.

The door to Willie's office bursts open and the gorilla roars and bounds into the colony. The wasps dissolve into a cloud, which reforms just a few seconds later and descends on the gorilla. He thrashes and screeches. He rolls on the floor in agony, lashing out at anyone stupid enough to be standing too close.

"In here!" says Tom, holding open the door to the office. I run in after him, and he slams the door behind us, shutting out all the noise and craziness from the club. Tom sinks to the ground. "We're never going to find out what happened to Slayden," he moans.

I sit down next to him. "Tom," I say putting my hand on his knee in what I'm hoping is a comforting way instead of a pervy one. "You know we're sitting in shit, right?"

He looks down and sees we are sitting in a big pile of ash. "Fuck," he says, running his fingers through it. "Who the fuck cares anymore." Then, from inside the scattered ashes, he finds a lump. When he holds it up to the light, it looks like a watch. A weird one with too many hands. The leather straps are singed and part burnt off. I'm a bit dizzy from the drinks, but I've seen that watch before. Slowly I realize the bouncer was wearing it earlier this evening.

He looks at me wonderingly.

"What?" I go.

"It's Slayden's time machine."

"Tom, it's a hipster's watch."

"No, no, it's a time machine, look." He taps its buttons. And nothing happens. He sighs, choking up. Maybe now he's starting to face the fact that all this time travel stuff is in his head. Poor, insane Tom. "You were right," he says, throwing the watch away from him. It lands on the floor on the other side of the room with a dull clunk.

"Bzzzt."

I look over at Tom. "Was that you?"

"Was what me?"

"Bzzzt."

"That!" I say. "Something is going bzzzt."

"Bzzzt. Katja to Slayden. Katja to Slayden. Come in, Slayden." A woman's voice is coming from the watch.

Tom grabs it back. "Yes! Yes, who is it?"

"Come in, Slayden. You're in the wrong time. Return to base. I repeat, return to base."

"He's gone," shouts Tom, but the woman isn't listening.

"The computer finished the temporal calculations. There is nothing wrong in your region. I repeat, *there is nothing wrong in your region*. It has always happened like that. It always will."

"What does that mean?" says Tom. "What about Andre's hat?"

"Slayden unresponsive after three attempts. Initiating emergency retrieval protocols. I am sorry, Slayden, but this will hurt."

Tom throws the watch away from him, farther this time, but still shouting at it, "But what are we supposed to do?"

There's a blinding purple flash and a thump. And the watch is gone, along with a six-foot chunk of the floor.

I say, "You know it's shit like this that's starting to give Aunty Bob's a bad name."

"We can never go back. We're stuck here. I'm sorry," he sobs. He's *crying*.

I put my arm around him. I am so bad at this. If he's crying, then I'm going to start crying, too.

ANDRE

2:01 a.m.

The paramedics are wheeling Amy out of Aunty Bob's on an ambulance stretcher. They don't seem to be in any kind of a hurry.

We're standing at the curb outside the club in the front of a straggly group of people watching the paramedics. I wonder how many of them knew her. How many times did she come to this club? How many of these people were her friends? I recognize some, but in the end I guess they weren't enough. *We* weren't enough.

I catch someone's face on the other side of the crowd, someone who didn't even know Amy, someone who's just standing around smoking and talking to his friend, and *smiling*, like he's going, "Who even does this? Doesn't she know what a fuss she's making?" And there's that look in his eyes. Cruel and uncaring, that makes you feel like it's your fault for even existing. I hate that look. And I remember now. I remember where I've seen it before. All those years ago when Amy pulled me off that bar and stopped me punching the bartender. I remember why I was trying to kill him. It was because he made her feel like she didn't belong here.

The paramedics shut the back doors of the ambulance and pull away. The siren's not even on.

Castro Street's still lit up like day. Some people are going home, but others are just beginning the night. Gutter punks are sitting next to the newspaper machines on blankets and sleeping bags with their dog and their guitar. They're trading a joint back and forth, drawing some strange shit on the pavement with chalk.

"Are we gonna say goodbye?" asks Tom.

"To who?" I say. "You don't know anyone. You don't have any friends. Stop being ridiculous." He hugs me, and I don't push him away. "Shut up. I hate you."

My face is pressed up against Tom's armpit. The slight shadow on my jaw brushes against his skin. It's smooth and warm. I shut my eyes. Maybe if I try to ignore it, I can make this moment last forever.

Tom lets me go gently.

"Do you want a chocolate penis?" he asks.

"Gross," I say with a sniff. "I knew you had a crush on me. It's that Jimmy Choo. You can't resist my pheromones."

"*Do* you?"

I nod and wrap my arms around my waist.

We walk up the block to the corner of Castro and Market. They're normally shut by now, but we've gotten lucky. Hot Cookie is late closing tonight, and they're trying to get rid of the last few cookies in the window. I get a good look at all the Rice Krispies squares, marshmallow cookies, and donuts splashed with cinnamon-flavored cum. At the end of the window is what I'm looking for—the last coconut macaroon penis on a stick, although this one looks like it has more testicles than normal.

"What do you call *that*?" I ask, pointing at the monster dong.

"We made too many testicles, so we had to get rid of the extras," says the guy behind the counter.

"That's fucking dirty," says Tom.

"It's beautiful," I say. "Like Frankenstein's mad dick biscuit. A genital frankencookie."

"Well, I don't want it."

"Shut up. You don't know what you want." I turn back to the server. "I'll get that one." The server hands it to me. I savor the smell of a freshly baked penis before I take a bite from the tip. "C'mon," I say to Tom. "Gimme a hand with this."

"I'm not putting that thing in my mouth."

"I can't eat it all on my own, Tom. I'm too beautiful to turn into a fat ass now. Here, shut up and have a testicle."

I break off one coconut-dusted ball and hand it to Tom. "You got your hat back," he says.

"It's all about hats with you. You're obsessed with hats. You need to discover masturbation and realize there's more important things in the world than hats."

Someone's not looking where they're going, because they run across the crossing at 17th & Castro and nearly knock the chocolate dick right out of my hand.

"Watch where you're going," I shout at him. "You nearly ruined my dick."

"I nearly ruined *your* dick?" Kelvin says. Oh my God, it's this guy. He's taller than me, and standing under a streetlight, so for a second I can only see his silhouette. I get an impression of something much bigger, something menacing. But then it's gone. It's only Kelvin. And of course, Lucien is with him. I can't even do this with them right now.

"You could have ruined *my* dick," Kelvin says. "Did you see what speed you were going? I have your license plate, young man. Don't talk back to your elders. Why, in my day this was all rolling green hills as far as the eye could see. Aye, they were simpler times, when men were real men and women were farmyard animals. Young people today don't know you're even alive."

"All right, I'm sorry," I mumble.

"Andre? What's wrong with you? I've never heard you apologize before."

Tom says, "You know that girl Amy who died at the club? She was his friend."

Kelvin's face falls, like he's almost having a human emotion. "Aw, I'm sorry, that sucks."

I take a nibble of my chocolate dick. "Want a testicle?" I ask, breaking one off for him. He says thanks and takes a happy bite out of it.

Lucien's tugging on Kelvin's sleeve and goes, "You should do your thing. You know," and he mimes doing like psychic powers.

I look at Kelvin. "I may or may not be psychic," he says.

"He totally is," Lucien whispers, while Kelvin subtly shakes his head at me. "Go on, get in contact with Amy. Reach beyond the mortal realm."

Kelvin sighs. "Sure, why not. Who are we contacting? Amy?" He nods wisely. "There's a very powerful presence right about here. I'm picking up something strong."

"Yes, herpes," I say. "Get on with it."

He shakes his head and sucks his teeth. "Oooh, lotta bad vibes around here right now. Lotta shade, if you know what I mean. It's creating a lot of fluff in the ether. My vision has gone cloudy."

"Oh good," I say. "Can we go yet?"

"Noooo," says Lucien, grabbing the sleeve of my blazer. "He's just attuning himself to the psychic wavelengths." Sure, that sounds like a thing that's real. "Go on," he urges.

"All right, all right," says Kelvin. He rubs his temples, and his eyes go distant. "I'm feeling you've lost someone very close to you. Is it…Mabel?"

"I just told you, it's *Amy*," says Tom.

"Mabel, tell us where you are. She says she's somewhere cold. She's all alone. There's a lot of money hidden in an old shoebox buried under the children's playset in Dolores Park. Hurry! You have to dig it up right now! Oh my God, someone else is here with us. It's…it's Hitler! Run now, you have to get the money before Hitler gets Mabel. He's chasing her!"

"He's eating her," whispers Lucien, covering his mouth in horror.

"He's eating her!" says Kelvin. I snort, but something

catches in my throat. It's half a sob. But it's also half a laugh. "There's an Amy here, too," he says.

"What does she say?"

"She says she's happier where she is. She says she's at peace. She says, 'The world is my oyster. And the oyster is my cupcake. And the cupcake is a *liar*. Fucking piece of shit cupcake. Lie to me, will you?' I'm not really sure where she's going with that last bit, but I assume you know what she means."

Lucien is giggling like crazy. The weird thing is, so am I.

"See," says Lucien with a nod, "I told you he's psychic." He's leaning on Kelvin's shoulder. Kelvin's got a head on Lucien, so Lucien's looking up at him, and there's this adoring glimmer in his eyes. Oh. Gross.

Tom shivers in the cold and asks if we can get going, so I pull out my phone with my free hand and start calling a car. "Seriously?" asks Tom.

"What? What seriously? I'm not walking all the way back home."

"It's like fifteen minutes."

"I know! It's practically on the moon."

"Come on," he says, and he starts walking.

We go up by Market and 16th where you can feel the bass from the Lookout pounding away in the distance. Someone is standing at the corner smoking a joint. It takes me a second to recognize the guy who stole my drink—Benny. He looks different in this light. I don't know why, but I had the impression he was a lot older than he is. He's with Marquis, Ashen, and the wonky-looking guy with a book in his pocket. Benny starts giggling when he sees us going by.

"Oh look," I say, "it's Benny and the Cunts."

Benny responds with, "Andre the Giant Dickhead."

Hmm. That's actually pretty good. But I'm not going to tell him that. "Where are you going from here?" I ask.

"Just relaxing," said Benny, indicating the joint. "Then probably home."

"Oh right, don't offer me any or anything." Benny holds out the joint to me and I say, "That's disgusting, why would anyone want that? You smell like smoke and a little bit of piss."

"Oh my God, did you see that guy get pissed on at the drag show? Best thing that ever happened at Aunty Bob's. Fuck, best thing that ever happened in the Castro."

"What? Someone got pissed on?"

Benny nodded. "Some guy just took a swan dive off the stage, tackled someone in the audience, and pissed right through his pants into the other guy's face. I already uploaded the video."

"Fuck, I missed it! How did I miss that? Nothing interesting ever happens in the Castro anymore. Do you know who got wazzed on?"

"No," says Benny. "But let me introduce you to the rest of the cunts. This is Kingsley, Marquis, and Ashen."

"Congratulations," I say. "*None* of you have real names. This is Tom, my extremely heterosexual friend who has a completely normal name like a goddamn human being. He's visiting from L.A."

"Are you really?" asks Benny.

"It's true," Tom nods. "I am extremely heterosexual."

Ashen interrupts to say, "Sorry, boys, but I've got to jet."

"I gotta go, too," says Marquis. "I dunno why, but I'm hella tired. Feels like…" He shakes his head to clear the weed smoke out of it. "I dunno."

"Is this about your bird AIDS again?" says Benny. "Because that's totally a thing, and you totally have it."

Marquis grins. "Imma sleep it off an' see." He catches Ashen before he goes and says, "Hey man, where you goin'? Kiss me love. And fuck me courage." He pulls him closer and kisses him, feeling Ashen's arm under his hand. Ashen is shorter but has a stronger build. Looks like that's Marquis's thing.

"Right, you two are disgusting and I never want to see you again," I say. "Come on, Tom. We're going home."

We wander back down 16th Street toward the Mission. It's

a chilly night, so I jam my hands into the pockets of my skinny jeans to keep them warm. I look up, but I can only see a couple of stars through the light pollution and the thin gray clouds. A pounding noise is coming from the Lookout behind us where the party's going late, and the sidewalks are crammed with people leaving the clubs, chatting and smoking on the curb, being loud and stupid and laughing and shouting and kissing. There's onions and sausages cooking on open grills in the Mission ahead of us mixed slightly with the smell of piss from the street.

I smile to myself, though I'm super careful to make sure Tom doesn't see it. *Kiss me love and fuck me courage.*

I like that.

About the Author

St John Karp is an ornamental hermit who likes to live near exciting things, so he can not go to them. He has an undying love for the unusual, the Bonzo Dog Doo-Dah Band, and toast. He spends his time writing about himself in the third person and trying to understand the milk aisle at the supermarket, often after one too many bottles of Château de Bauchery. *Quake City* is his third novel.

Books Available From Bold Strokes Books

Quake City by St John Karp. Can Andre find his best friend Amy before the night devolves into a nightmare of broken hearts, malevolent drag queens, and spontaneous human combustion? Or has it always happened this way, every night, at Aunty Bob's Quake City Club? (978-1-63555-723-7)

Death Overdue by David S. Pederson. Did Heath turn to murder in an alcohol-induced haze to solve the problem of his blackmailer, or was it someone else who brought about a death overdue? (978-1-63555-711-4)

Every Summer Day by Lee Patton. Meant to celebrate every summer day, Luke's journal instead chronicles a love affair as fast-moving and possibly as fatal as his brother's brain tumor. (978-1-63555-706-0)

Everyday People by Louis Barr. When film star Diana Danning hires private eye Clint Steele to find her son, Clint turns to his former West Point barracks mate, and ex-buddy with benefits, Mars Hauser to lend his cyber espionage and digital black ops skills to the case.(978-1-63555-698-8)

Cirque des Freaks and Other Tales of Horror by Julian Lopez. Explore the pleasure of horror in this compilation that delivers like the horror classics…good ole tales of terror. (978-1-63555-689-6)

Royal Street Reveillon by Greg Herren. In this Scotty Bradley mystery, someone is killing the stars of a reality show, and it's up to Scotty Bradley and the boys to find out who. (978-1-63555-545-5)

Death Takes a Bow by David S. Pederson. Alan Keys takes part in a local stage production, but when the leading man is murdered, his partner Detective Heath Barrington is thrust into the limelight to find the killer. (978-1-63555-472-4)

Accidental Prophet by Bud Gundy. Days after his grandmother dies, Drew Morten learns his true identity and finds himself racing against time to save civilization from the apocalypse. (978-1-63555-452-6)

In Case You Forgot by Fredrick Smith and Chaz Lamar. Zaire and Kenny, two newly single, Black, queer, and socially aware men, start again—in love, career, and life—in the West Hollywood neighborhood of LA. (978-1-63555-493-9)

Counting for Thunder by Phillip Irwin Cooper. A struggling actor returns to the Deep South to manage a family crisis but finds love and ultimately his own voice as his mother is regaining hers for possibly the last time. (978-1-63555-450-2)

Survivor's Guilt and Other Stories by Greg Herren. Award-winning author Greg Herren's short stories are finally pulled together into a single collection, including the Macavity Award–nominated title story and the first-ever Chanse MacLeod short story. (978-1-63555-413-7)

Saints + Sinners Anthology 2019, edited by Tracy Cunningham and Paul Willis. An anthology of short fiction featuring the finalist selections from the 2019 Saints + Sinners Literary Festival. (978-1-63555-447-2)

The Shape of the Earth by Gary Garth McCann. After appearing in *Best Gay Love Stories*, *HarringtonGMFQ*, *Q Review*, and *Off the Rocks*, Lenny and his partner Dave return in a hotbed of manhood and jealousy. (978-1-63555-391-8)

Exit Plans for Teenage Freaks by 'Nathan Burgoine. Cole always has a plan—especially for escaping his small-town reputation as "that kid who was kidnapped when he was four"—but when he teleports to a museum, it's time to face facts: it's possible he's a total freak after all. (978-1-163555-098-6)

Death Checks In by David S. Pederson. Despite Heath's promises to Alan to not get involved, Heath can't resist investigating a shopkeeper's murder in Chicago, which dashes their plans for a romantic weekend getaway. (978-1-163555-329-1)

Of Echoes Born by 'Nathan Burgoine. A collection of queer fantasy short stories set in Canada from Lambda Literary Award finalist 'Nathan Burgoine. (978-1-63555-096-2)

The Lurid Sea by Tom Cardamone. Cursed to spend eternity on his knees, Nerites is having the time of his life. (978-1-62639-911-2)

www.ingramcontent.com/pod-product-compliance
Lightning Source LLC
Chambersburg PA
CBHW030511020726
47494CB00004B/1055